The Retreat

The Retreat

The Retreat

Dijorn Moss

www.urbanchristianonline.net

Urban Books, LLC
78 East Industry Court
Deer Park, NY 11729

ISBN 13: 978-1-60162-883-1
ISBN 10: 1-60162-883-8

First Printing December 2010
Printed in the United States of America

10 9 8 7 6 5 4 3 2 1

Distributed by Kensington Corp.
Submit Wholesale Orders to:
Kensington Publishing Corp.
C/O Penguin Group (USA) Inc.
Attention: Order Processing
405 Murray Hill Parkway
East Rutherford, NJ 07073-2316
Phone: 1-800-526-0275
Fax: 1-800-227-9604

The Retreat

Dijorn Moss

Dedication

To my father:
who never accepted anything
less than my very best.

To my mother:
who always reminded me to enjoy life
because you only live it once.

To my wife and muse, Trinea:
you remind me that without love,
everything we do would be in vain.

And in loving memory of Reggie Dottson:
a great man who will never be forgotten.

Acknowledgments

Thank you, Lord Jesus Christ, for blessing me to write this story. It has been a remarkable journey both mentally and spiritually. To my Uncle Richard and my Aunt Denise, you guys were instrumental in my spiritual growth. Thank you for always being willing to go the extra mile for family. I thank God for my awesome team of readers: Wanda Camp-bell, Mark Porrovecchio, and Dawn Gibson. You guys have pushed me to deliver my best work, and as a result, I am a much better writer. To my mentors: Scott Sublett, Ethel Walker, and Floyd Salas, God gave me the gift and you guys gave me the instructions on how to use it. And I cannot forget my editor, Joylynn Jossel. Thank you again for this opportunity to write for Urban Christian. Thank you for always seeing ways in which my writing can become better. To my uncles Jeryle and Julius, you guys are the epitome of conquerors. Sistahs in Conversations book club, you ladies are amazing, and I am grateful for all of your hard work. To my grandmother, Ruth Jonice, you continue to personify strength. To my grandparents in Miami, Nana and Grandpa Moss, I love you guys. I consider myself blessed to have two great stepparents in David and Elainna; thank you guys for all of your love and support. To City of Refuge, Bible Way Christian Center, and Alondra Church of Christ, thank you for being great church homes, both past and present. To the men who labor tirelessly for the will of God, I see you. Your efforts are not in vain and

Acknowledgments

this book is for you guys. Finally, to you, the reader, thank you for taking this journey with me. I love you, and may God bless you!

What are people saying about *The Retreat*?

"*The Retreat* is a realistic and comical look into the hearts of men. Dijorn Moss masterfully dispels the myth that men don't have issues and guides them to a breakthrough."
—Wanda B. Campbell, author of *Illusions*

"*The Retreat* is an interesting, entertaining and intriguing story. I am so glad to read a refreshing story like *The Retreat* literally because of its welcoming change by a man's point of view. You wrote a believable tale using captivating, everyday men."
—Shelia E. Lipsey, author of *My Son's Wife*

"Soul stirring! Finally, a story about men by a man. Dijorn Moss has developed memorable characters facing tough situations whose journeys all lead them to God's truth. He has easily earned his place as one of Christian fiction's best storytellers."
—Rhonda McKnight, author of *Secrets and Lies*

Prologue

No matter how much the congregation of Greater An-ointing Christian Center danced and shouted, when Bishop Dawkins approached the pulpit in his traditional black robe, everyone within the 2,500-seat sanctuary pushed the noise level higher. Standing there, taking the celebration in, it seemed as if there wasn't a pulpit big enough to balance his six-and-a-half-foot frame.

A former college basketball player, Bishop Dawkins leaned in with his left elbow on the pulpit as he held a microphone in his hand. His right hand scratched his white beard as his hazel eyes peered out into the vastness of the crowd. The choir positioned behind Pastor Dawkins took their seats. The musicians to the right of him started to phase out their play.

"It's marvelous that in spite of all that we go through in our lives, we can come together and show God that He is still number one in our lives," Pastor Dawkins said.

The congregation responded with a shower of "Amen's." It was a largely, and frustratingly, feminine chorus. Low male membership was a common problem in most pre-dominantly African American churches. Men found all kinds of excuses for not being present in church on Sunday mornings. Football, baseball, and now even—God forbid—mixed martial arts.

They did not mind if their wives and girlfriends attended church, so long as they did not boast about their male pastors too much. Men are very territorial and competitive by nature; that is why Bishop Dawkins took pride in the fact that, though low, the male membership was still higher at Greater Anointing than at other churches in the area.

His flock was the result of his approach. His teachings were sound, scripturally based, and community focused. He demanded accountability, especially from men. As a middle-aged, single pastor, he was mindful of his interactions with the women in the congregation, avoiding any hint of impropriety that would tar him with the whisper of "womanizer" or "hypocrite."

"As you know, around this time of the year, the men of Greater Anointing get together for our annual Men's Retreat," Pastor Dawkins's raspy voice bellowed.

The men in the congregation started to clap and shout praises to God. The first weekend in October brought forth the rebirth of the sanctified male. With one hand on the razor-thin Bible pages, Bishop Dawkins took a look back at the few men in the choir.

"Our theme for this year is 'Stand Up and Be Accounted For,'" Bishop Dawkins said.

Men stood up, they smiled and clapped. Bishop Dawkins turned back toward the congregation. To his delight, there were men and women who stood up as well to cheer him on.

"Sisters, I need your help. I want you to sign up your husbands, your sons, and your crazy uncles." Bishop Dawkins paused to laugh for a moment and rub his copper, bald head.

"I want them to come and join us this weekend. We will experience a move of God unlike anything we have ever seen, and the men you knew will return on fire for God, ready to take back their homes and their communities."

A joyful ovation punctuated his pitch. And he needed to be pitch-perfect this weekend. As the congregation's approval died down, Bishop Dawkins said a prayer to himself: Father, watch over my brothers. There will be numerous snares that will try to prevent them from coming, but I pray that your angels will protect them and that your perfect will will be done. Amen!

Chapter One

Quincy could not think of a better way to spend a Monday than under a clear October sky, playing a round of golf. After an early lunch with his business partner, Gregg, they both decided to forgo the rest of the day and get eighteen holes in. First, Quincy would need to go home and change out of his power suit into something more casual.

"Tee off is at two o'clock." Gregg pointed at his watch.

"The 405 shouldn't be crowded." Quincy patted his stomach. "That'll give me plenty of time to work off the roasted crab and garlic noodles. I'll be there."

Gregg gave Quincy a fist bump as Quincy walked over to the driver's side of his Range Rover. He met the valet and exchanged a fifty dollar bill for the keys to his SUV.

"Thank you very much, sir," the valet said.

Once in the driver's seat, the noise that defined a busy Southern California day was now neutralized by the sound of contemporary R&B. Quincy worked his way through the surface streets and entered the nearest 405 freeway ramp. Eighty-five miles per hour didn't feel like a moving violation as Quincy maneuvered his way through light traffic.

The time on the touch screen read 12:45 P.M., and still there'd been no word from Karen, his wife. Quincy and Karen would talk frequently throughout the day, but the conversations were trivial and contributed more to their stagnation as a couple than to their actual growth. Their routine was monotonous, but it remained safe and secure. Quincy relied heavily on security, so he attached his Bluetooth ear piece and placed a call.

"Hello?" Karen said.

"What up, babe? I haven't heard from you today. I was calling to see what's up."

"Nothing, I'm just very busy. Quincy, you sound like you're in the car."

"Yeah, Gregg and I grabbed a bite to eat at Crustaceans. I'm leaving."

"It's been a long time since we ate at Crustaceans."

Already Quincy regretted the call. It was as if Karen looked for every opportunity to remind Quincy that he was not up to par in his husband duties.

"Anyway, Gregg and I are heading over to Virginia Country Club to play a round. I'm going to stop by the house first."

"You're headed home?" Karen's voice fractured.

"Yeah, I need to change first."

At first, the silence seemed like an indication that the call had dropped.

"Hello?" Quincy asked.

"I'm here. What about work? What about the Culver City project?"

"That's the beauty of being your own boss: you make your own hours. And the Culver City project is a slam dunk. We close this deal by the end of the week."

Her silence grew more awkward and teetered on sus-picious. Suspicion brought forth his acute hearing.

"Where are you?" Quincy asked.

"I'm at work."

Lie. As an architect, Quincy built his empire around the

principle that the devil is in the details. It could be something as small as the sound of Karen's Swiss clock that echoed throughout her subdued office, or something as big as the sound of their retired neighbor, Daryl, mowing his lawn.

The absence of one sound and the presence of another brought Quincy to the conclusion that his wife was not at work, but at home.

"I'll tell you what, why don't I come pick you up and we have lunch together? I'm still a little hungry for something sweet. Perhaps we could share something on the dessert menu."

"Oh, no no no! You go and play your game. I'll probably go to lunch with Amber."

Karen's certain spike in her voice indicated that she was frantic.

"Humph. Okay, I'll see you later," Quincy said.

"Okay, babe, have a good game," Karen replied.

The call ended. Quincy imploded and the Range Rover hit one hundred miles per hour. This is not happening; Karen is not having an affair. Quincy was certain that he would have to apologize for his overreaction. There were only two reasons why his wife of twenty years, this devout woman of God, would lie to him, her husband: either she was throwing him a surprise birthday party (but Quincy's birthday wasn't until April 28), or she was having an affair.

"Come on, man! Move out of the way!" Quincy's horn signaled for the slow cars to move out of the way. He kept his eyes locked on the rearview to make sure the police were not in sight. It was inevitable that during the forty-minute drive from Beverly Hills to Signal Hill, Quincy would pass a police car or two. He just had to get home.

When Quincy finally did get home, it was empty. Karen's car was not in the garage. No sense in being coy, the bedroom was the place that would tell him all he needed to know about why Karen had been home.

He removed his smoky gray business suit as if he were about to make love to his wife, laid the coat at the foot of the winding staircase, and began his ascent of the stairs to the master bedroom. It was questionable why the sheets on the bed had been changed, why the coconut scent was forceful throughout the room. It all could mean nothing more than just Quincy's mind in overdrive. Karen would never let him hear the end of it if he made his suspicions of her infidelity known. This wasn't a movie. The mirror in the bathroom was not fogged from a recent shower. The closet doors were open and there was no one who lay hidden. He had overreacted, and the best way to shrug off the minor embarrassment was to remember the reason he came home in the first place. Karen would kill him for coming home and tossing his clothes on the bed, but he was pressed for time.

Quincy walked into the closet in their bedroom. He loved clothes and shoes as much as Karen did. He pulled his golf bag out of the closet, and several white golf balls fell out and rolled over to Karen's lavender purse. Karen had a plethora of purses in every color, shape, and size. Quincy put the golf balls back in his bag. He went to set Karen's purse back on the wooden shelf next to her dresses when a cell phone fell out. Quincy had never seen this cell phone before. His suspicions had returned. He flipped open the pink phone and discovered that the phone was on silent mode with the "new text message" symbol blinking on and off. He viewed the message from a nickname A-MOG:

> Where are you? I've been trying to contact you. I left my cuff link by the bed. By the way, at Bible Study last week you looked so hot in that pink miniskirt, it was hard for me to concentrate.
>
> –A-MOG

Pink skirt! Cuff links by the bed? This had to be a joke. Quincy walked over to his bed and looked underneath their California king–sized platform bed. He did not see anything on Karen's side, so he walked around to his side, and there on the floor was a gold cuff link. Though everything started to add up, it still did not make sense. Quincy could not remember Karen wearing a miniskirt in years, and when he'd left for work this morning, she was dressed in her conservative business suit. The coconut scent, the mysterious cell phone, everything was pointing to one thing: Karen was having an affair, and he suspected that it had to be someone from the church.

To appease Karen, Quincy would occasionally make an appearance at Greater Anointing. He did not attend last Sunday, and, as far as remembering what Karen had on, Quincy could not remember what he had for breakfast. He checked her inbox to find more messages from A-MOG. This one was dated two weeks prior:

Last night was off the chain. I know you couldn't spend the night, but it was still good to see you. The sheets still carry your scent. See you Sunday.

–A-MOG

Quincy sat down in disbelief. He stared at the wall, confused. Karen was having an affair. He scrolled through the text messages, and anger arose as he discovered that Karen was involved in an affair with someone from the church.

I know sex in the car was not comfortable, but you looked so hot last night during choir rehearsal that I had to pull the car over and have you right then and there.

–A-MOG

***

Karen was not an unattractive woman. But this A-MOG guy talked about her like she was Beyoncé or Vivica Fox or someone! It disgusted Quincy that a so-called man of God could leave her such perverse messages. Quincy dialed the phone number associated with the text message and got an answer.

"What up, ma? Did you find the cuff link?" a male voice asked.

"Ma can't come to the phone right now, but pa is available," Quincy replied, struck by the youthfulness in the guy's voice. He was also now aware that the intense scent of coconut was to cover up, and not to freshen up, their bedroom.

"Ma?" The man let out an expletive word before he hung up.

Quincy did not even bother to call back. He didn't want to get answers from this individual. He wanted answers from his wife, so he would have to go to the source. Quincy could not wrap his head around the fact that his wife and her lover had been here as early as today. In his home, in his bed. This was all playing out like a bad movie.

Quincy ignored the call from his business partner, who kept trying to get in contact with him. Karen had played him and made herself seem like the perfect wife. If there was one thing Quincy did not appreciate, it was being made a fool; so now it was time for him to act a fool.

His brain ran through numerous scenarios. If he were a woman, he would set all of Karen's clothes on fire like in the movie Waiting to Exhale. Better yet, he would do what Mary Woodson did to Al Green and throw some hot grits at her, or just pull a Mrs. Lionel Richie on her tail and administer a beat down. Worst yet, he would pull a Bobbitt. But he was not a woman.

He was Quincy Page, and Quincy Page was too cool to lose control. So the game was definitely on, but it had nothing to do with a golf ball. Quincy slid both the cell phone and the cuff link into his pocket, and he stormed out of his closet and house with his sights set on his wife's job.

With a 9 iron in his hands, Quincy parted through Karen's coworkers like the Red Sea, ignoring the greetings and the chatter. He started to shake as he got close to Karen's office. He wanted to kick down the door, but settled for a more civilized approach, and knocked.

"Yes," Karen said from inside her office.

Quincy opened the door and slammed it shut behind him.

"What's wrong with you?" Karen stood up and took off her glasses.

Quincy reached into his pocket and pulled out the cell phone. The look of shock on his wife's face gave him all the confirmation he needed. Quincy threw it at Karen. She ducked, and the phone just missed her head as it ricocheted off of her glass window.

He then pulled out the cuff link and chucked it toward Karen; the cuff link landed square on Karen's shoulder.

"Baby, I can explain," Karen said.

"You had him in my house, Karen! My house! You've been creeping on me behind my back."

Quincy watched her whole being crumble, and he knew she could not even search the rubble to find an explanation that would suffice. For once, Quincy needed her to find an explanation. He needed her to say something that would make sense.

He needed her to win. Instead, what he found was a diminutive will that could not even go on to fight.

"I've forwarded the messages to my phone. Tomorrow I'm going to see a lawyer," he told her.

"Baby, we just need to talk. Let's not let our emotions get the better of us," Karen said with tears in her eyes.

"I left my emotions at home. Now all I have is my resolve to send you to Wal-Mart to shop from here on out."

"I'm so sorry." Karen's voice quivered.

"You know I wasn't particularly happy in this marriage. I haven't been happy for a long time, but I know that I promised to be faithful and loyal to you. I've kept my vows despite countless opportunities to break them." Quincy took a moment to catch his breath and grip his 9 iron.

"What are you going to do with that?" Karen looked at the golf club her husband gripped in his hand.

"I haven't decided. Is he someone I know?"

Karen's silence admitted her guilt.

"He is, isn't he? It has to be someone from that church." This time, Karen's tears admitted her guilt. "Who is it?"

"Listen, baby, we can work this out."

The levees that held back Quincy's anger broke. He swung the golf club down on her glass table like an axe, and shattered a piece of glass.

"Have you lost your mind?" Karen yelled.

"Who is it?" Quincy voice had a demonic rage to it.

He turned toward her picture display case. He hated to have to destroy their wedding pictures. Quincy looked real good in his black tux with the buttercream-colored tie, but that picture represented the sham that had become his life, so it had to go. With one swing, he started to destroy the pictures on Karen's shelf, including the high school graduation picture of their daughter, Sasha, who was now a student at UC Berkeley.

He knew he would regret his actions, but he was too caught

up in the sounds of broken glass and Karen's screams. The two entities sounded like thunder. Two men wearing navy blue blazers entered the office.

"Sir, you have to leave right now!" one security guard said while pointing toward the door.

"What you going to do with your flashlight, your clip-on tie, and a jacket that's two sizes too small?" Quincy now raised his bent 9 iron like a samurai sword.

The second security guard emerged from behind the first. He was almost a foot taller than the other security guard.

"I guess you choose to do this the hard way," the second security guard stated.

With that said, both security guards rushed Quincy before he could get a good swing, and wrestled him to the ground. They lifted Quincy off the ground, and he kicked his feet up to try to get loose.

"Get your hands off me!" Quincy yelled, but to no avail. The men escorted him out and he endured the dropped jaws of his wife's coworkers.

The elevator doors opened, and then sealed in Quincy and the two behemoth security guards.

The compacted space and elevator music did nothing to loosen the guards' grips around Quincy's arms. This would be the part in the movie when the hero disables the guards and walks out of the elevator, with the guards left unconscious on the floor. This would not be the case for Quincy, because these guys were pretty strong.

The elevator reached the bottom floor and the doors slid opened. The two men carried Quincy out on the tips of his toes.

"We could let you go if you were going to go in peace," one of the security guards said.

"No, I still want to do things the hard way," Quincy replied.

"Suit yourself," the security guard said.

There was light foot traffic in the lobby, and Quincy was too furious to be embarrassed. If he got a second crack at Karen, he would cause more damage and the real police would be escorting him out. The guards released their hold from Quincy as soon as they passed through the front sliding doors. The sky was still beautiful, but Quincy's soul was cloudy. He'd heard about out-of-body experiences. Up until this point, he viewed the notion as a load of crap. Quincy had to come to grips with the fact that he just might be having an out-of-body experience. Karen? Karen having an affair?

Quincy could not begin to fathom that his wife of twenty years was capable of such actions, capable of being unfaithful. Quincy had had his share of perspective rendezvous that he reneged on at the last moment for the sake of his marriage. He thanked God for the fact that he had not engaged in infidelity. Now that very same God had betrayed him. There was only one thing Quincy could do: call up a friend and borrow a G-5 jet. He needed to leave town.

Chapter Two

Chauncey pulled his champagne-colored Cadillac into the parking lot behind the baseball field. His New International Bible, just a touch lighter than his chestnut skin, seemed like an extension of himself. As he exited the car, Chauncey was greeted by a gust of wind that pushed the autumn leaves into his path. After locking the door, he turned and started his walk along the cemented path of the park.

Chauncey passed by an empty playground. He could remember a time when this playground was full of children at play. That was another time. In the distance Chauncey could make out a group of thugs, petty neighborhood gang-bangers, hanging out under a tree, blasting god-awful rap music.

They, he surmised, were the reason there were no longer children at this park. Drinking, smoking, cussing, and carrying on. Well, that stops now. Chauncey was mighty and strong in the Lord. He was going to take back the park by reclaiming some lost souls. As he continued down the path, he passed a derelict water fountain. It stood in the middle of the park between the soccer field and the basketball courts.

In the old days, kids would take a break from shooting hoops or kicking around the ball, and gather here. Now it just stood idle. The fountain had a two-step platform. Chauncey walked over and positioned himself on the second step. He opened his Bible. The wind blew the pages over, but the

Bible was more for the look and less for the actual message. Chauncey knew the passage by heart, knew every line and the cadence it deserved.

"Oh yes, Jesus! Thank you, Jesus! Lord, you declare in your Word that you're the way, the truth and the light. Those who believe in you shall not perish, but have everlasting life. I pray that everyone under the sound of my voice will choose life today," Chauncey prayed.

Chauncey's voice must have carried over the sound of their music; the thugs underneath the tree were now eyeing him.

"Those who practice sin shall not inherit the kingdom of heaven. You have to be born again." As he said this, Chauncey felt his voice crack. It was their attention that he wanted as he tried to project his message over the din of their music. "I'm that voice that cries in the wilderness, 'Make it straight!'"

"Make it straight with the Lord," a homeless man shouted from behind him.

Chauncey turned around. The man had salt-and-pepper dreads that caked his shoulders and reached down his dirty army jacket. He was pushing a shopping cart filled with bags of cans and plastic bottles. As he approached the fountain he continued to speak, but it was low and slow and sounded like gibberish. The smell of caked-on liquor was oppressive, sweet and sour at the same time. It stung Chauncey's nose.

Chauncey did not have time for this deranged man. So he broke from the fountain, walking in the direction of the thugs under the tree. Halfway there, he spied a young black girl who lay on top of a blanket. She wore sunglasses and a tie-dyed bikini top with white shorts. Chauncey maneuvered around her to step in her shade, and the girl immediately used her hand as a visor.

"Hello," she said.

"Hello, God bless you. I saw you from over at the fountain," he replied. "Enjoying this beautiful weather?"

"Yeah, I'm supposed to be studying." She pointed to a casually opened philosophy textbook tattooed with garish highlighter and random notes.

"I would like to talk with you about making Jesus your Lord and Savior."

"No, thank you," she said, curtly picking up the textbook.

Fair enough. Chauncey did not feel any desire to press the issue. He wasn't here to witness to some college student. The group of thugs who hung out under the tree needed his attention more than some blasé undergraduate.

"Yea, though I walk through the valley of the shadow of death I will fear no evil," Chauncey muttered under his breath as he arrived at the group and broke the circle the gang had formed.

The group started to reposition themselves to size up Chauncey. One guy was as big as the tree. Shirtless, he showed off his coil skin and stretch marks. With a pot belly, his physique was not desirable. Chauncey set his sights on the young man who appeared to be the leader, since he was the only one who did not move.

"Could you turn it down?" Chauncey asked.

"What?" the leader said.

"I said could you turn it—"

"Speak up! I don't like all that mumbling," the leader said.

The leader who commanded this motley pile of thugs looked to be no more than eighteen. His body was like a memorial: tattoos of "rest in peace" followed by the names of what Chauncey assumed were his fallen comrades covered most of his golden skin.

"I just want you to know that you should be ashamed of yourselves for doing the devil's work," Chauncey said.

His comment caused a nod from the leader, at which point one of the other thugs reached over and turned the music off.

"Say that again, old man?" the leader urged, spitting out the last two words.

"I said you're doing the devil's work and you need to repent. I have the Lord on my side and I refuse to be intimidated by you thugs."

Chauncey felt an object press against his temple. He held on to a fool's hope that it was not a gun until he turned ever so slightly and caught a glimpse of the muzzle.

At that moment, Chauncey's raven-like eyes burst out of his skull.

"Oh, Jesus, Jesus, Jesus!" Chauncey's facade crumbled as he cried out the words.

"You better get up out of here with that church crap before I have the homie bust a cap in you," the leader warned.

Chauncey backed away from the group and started to walk as fast as his heart beat. Even the wind terrified him, as if at any moment he would be shot in the back. These gang members are ruthless cowards, Chauncey thought, not noting the irony.

As he got back into his car, Chauncey peered out of his front window. In the distance he could see the gangsters laughing at him.

He was jolted back to attention by his cell phone vibrating in his coat pocket. The caller ID showed that it was his sister, Nicole. She lived in Sunnyvale, a small city in Northern California. It was about an hour away from Monterey, where the Men's Retreat would be held this weekend. Chauncey planned to get to the Retreat on Thursday evening, a day before the official start.

He wanted to help set up and spend some quality time

with his pastor and some of the brethren. Of course, there was also a professional matter that Chauncey needed to secure. Pastor Dawkins had been reviewing applications for the minister's class. Chauncey's application was among them. When Chauncey was twelve, a prophet had spoken about him becoming a preacher, and how yokes would be broken by his testimony. Chauncey believed that his time had come to become a minster, and being at the Retreat would show Pastor Dawkins his commitment.

"Sis, thank God you called. I just wanted to tell you that I love you," Chauncey said.

"Did you forget that you're supposed to visit your brother today?" Nicole asked.

"No hello . . . just right into criticism. Sister, you would've made a great Sadducee, because you love to judge people," Chauncey said.

"So now you think you're Jesus?" Nicole snapped back.

Whatever excitement Chauncey felt to talk to his baby sister had left by the time she started talking. He had just escaped a life-or-death situation, and his sister's accusatory attitude was not the response he needed or wanted.

"Oh no, I'm supposed to see him, I just had something more important to take care of," Chauncey said.

"Just get over here. You know how bad traffic is on the 405 around this time," Nicole said.

Chauncey hung up the phone as he sped away. He wondered how in the world he would ever truly be able to do God's will when his family was in constant need of his help.

Chapter Three

"Not the response that I expected." Melvin, Jamal's boss, adjusted his platinum Day-Date Rolex.

Jamal began to loosen his tie and unfastened his top button. "I am happy. I'm ecstatic. This is what I want."

"I remember when you sat in that chair five years ago, nervous and scared. It was like your entire future rested on you getting this job. But day in and day out I've seen you hustle your butt off to get results."

Jamal had worked for that promotion every day for the past four years. To become a senior marketing exec for Pinnacle Sportswear was his goal. He was sick and tired of living from dime to dollar. Jamal's family raised him on the idea that if a person wanted something, he had to be willing to work harder than the next man to get it. That meant that when everyone else was asleep, he needed to be at work.

So he made a solemn promise to work while everyone else was at the water cooler, engaged in gossip. Jamal would work while his coworkers complained about their salaries. He never lost sight of his goal and purpose. With his faith in God, he now had everything he wanted career-wise, but his mind could not allow him to savor his victory.

Jamal thought about his son, Jamir, and how every day Jamir resembled him less and less. His life was at a crossroads, and with so many life-changing decisions at his feet, Jamal turned to the only one who knew what the best course of action was for his life.

"Father, open my eyes so that I might see the wonderful plan you have for me. I don't want to be outside your will, and I pray that the results today will bring you honor and glory. In Jesus' name I pray, Amen." Jamal prayed.

"If I had your wisdom at my age, I would be a billionaire by now. But understand we are not going to pay you this salary for a nine-to-five, forty-hour workweek. We are going to need you to be a machine. Can you live with that?" Melvin asked.

Jamal locked into his problem: a $100,000 salary in exchange for time with his most precious resource, his son Jamir.

"Can you?" Melvin asked.

"I know I can, I just need a minute to get my affairs in order."

Melvin pulled the cigar out of his mouth. "I'll tell you what, take until next week to think about it, and on Monday I expect your answer."

"Thank you, Mr. White."

This weekend was the Men's Retreat, and Jamal would have a lot to think and pray about. He walked back to his cubical, where he had a decent view of the parking lot. He also had a view of his car: a white Honda Civic with a dented front bumper. This is where he was. Mr. White's offer was where he could be.

"How did it go?" Mylessa asked, interrupting Jamal's thoughts.

Mylessa was a five-foot-six-inch-tall, chocolate-complexioned beauty with a curvaceous frame. She commanded the attention of every man in the office, including Jamal.

"It went great. He offered it to me." Jamal leaned back in his chair.

Mylessa wore a smoky gray skirt that was sprayed to her hips. Her complete body of work was punctuated by the sound of her four-inch stilettos. "Well, that's great. So you're going to celebrate, right?" Mylessa tossed some of her shoulder-length hair behind her shoulder.

Jamal was certain that it was a weave, but with the advancements in hair technology, it was becoming more and more difficult to differentiate real hair from a weave; such was the case for Mylessa.

"I might do something, I don't know yet," Jamal said.

"Well, a couple of us from work are heading over to Club Infusion tonight, and I would love to see you there." Mylessa finished her pitch with a seductive licking of her lips, as her eyes scanned Jamal from head to toe. Jamal was feeling her. She was beautiful, intelligent, and had a great body. Jamal was certain that by the end of the night, they could be at his place eating cheesecake while listening to Sade, right before they headed to the bedroom and made some music of their own. The thought alone awoke some urges within Jamal.

"I would love to, but I'll have to pass," Jamal declined.

Mylessa slumped down from his news. "Well that's too bad. Maybe we could get together for a drink one day?"

"I'm sorry, but I don't drink."

"Oh, so you're just a good little church boy."

"I go to church, but I wouldn't necessarily say I'm good."

"You're better than most men," Mylessa said as she looked back to a group of guys who had been eyeing her and chuckling ever since she'd walked over to Jamal's cubicle. "Some other time."

"Have fun tonight and be safe," Jamal said as he returned to his computer. But he was unable to shake thoughts of the curvaceous Mylessa.

Terry, Jamal's coworker, walked past Mylessa and stared at her from behind. Jamal saw Terry coming and decided to turn on his iPod with Marvin Sapp playing.

"What's up, pimpin?" Terry asked.

"Nothing, just trying to get work done," Jamal said while typing on his computer.

"So what did big-booty Mylessa want?"

"She invited me to Club Infusion." Jamal shrugged.

"You're going to go, right?" Terry leaned in.

"Naw, I have plans."

"What plans could you possibly have that beat getting the hottest girl in the office to make you grits butt-naked?"

Therein lay the reason Jamal did not like to interact with Terry. Thirty years old and Terry was still mistaking the office for a school playground. Jamal ignored him, and eventually Terry left. The day was almost over, but it was only Monday and the week was still young. Jamal felt the vibration from his cell phone, and a familiar number appeared. Jamal pressed talk to answer the phone, but held it down by his black slacks until he made it to the lounge, which was across the way.

"What's up?" Jamal asked.

"The results came in," Chantel said.

Jamal's heart nearly jumped out of his chest. He knew the results would be in today, but he was not sure if that was good news or bad.

"I'm on my way." Jamal hung up the phone. Two pieces of news in one day.

Jamal left the lounge and went back to his desk to shut down his computer and grab his black messenger bag. He made his way toward the elevator and passed by his coworker, Christal.

"You leaving early?" Christal asked with her mouth open.

Christal reminded Jamal of Serena Williams. She had both Serena's facial features and curves. Even though Jamal found her attractive, she spent way too much time in the club, and while at work, she made gossiping her full-time job.

"Yeah, I got to take care of something," Jamal replied.

"But the sun is still out." Christal pointed toward the window, where a gorgeous blue sky awaited Jamal.

"Oh, so you're trying to shoot?" Jamal asked.

"No, I'm not trying to clown you. I'm just saying that I hardly see you leave when the sun is still out."

"Have a good evening." Jamal turned away from Christal and headed toward the door.

From the elevator, Jamal made his way to the parking lot. Jamal opened his car door and tossed his messenger bag in the passenger seat. He put the key in the ignition and tried to start the car. The engine sounded like a record being scratched.

"Come on, don't do this now. Please, God!" Jamal pleaded.

Jamal tried to turn his car on several more times, but he could not get the engine to start. He assumed that the battery had died and he would need a jump. For now, the most important results in his life were on hold.

Chauncey knew he was not supposed to find pleasure in his brother Henry's death. Well, technically, his brother was not dead yet.

But the air was thick with the putrid smell of Henry's frail body as Chauncey pushed open the hospital room door. Chauncey had forewarned his brother that the path he chose in life would eventually lead to destruction. Henry did not heed his older brother's advice, and indulged in sex and drugs until he alienated everything and everyone around him; all except for sin.

Now Chauncey stood over his brother a proud champion of the faith, with no trace of the fear he'd displayed in the park. Whenever Chauncey would visit his brother, he would bring his blue leather-bound King James Version Bible. This was the Bible out of which he had prophesized to Henry numerous times that the wage of sin was death. With only a thin layer of auburn skin over Henry's bones, it was clear that sin would complete its work.

Chauncey finally acknowledged his baby sister, Nicole, sitting across the hospital bed from him. The darkest one of the siblings, Nicole's mocha complexion made her the desire of all the boys in Chauncey's neighborhood. She did, however, have the signature McClendon lips, which seemed to be permanently in pout mode. At this moment, the pout almost seemed like a grimace. Chauncey turned his back to his brother. The Bible was so thick that it required him to hold it with both hands. He held the Bible midway toward his chest.

"I'm having trouble keeping food down. All I feel is pain all the time," Henry said before he swallowed hard.

"That's because you don't know that by His stripes you are healed," Chauncey said.

"Chauncey," Nicole pleaded from the other side of the bed. She shook her head as a sign for Chauncey not to get on his soapbox. Chauncey did not know how long he could stay in this room without being able to speak his mind.

"The doctors ain't saying nothing either, and when that happens that's not good. I'm having visions that in the end I'm alone in this hospital bed with the cancer and my demons," Henry said, trying to hold back tears.

Nicole got up and rubbed her frail brother's bald head,

bending to give him some water in a beige cup with a straw. Chauncey could see Henry's throat take in the water.

"They aren't the ones who have the final say. God is the author and finisher of your faith," Nicole said with a forced smile that highlighted her full ruby lips.

"Nicole, don't give him no half-truths. God is the author and the finisher of his faith. But you have to have faith first." Chauncey's eyebrows arched.

Nicole used her dark brown eyes to cut into Chauncey's chest. His little sister had a mean side, but this was about souls. For the sake of the Gospel, he could not be moved on what was the truth.

"Chauncey, could I talk to you outside for a moment?" Nicole stood up and headed toward the door.

Chauncey extended his hand like an usher and followed her outside.

"Would it kill you to come down from your mountaintop and show your brother a little compassion?" Nicole asked.

"What do you want me to do, lie to him? You and I both know that if he ain't saved, then none of the Bible's promises apply to him."

"You're not God, so you can't judge him. God sees his heart and Henry knows better," Nicole said.

"You Baptists are nuttier than fruitcakes. I don't know what they teach at your church, but at my church we teach that unless you are born again, you will not see the kingdom of heaven."

Nicole put both of her hands up in a choking motion and grunted in disgust. "You act so high and mighty!"

"High? He stole from both of us to get high! You act like

he didn't steal from you or mess up your credit. I can't get a Macy's credit card because my brother got high. All I ever wanted from him was for him to get his life straight with the Lord. Even now, in the midst of his sin and illness, he lies up there unrepentant and wanting someone to pity him," Chauncey said with frustration.

"Those things we can get back. We have one brother and right now he's scared, and we're the only family he's got." Nicole pointed toward Henry's room.

"I've sat in AA meetings and therapy sessions just to hear my brother use me as a scapegoat for why he couldn't get clean. I'm tired of it and I don't have time." Chauncey looked at his watch.

"Where you got to go now?" Nicole asked.

"The Men's Retreat is Thursday; I got a couple of things before then to take care of."

Nicole let out a sarcastic laugh, and with her hands on her hips, she started to tap her black leather flats on the hospital's mint checkered floor.

"Are you serious? It's Monday, bighead! You have all week. What's more important? Being a good deacon or being there for your brother when he needs you the most?" Nicole asked.

Chauncey did not even bother to dignify Nicole's question with an answer. He brushed by her and went back into the room. Henry's eyes were full with tears, and Chauncey was certain that he had caught most of the conversation.

Chauncey placed his hands over his brother's head. His brother closed his eyes as a sign of pleasure. "Father, we ask that you touch my brother's body. In the name of Jesus that you heal him. I ask in the matchless name of Jesus, Amen." Chauncey turned and headed toward the door.

"Don't leave," Henry pleaded.

"I've got to go. I've got some important matters to attend to, but you don't need me; you need the Lord."

"Please," Henry said with his eyes full of tears.

Chauncey should have been moved by this pathetic display, but he wasn't. All he could think of was how Henry was the most stubborn person on the planet. Instead of making it right with the Lord, he preferred to call on his brother to save him. But even Chauncey could not save his brother. Chauncey walked past Nicole, who was still at the door, and did not bother to say a word.

"Bye, bighead," Nicole shouted.

The nickname Nicole used to call Chauncey when they were kids still conveyed a sense of love and affection.

Chauncey did not break his stride as he continued to walk, and held up his hand as a sign that he had heard his younger sibling. He was always treated as the enemy. All Chauncey ever tried to do for his brother and sister was equip them with a spiritual foundation. As far as he was concerned, both his sister and his brother might end up in hell.

Chapter Four

In school, Chantel had been fascinated with Japanese culture. She welcomed the rumors that she was half black, half Asian. Her tight lids gave weight to the rumors. So the fact that the living room of her two-bedroom apartment was decked out in Japanese decor was not a shock to Jamal.

The answer to a two-year mystery lay in a manila envelope that sat on a Japanese-inspired table. Every day doubt grew while certainty regressed. Truth was abstract, and while Jamal could coach himself into believing that the results did not matter, deep down inside he knew that the result made a world of difference.

Chantel placed her petite hand on top of Jamal's stony hand. When she smiled, her cheeks looked like she had swallowed golf balls. Jamal considered it an honor to even be in her presence. Timing and guilt had so much to do with why they were not together; it had everything to do with where they were now.

She broke the seal of the envelope and removed the contents from inside. She held her breath as her almond eyes scanned the document. Chantel took in a deep breath and did not exhale as she handed the document over to Jamal. It was confirmed. The mystery had been solved, and like many mysteries, the truth left Jamal and Chantel more confused than they were before. He was not sure if ignorance was bliss, but what he was sure of was that his world would never be the same.

"Daddy." Jamir ran from his room and sat on Jamal's lap.

Jamal and Jamir both had bronze skin. They both had jet-black hair. Jamir was everything that Jamal desired in a son, and for Jamir he would give the world. But no matter what Jamal would sacrifice for two-year-old Jamir, he would never be his son.

"High five!" Jamal stuck his hand out.

Jamir smacked his hand with glee.

"Here you go." Jamal gave Jamir some building blocks from a playpen near the TV.

He sat Jamir down on the carpet. Jamal sat down behind Jamir and pointed to the block he wanted him to pick up. Jamir reached for a building block and played with it. Jamal placed a kiss on top of Jamir's head. While Jamir's attention was on the building blocks, Jamal turned his sights toward Chantel, and followed her into the kitchen. She'd retreated to the kitchen to weep. With her back turned, Jamal approached her and wrapped his arms round her waist. Chantel turned around and embraced him. Her damp face pressed against Jamal's beard.

"How could this happen?" Jamal whispered.

"I don't know," Chantel whimpered.

Jamal broke away from Chantel, but he maintained his reserved tone. "It doesn't make sense. You were six weeks pregnant when Clay died, and you said that you two had stopped sleeping with each other two months prior."

"That's because he liked to sleep with any little skank who winked at him. I didn't want to risk catching something."

"Meanwhile, you and I continued to have sex, so you must have a messed-up calendar."

"I didn't, I'm sure of it." Chantel diverted her eyes.

If Chantel was sure, then Jamal was certain that he had been kept out of the loop. Was it possible that Clay was the father? Yes, but the improbability of that scenario was what had Jamal perplexed. For two years, he'd allowed the death of Clay and the life of Jamir to blind him from seeking the truth. For two years, Jamir's physical features favored his mother more, and Jamal could barely find anything that resembled him. Now, with so much at stake, he had to probe and get to the core of the issue. Jamal could not go into the next phase of his life with doubt.

"Let me ask you something." Jamal paused to see Chantel's eyes lock in with his. "You knew, didn't you?"

Jamal watched Chantel's eyes and saw that she did not respond in outrage, but stood there frozen, as if she was searching for a lie to tell but had drawn a blank.

"You did, didn't you?" Her silence took the wind out of Jamal as he sat down on the chair next to the kitchen counter.

"I knew that more than likely you were not the father. That was wrong and I'd understand if you didn't want to have anything to do with me or my son. But everything I did, whether foul or not, I did for my son." Chantel pointed at Jamir, who was still in the next room, playing.

"I didn't want my son to grow up hearing about his father being killed in the streets. I would rather have his father be a hardworking man of God. That's the example I wanted for Jamir."

Chantel was not a churchgoer, but she always respected Jamal and his faith. Despite her deception, her reasoning was well placed.

"I'm sorry; I didn't want to hurt you. I just hoped that maybe things would work out." In a faint voice, she added, "Why is this happening?"

Jamal clenched Chantel closer. His heart did not even register the fact that she had deceived him. He knew that deep down Chantel never wanted to hurt him. She wanted the best for her son, and because of her mistakes, Chantel did not feel worthy of love. Jamal felt that she was worthy of his love and redemption. He hoped he could squeeze all of the sorrow out of her and replace it with the love that he had for her.

It was a love too strong to ignore, but not strong enough to trump principle. There was a shortage of good women in the hood. The same could be said for men, but Jamal was certain that the woman whose arms were firmly wrapped around his shoulders was one of a kind. Jamal broke away from her grip and reached into his front jeans pocket. He removed a white envelope.

"This is for Jamir's day care." Jamal extended the envelope to Chantel.

"I can't accept this." Chantel pushed the envelope against Jamal's chest.

Jamal did not even attempt to put the envelope back in her hands; he just laid the envelope on the white kitchen counter.

"I still want to be in Jamir's life, and if Clay were here, I know he would want the same."

Clay had been Jamal's best friend, and the test results showed that Clay was probably Jamir's father. He wished Clay were here, even if that meant things between him and Chantel would be different. The test results brought forth another frustrating matter. Jamal and Chantel would have to have a candid talk with Clay's parents and let them know the truth.

"I can't ask you to take on a responsibility that's not yours," Chantel said with her hands on her hips.

"Look, Momma!" Jamir said from the living room.

Both Jamal and Chantel turned to see that Jamir had started to put together a tower.

"That's great, baby." Chantel wiped more tears from her eyes.

Jamal now knew that part of his best friend lived on through his son. Maybe in Jamir, Jamal would get a second chance to right a wrong.

Sometimes God's opportunities for redemption came in the most unique packages.

"You want some coffee?" Chantel asked.

"Sure," Jamal accepted.

Chantel's eyes were edged with tears. She put a teapot on the stove, then went into the cabinet next to her refrigerator and produced two fire engine red cups. Moments later she handed Jamal a cup with the steam evaporating like a snake.

"There's something else," Jamal said after he took a sip.

Chantel started to wipe down the counter to appear busy. She looked up to let Jamal know that he had her full attention.

"They offered me the promotion."

Chantel gave Jamal a look like her world had just spun off of its axis. "Well that's great, isn't it?"

"I don't know. It would mean that I wouldn't be able to spend much time with Jamir."

"Don't throw your future away," Chantel said as she looked at Jamir.

Jamal gazed at her profile. Her hair was in a ponytail with bangs like curly fries.

"You look—" Jamal started.

"I know." Chantel shot Jamal a smile.

Chantel put her palm underneath her chin as her eyes rotated up and down at Jamal. He recognized that smile as utter content, but he could not find anything that she would be content about in this moment.

"What?" Jamal asked.

"Look at you, all grown up. I'm proud of the man you've become," Chantel stated.

"You act like I was a player or something," Jamal said with a smile.

"You were a player. You and Clay used to run around school thinking y'all were some pimps."

"You got with Clay," Jamal reminded her.

"That's because he had better game than you." Chantel followed her comment with a laugh.

Jamal put his hands over his heart, as if he were going into cardiac arrest. "I didn't want you anyway, chickenhead," Jamal said.

"Oh, you know you did." Chantel stood up and walked over to Jamir.

Jamal followed Chantel to the floor where the two sandwiched Jamir.

"Here!" Jamir handed Chantel a building block.

Chantel played with the block in her hands before she handed it back to Jamir.

"So Friday is the big day? Isn't it the Retreat?" Chantel did not divert her eyes from Jamir.

"Yeah, so I need to make sure I go see my father this week before I go."

"Humph! Is he going?" Chantel grunted.

Chantel and Otis, Jamal's father, did not get along. Otis saw Chantel as a complete waste of Jamal's time and he made sure to treat her with as little respect as possible. While Chantel remained respectful, she made it abundantly clear that she did not like Jamal's father either.

"I don't know. To tell you the truth, I haven't seen him in a while now." Jamal checked his phone for any missed messages.

"Well, don't let that stop you from getting what you need to get this weekend," Chantel said.

"Oh, for sure." Jamal put his phone away.

Jamal did not know what to make of today. He wished it were that simple that he could go from loving a child like a son, to that child feeling foreign to him in a matter of moments. He hoped that this weekend's retreat could provide him with some much-needed answers.

Chapter Five

The ice in Quincy's glass melted with the warmth of the Glenfarclas single malt, slowly dissolving into an oval shape. The coffee brown ballpoint pen matched the color of his complexion and stood suspended between his recently and expertly manicured fingers. It was the same pen he'd used over the years to close multiple deals that made him and his business partner embarrassingly rich. This pen, he thought reflectively, this pen. It had paid for itself and would keep on paying.

This pen would also come in handy when Quincy began the divorce process on Thursday when he returned home. For the last two days he had indulged in the aphrodisiac that only Sin City could provide. For two decades he had regulated his trips to Las Vegas. A little gambling and a lot of booze. But since Karen was not going to honor her marriage vows, this time neither was Quincy.

Of course it was not as easy for Quincy to disregard ethics. He had been faithful to a wife for twenty years. Quincy was not an avid churchgoer, but he did believe in God and he did see a simple prayer go a long way. Even though he used Karen's affair to justify his actions, Quincy's principles vexed him. His train of thought was derailed by a knock on the door.

"It's open," Quincy called out, gently placing the pen back on the stand next to his drink.

Candy walked in with a silver dress that hugged her curvaceous body. The springs in the hotel room door slid the door closed quietly behind her. As she approached, Quincy casually leaned forward and flipped the chrome top off of the ice bucket.

With acrobatic ease, he used the tongs to gently place a couple of cubes into his glass, all the while making a drink for her. Some said the ice diluted the flavor. Well, single malts were his drug of choice, and he bought it, so he was going to do what he wanted.

"What's the occasion?" Candy asked.

"We're celebrating." Quincy handed Candy a drink.

"If there's one thing I love to do, it's celebrate," Candy replied.

Quincy squinted and exhaled lightly as the warm liquid spread across his palate. "You're looking at the man who develops new lavish condos in Culver City. Did I mention that I'm also back on the market?" Quincy flashed a LeBron-sized smile.

"How come you're not celebrating with the Mrs.?" Candy nodded toward Quincy's ring finger.

Why did she have to call his attention to his wedding band? Quincy was not in the wrong. Karen cheated first, and as a result, it was only fair that he got a little something on the side.

"That's not something that I care to talk about." Quincy removed his wedding band and placed it on the nightstand next to his bed.

"That's fine; we don't have to talk about anything that you don't want to talk about. Okay, baby?"

Quincy loved the sound of her voice. He took Candy by the hand and spun her around, almost spilling her drink. He placed her honey blond hair on one side of her neck, as he leaned forward to kiss her shoulder. Both gazed out of his Wynn Hotel Fairway apartment. He loved the seclusion that the room offered.

There were no views of the luminous Mirage Hotel or the kiddy Treasure Island. This room offered a view of the Las Vegas desert at night and of the golf course. He just might take her out on the balcony and have his way with her on the outdoor dining table. How could a woman not be impressed with a man who could provide her with such an awe-inspiring view? Why wasn't this life enough for Karen?

"My wife and I are going through a divorce," Quincy muttered in Candy's ear.

Candy turned around and pulled back from him a bit. "You seem very happy for a man who is about to split from his wife."

Quincy tenderly broke her grasp, took a quick pull from his glass, and walked deliberately back to the wet bar to pour himself another drink. Quincy took a sip, regaining his composure, as he surveyed her from across the room. "Why shouldn't I be? There is nothing that she can use to keep me."

"Money! Money always talks." Candy took another sip of her drink.

Money was not the issue. Karen was unfaithful and she would not be entitled to a dime. Of course, admitting the truth surrounding his pending divorce to her would be a massive blow to his pride.

"It's only money. There's a ton of it out there that I can make and I have made. I couldn't care less about the house. Too many bad memories."

"I hope she is taking it as well as you."

"What's that suppose to mean?"

Candy crossed the room deliberately. She lifted the glass effortlessly out of Quincy's hand and took a hard swallow before setting the half-empty glass on top of the TV.

"I deal with married men all the time. Most of them love their wives very much, but they desire something different every now and then. I can't imagine being married for as long as you have and it being easy for me to walk away," Candy surmised.

An image of Karen in her two-piece turquoise bathing suit popped into Quincy's head. The image came from a trip to Jamaica two years ago. Karen had a flat stomach with caramel skin and brown hair with blond highlights in it. Most men would die to be with a woman like that. But when he thought of her it was in abstract terms, like she was a house he had paid to renovate.

All he could see was all the money he had paid to keep her forty-two-year-old frame looking like a twenty-five-year-old. He could not explain why such a random image had an emotional impact on him. Maybe it was because, for the first time, he felt lucky to be with her.

"What do you know about what she's going through?" Quincy asked.

"I don't know. In fact, I'm the last person to give advice about marriages and relationships."

"All I know is that I'm having too much fun. I got a hotel room, I called you up, and we're about to have a good time. Then I'll go to the casino, and hit up the blackjack table before I fly back to LA to work with my architect firm. Whatever joy or fulfillment I find out here, it will be gone by the time I reach LAX."

"Well, I don't want to hold you up, so if we could . . ." Candy held out her hand.

"Oh, of course." Quincy pulled out his reddish-brown leather wallet and removed a stack of one hundred dollar bills. The money was so crisp that some of the bills stuck together as Quincy counted out $1,500.

"Hopefully, we'll still see each other after the divorce. You're lots of fun," Candy said as she placed the money in her matching silver purse.

"We'll always have Vegas."

Candy put the cash in her purse and started to take her dress off. With her standing there naked, Quincy had an epiphany: for twenty years he had paid to be with a woman he no longer wanted, and he was about to pay for a woman he could never have.

Quincy checked the two jacks he had in his hand. Candy had done her job and relaxed him, but the night was far from over. He tapped on the table with his fingers as signal for the dealer to hit him.

The dealer flipped over the card, and before he knew it, Quincy was up ten grand and the envy of the entire table. It was just as well, he could have been down ten thousand and that would not have mattered. Quincy was wired differently than most people.

He either had to be the richest guy in the room or the poorest. Quincy had an either/or personality; no room for moderation. Quincy avoided contentment at every turn. His inner circle did not consist of people who were satisfied with being able to pay their rent on time and take an occasional vacation. He enjoyed the company of people who wanted to purchase a Lear Jet or an island.

Quincy checked his cell phone and noticed that Gregg had called, probably to discuss one of the pending deals.

Gregg remained in a constant state of worry. The Culver City deal was scheduled to happen on Monday.

Quincy was not about to waste a Wednesday night worrying about something that would not take place for several days. He was too busy trying to live in the moment. Quincy took a sip of his drink and tossed some more chips onto the table. Gregg can wait. And Karen could too, for now. Besides, she would suggest a prayer and a fast for an occasion like this. All Quincy needed to close the deal was a cranberry and vodka and a modest game of blackjack.

"You are being too kind to him, Dan," a white woman in a blue evening dress said to the dealer.

"I guess it's my lucky night." Quincy took a sip of his cranberry and vodka.

"Not mine; half of my kid's college tuition is on the table," she replied.

Quincy had seen the woman before. She seemed to know the dealer on a first name basis and she would beg him to go easy on her and let her win once in a while. It seemed like a pathetic sort of friendliness; one side always asking and giving, the other side always taking.

Lost in his train of thought, Quincy was unaware he'd won until he saw the dealer push more chips toward him. The woman's head dropped in despair. She began to comb her fingers through her hair, as if she were searching for loose change.

"I think I'm going to quit while I'm ahead." Quincy gathered up his chips and walked away from the table. He turned in his chips and checked his voice mail. There was a message from Karen.

"Quincy, I don't know where you are, but please call me," she'd said.

Quincy felt the buzz of the alcohol, but still had good

control over his faculties. Thursday he would fly back to Los Angeles with a divorce to finalize.

This had been a long week, and one that he still could not completely wrap his head around as he entered his hotel room and laid across the bed on his back. As he stared at the ceiling, his BlackBerry started to vibrate. He had a dinner planned tomorrow with his prayer partner, Jamal. They'd met at last year's Men's Retreat and were assigned to be prayer partners by Pastor Dawkins.

They barely spoke, but, occasionally, Quincy would take the young man out for dinner. He liked Jamal and thought he had a lot of promise. Quincy wanted to cancel the dinner, but Quincy had given Jamal his word. His father taught him that when a man gives a person his word to do something, no matter how small or insignificant it may be, it better be a matter of life and death that causes him to not make good on it.

Quincy started drifting off to sleep. He knew that tom-orrow would require him to have fortitude. He would start to put the final touches on the Culver City deal and work with his lawyer to get the divorce papers filed. It was a good thing he'd had fun tonight with Candy and the roulette table, because it would be some time before he had fun again. Emptiness and heartache were what awaited him.

Chapter Six

Stealing a car was not that difficult. Will's father was a smooth car thief and Will had become an able apprentice. By the time Will's father had gone to prison two years ago on a seven-year sentence, he had taught Will how to steal everything from cars to a girl's heart. Odell had also taught Will another trick, how to be invisible, since he was barely around for Will and his two younger siblings. Will's mother did not mind Odell's absence so long as she was able to maintain a comfortable lifestyle that did not require her to work.

Will got an adrenaline rush whenever he stole an exotic car. He loved to speed down the highway and test how fast a car could go before he turned it into Tony's chop shop or his gang leader, D-Loc. The job, like all other jobs, had its down moments. Boredom grew from a lack of a challenge.

Like this Mustang GT that Will was about to steal. It was jet-black, with gold racing stripes along the top of the car. It had R1 drifting rims to match. The owner obviously cared more about the look of the car than its safety, because Will didn't see any car alarm.

Will leaned into the window to double check the interior, but no red light flashed in the midst of the darkness. Will had had this car in his sights for a few weeks now. The occasion had arrived where he could finally claim it. Will removed the dealer-issued key from his pocket. It was amazing what a car thief could accomplish with a VIN and a stack of money. Car dealers were willing to part with dup-licate keys to the cars Will planned to steal, which made stealing cars a lot easier, but more boring. It wasn't the same as hot-wiring a car.

His suspicion was confirmed that there was not a car alarm as he entered the car. After he inhaled the vanilla-scented air freshener, he revved up the V8 engine. Will pulled away and got halfway down the block before he turned on the radio and was engulfed by Kelly Clarkson.

"What kind of crap is this?" Will said to himself.

He scanned the radio stations and found a hip-hop station that played the latest Jay-Z song. The music put him in an aggressive mood. So he scanned the stations until he found a jazz station. Will would not consider himself a jazz fan, but the slow melancholy sound of a saxophone or trumpet was soothing, checking any adrenaline that lingered after a boost.

Will had been a car thief since he was eleven. At fourteen he joined a local gang called the Untouchables. They found his skill helpful and lucrative. Now he was barely nineteen and he was already restless, ready to do something different. What, he was not sure of yet.

Lost in deep thought, Will neglected to stop at a red light, which prompted a siren to flash from a police car. The police siren grew louder as it approached Will and pulled just behind his rear bumper.

"Oh, shoot." Will turned off the music.

"Pull over!" the officer said from the loud speaker.

Will's size eight black-and-white shoe pressed on the ac-celerator. The Mustang GT went from sixty-five miles per hour to ninety in a matter of seconds. The police were in hot pursuit. The engine roared as the Mustang cleared one hundred miles per hour, leaving the scent of burnt rubber in its wake. He maneuvered around cars that obeyed the thirty-five-miles-per-hour speed limit, and cleared the intersection right when the light turned red.

As the speed increased, so did the interest in his activities. One police cruiser quickly became three. Will's adrenaline, no longer under the spell of Coltrane, spiked. A blur of jagged thoughts crisscrossed his mind before he pulled things into focus: he had to shake the police. The three behind him would be matched by the flying "Squirrel," the Eurocopter AS350 training its infrared on him. Once the Squirrel had him in its sights, Will's fate would be sealed.

Will approached another red light and hooked a right. If not for the aftermarket sway bar that held the 'Stang to the ground, the chase would have been over. Instead, it created a small window of opportunity.

A black SUV, lurching to avoid him, collided with a rust bucket Honda. The damage was enough to stop the police cars dead in their tracks. Will did not have time to worry about the mess fading in his rearview. Instead, he gained a mile of distance and then darted into a residential neighborhood. Turning off the lights, he slid into the curb, a not-so-anonymous car at rest in a very anonymous suburban neighborhood. The sounds of the sirens grew faint, but then seemed to be picking up. No time for reflection. Will turned the car off, got out, and chucked the keys across the street. Time to move.

His baggy pants hung low and made him feel like he was entered into a sack race. But Will pushed on, running until he could not run anymore. No matter. Will was not that much taller than a bar stool, so it was easy for him to hide. Wait! What was that? Will heard the helicopter in the distance. No time to hunker down. He needed another set of wheels. Running alongside the edge of the neighborhood, he reached the back end of a commercial building. He saw a late model minivan idling in the empty side lot.

As Will drew closer, he could make out the words "Celebration Christian Center" stenciled along the side of the van. About fifty paces out, Will slowed down and started to advance on the van, crouching as he moved toward the driver's side door. The door was suddenly thrown open. Will pressed hard against the side of the van. The guy who got out was head and shoulders taller than Will, so Will had to act before the guy turned around. The guy moved to close the door, and with his profile exposed, Will tackled the guy against the door. While the guy was stunned, Will delivered several swift hooks to the guy's chin. While the punches staggered him, they did not render the man helpless.

The guy braced himself against the van and used his free hand to grab the nape of Will's sweatshirt, swinging him to the ground in a heap. Now Will was at a disadvantage as his much bigger opponent towered over him.

"Are you out of your mind?" the man asked, his voice a loud but nervously cracked baritone.

Will managed to right himself, and kicked the man in the groin. He howled like a wolf. Back on his feet, Will followed his kick to the groin with a knee to the face. Now the guy was on the ground, and Will stomped on his stomach until the man yelled out in pain. Will then gave the man a punt to the head.

There was no more resistance. Will patted the man's pockets. He grabbed the keys from the front pocket and drove off in the van. He exited the parking lot and merged onto South Street. Will tried to shake off the events that had just unfolded, but that was foolish on his part. He embraced a smooth ride until he flipped on the radio. He heard a lot of rambling and hollering.

"What's this he listens to? Lil' Jon?" Will turned up the stereo. It became clear that the speaker was not a rapper, but a preacher with a thick Southern accent.

"One sin! One sin is enough to get you tossed into the fires of hell. So you have to ask yourself before you commit that sin, is it worth it? Is it worth it to burn in hell for all of eternity?"

Somebody should have told the preacher that we're in hell already, Will thought. Preachers who spent all their time talking about a better life after this life were basically admitting that this life was a mess. Will did not know what would happen after he died. He really didn't care. All he wanted was to be away from this world.

"These chicken-neck pastors want to teach milk and honey. Well, you can't get to heaven living like the devil. It's either holiness or hell," the preacher roared.

Will tried to recall what would qualify as a sin. He used profanity, but then he thought about the Bible and it didn't say anything about profanity being a sin. He smoked weed, but that came from the ground, so it was natural. If God did not want Will to smoke, he should not have created weed. He could not put his finger on any sin he could have possibly committed.

He had sex, but he always used a condom, so God would appreciate safe sex. Besides, sexuality was normal and natu-ral. He could not wrap his brain around any outright sins, but he could not fathom why, on the inside, he had this burning desire to confess. It wasn't the type of burn that consumes, but the type that lingers until it becomes a gray cloud in one's soul.

Will changed the station, but came across another fire-breathing Christian.

"Jesus comes like a thief in the night. You never know when. It could be at this very moment and you want Him to say, 'Well done, good and faithful servant.' You do not, and I repeat, you do not want Him to say, 'depart from me, I never knew you.'"

Will's body temperature shot up 400 degrees. His pores started to open up and drops of sweat started to leak out. Will turned off the radio. That last line stuck with him. He could not understand what would make Jesus say He never knew someone. What could a person possibly do that was that consequential? That was when Will came to the conclusion that God was a cold piece of work.

He patted his pocket for a blunt, found one, and inserted it between his black lips. He patted his pocket again for his nickel-plated lighter, but to no avail. The events of tonight had been too much for Will to deal with without smoking.

"Where my lighter go?" Will said to himself. He never left the house without his lighter, so the fact that he had a blunt in his mouth with no lighter was very strange. What was also strange was that the cigarette lighter in the car had been removed. So he assumed that Christians did not smoke. Just then, he spotted a liquor store beyond the intersection. The dirty neon sign was popping on and off like a beacon.

Will pulled off of South Street and into the parking lot. The liquor store sat on the corner of a strip mall, next door to a Mexican restaurant and cleaners. Will entered the liquor store with purpose, but got sidetracked.

From the corner of his eye, he saw a magazine with a girl

who had a behind the size of two basketballs on the cover. The magazine stood out in the midst of the other adult material. Above the magazine section stood a sign that gave a five-minute time limit for reading the material.

Judging by the condition of the magazines, the liquor store's clientele either didn't see the sign or didn't care much for the rules. He scanned through the magazine, then placed it back on the shelf as he made his way to the cash register.

"Lighter," Will said as more of a demand than a request.

The white guy at the cash register handed Will a lighter in exchange for a five dollar bill. Will took the change and made his way back to the van. He got back inside, felt his pocket, and retrieved his blunt. Blunt in his mouth, Will was ready to smoke, but he hesitated. He felt the urge to turn the radio back on.

Will had never heard preachers speak with such passion and conviction. Most of the preachers he encountered were what he liked to call the Liquor Store preachers. They would preach the gospel and then ask for an offering so they could buy beer. Will turned on the radio and a more mellow voice spoke.

"We all mess up sometimes. Lord knows I do, but the scripture says that the Lord makes us new mercies every day. So you do not have to carry your past into your future. You can decide to land anew and God is waiting for you. No matter what you've done."

Tears started to well up in Will's eyes. He came face-to-face with the person he had become: taking things that did not belong to him and using a survival-of-the-fittest mentality that rationalized his actions. But in this hot van he was struck with the realization that his petty crimes had impacted countless lives.

Who knew what that man with the van was about to do? Now he lay in the middle of the street, beaten, and for what? Who knew how much debt people accumulated to buy a replacement car because their insurance policy may not have covered the ones he'd stolen from them? Who knew how many jobs were lost because of the cars he'd stolen? What if someone was one tardy away from being fired by an inflexible boss, and Will had stolen his only means of transportation? Will had become (it would be funny if it weren't so sad) a menace to society.

"Don't wait, tomorrow is not promised. Make a choice to accept Jesus as your Lord and Savior, and He will remove your sins. You might not feel like you deserve it, but the scripture says that His ways are not your ways."

Will crossed Paramount Street and turned down a poorly lit alley. A group of guys hung out underneath a streetlight. They wore all black, with beanies. A little flicker of light indicated that they had been smoking. Will pulled up and turned off the lights when he got near the group. He hopped out of the van and exchanged fist bumps with the group.

"What's this?" D-Loc asked him.

D-Loc was the Untouchable's leader. He put in enough work to get everyone's respect in the hood. Even though he was only twenty-four years old, Will saw him as a father figure. Shaped like a bowling pin, only the whites in D-Loc's eyes stood out. A chill swept through Will's body whenever he stared at D-Loc for a long period of time.

"I had a problem with the other car," Will said.

"Oh, so you steal a church van?" D-Loc said.

Will couldn't care less about stealing a church van, as he thought about the Mustang GT he had to abandon in order to keep from being caught. "Look, I can get you another whip. Just give me a minute."

"It'll do," D-Loc said.

Of course Will knew that a minivan and a drive-by were exclusive concepts. They needed something with some muscle and a little bit of a pickup.

"Give me twenty minutes; I'll find you something better," Will said.

"We don't have time to waste, so you got twenty minutes before we leave." D-Loc looked at the minivan.

Will watched as D-Loc scanned his crew's eyes. J-Rock had just been put on, and the drive-by that was about to occur was his initiation. Droopy was a veteran street soldier. D-Loc handed Will a chrome pistol.

"It ain't a fancy tool kit, but it'll get the job done," D-Loc said.

Despite being in a gang, Will did not like guns. Guns were a magnet for trouble; however, he could not afford for his crew to do a drive-by in a church van. So Will took the gun and wedged it into the front part of his pants.

"We ain't called Untouchables for no reason. We live this, we breathe this, and each and every one of us is willing to die for the set. So when I look into your eyes, I better not see fear. There ain't no room for fear," D-Loc said.

D-Loc could inspire the smallest guy in the room to feel like a giant. D-Loc had given Will's father his word that Will would never have to kill anyone. He used Will to steal cars and allowed his other compos to put in work.

"Nobody messes with the Untouchables because they know that we ain't the ones, man. We strike fear in their hearts, and you know what?" D-Loc pointed to his head. "That stays with them longer. It messes with their head, man, they because know when they see you on the streets, they see death."

While D-Loc spoke, guns were passed like an offering

plate. From sawed-off shotguns to nine millimeters, this looked more like soldiers going to Iraq than doing a drive-by. Will was not off the hook for the evening. After some mumbled good-byes, Will made his way back toward South Street on foot. The wind started to make its presence known as it began to shake the trees. Will always tried to see what lurked in the shadows.

He never knew what could prey on him as he tried to walk toward the intersection. Maybe the preacher man's devil lurked in the shadows. He approached the corner of South and Paramount. The plan was to jack the first car he saw and get off of the creepy block. He waited for the right car to stop by the gas station across the street, where the gas attendant never got involved with any carjacking. The owner didn't even have security cameras to turn over to the police. A few minutes later, a champagne Cadillac pulled into the gas station, and a robust man in a wool jacket got out and began pumping gas.

"That's what's up," Will said to himself.

Will crossed the empty street and made his way up to the gas station lot. The guy had his back to Will, and he had no clue what was about to happen. Will grabbed his gun, pulled back the handle, and got within inches of the guy. The guy turned around with a weird, contorted look on his face.

"Check this out, playboy, we can either do this the easy way and you give me the keys, or I can go old school and put the gun in your face," Will said.

Fear was evident on the guy's face, to the point where he froze up. In Will's peripheral, he saw a black-and-white squad car approaching the gas station.

"Can you believe this?" Will pointed the gun at the guy's chest. "Get in the car. Now!"

The guy got into car from the driver's side, and slid his way into the passenger seat. Will entered the car on the driver's side with his gun in hand, and pointed it toward the guy's abdomen.

"Oh, Jesus, please don't shoot me. Jesus. Oh, Lord!" the guy yelled.

"Shut up!" Will placed the gun on his lap and turned on the ignition. The police car was at the pump behind Will. This would have to be Will's worst string of bad luck.

The Cadillac slowly pulled away from the gas station. Will could see the dashboard glow of the cop's computer. Two pros, he mused, going about their work. One jacking and the other filling out paperwork. The night was unusual to say the least.

"What's your name?" Will asked.

"Chauncey. Deacon Chauncey McClendon," Chauncey replied. He had a look of utter terror in his eyes. "If you need money I would be happy to give it to you."

"I do need money, but I don't want your money." Will looked at him in a way that started to freak the man out. "Listen, I need you to be cool. I don't want to hurt you. I just need your car."

Will could tell that statement relaxed Chauncey a little.

"Listen, I know this is awkward, but I really am trying to get to this church event. I should've left hours ago, but I was held up."

"You're real religious?"

"I'm not religious; I have a relationship with God."

This statement raised an awkward look from Will. "How's that?"

"Well, religion is based on a set of rules used to control people, and God is about setting people free."

"I'm not sure I understand," Will said.

"Well, maybe you can come with me to the Men's Retreat," Chauncey said joyously.

"Men's Retreat!" Will said, almost bursting a seam from laughing so hard.

"Yes, it's a time when men get together to get close with God."

"Let me get this straight, you claim to be in a relationship with God, and now you want me to go away with you to a Men's Retreat with nothing but men?"

"Yeah!"

"That sounds a little suspect."

Silence set in as neither one of them could figure out what to say or where they were going. Will appreciated the moment of quiet.

This guy is definitely in a cult or something.

"Are you going to kill me?" Chauncey asked.

"If you keep asking stupid questions, then yes, I will."

"Can I at least ask where we are going? South branches up ahead."

Pops had a point. Will did not have a clue where he was going. But the farther they drove, the more he felt the flux of the night churning in his stomach: the preaching, the tacky minivan, the liquor store, D-Loc, the gas station, this guy sitting next to him. Things were too hot for Will. It was too much for this nineteen-year-old to process. But a chance to get away from it all was more appealing. Will would go anywhere if he could be free from worry for just one night. A church event didn't seem too bad.

"I got to make a stop before we go to this Men's Retreat." Will was shocked by his own words.

This Cadillac was definitely a getaway car, but for whom?

For the first time, Will considered that there may be a force greater than himself that was moving him away from his surroundings and into the unknown.

Chapter Seven

Jamal dreamt of one day being able to afford to eat at the Gardens restaurant inside of the Four Seasons. The ambiance of the room, which was decorated with contemporary art-work and natural lighting, made Jamal feel a little out of place. His prayer partner, Quincy, was generous enough to take him out for a celebration for being offered a promotion. Jamal was not sure if he was being completely honest with Quincy, since he had not decided to take the promotion yet.

The other day, the DNA test results threw Jamal's entire world off of its balance. He searched for a way to put everything back into perspective while he indulged in a juicy, medium rare, sixty-day dry-aged rib eye steak.

"I've seen a lot of sports companies crumble, but Pinnacle Sportswear has a strong foundation. You'll do great in their marketing department." Quincy held up a glass of Chianti. "To a skyrocketing career." Quincy took a sip.

Jamal gave Quincy a toast with his iced tea. He did not mind that Quincy was a social drinker, but bad things happened whenever Jamal drank. For the most part Jamal was mild mannered, but whenever he drank, his temper became short, so he just avoided alcohol all together.

"So you know the Men's Retreat is this weekend." Jamal was unsure if Quincy had even signed up.

"You know I just got back in town and I am about to close a major deal. I'm thinking about kicking back this weekend and maybe watching the football games."

Quincy had not been to church in a few Sundays, and just this week there had been rumors swirling about Quincy and Karen's marriage being in trouble. Karen had walked around Wednesday night's Bible Study like a woman who lost her husband to the world. Jamal noticed her asking for prayer from Pastor Dawkins. He even noticed her with Pastor Dawkins and other ministers, seeking counseling.

He knew his buddy was always busy, but even the task of rebuilding Long Beach was not big enough where Quincy could not squeeze in a few hours for church. Jamal was not married, so he did not know if the conversation may have been above his pay grade, so he simply asked, "How's Karen?"

Jamal knew the question threw Quincy for a loop, because Quincy contorted his face in disbelief. Something was definitely wrong, and Jamal was curious to get to the bottom of it.

"I don't know." Quincy shrugged and took a bite of his salmon.

How come he doesn't know how his wife is doing? Jamal thought. Something must have been wrong on the home front, but Quincy seemed indifferent. "Man, what you mean you don't know? She's your wife."

"I don't know!" Quincy looked around the room. Jamal saw that Quincy's aggressive tone did not startle any of the dinner guests. "I haven't been home the last couple of days. I don't know how Karen is and I don't care."

"What's going on, man? Talk to me. I'm your prayer partner."

Jamal was not offended when Quincy laughed at the term "prayer partner"; in truth, Jamal only saw Quincy pray over food.

"Look, Jamal, I like you. You're a good kid. But I have to be honest with you; all those times I attended those Men's Retreats and prayer breakfasts was all for show. I mean, I believe in God and all, but I'm not as into it as you are."

Nothing about what Quincy just said came as a shock to Jamal. Most men who attended the events at church did so to appease their wives. Quincy was not the exception.

"Look, J-Money, I'm not going to play games with you. Karen and I are getting a divorce." Quincy's voice was very callous.

Jamal was not stupid as much as he was hopeful. He may have even been a little naive. He was not surprised by Quincy's announcement, but disappointed. He wanted to believe that marriages in this day and age ran the distance. He wanted to believe that when two people made a vow before God, that that vow was stronger than any force on earth. No, Jamal was not surprised by the news of Quincy's divorce to Karen. The news was just a punch in the gut.

"It's not something I really feel like talking about. You know, we're both adults and we just have to take responsibility for our actions."

Another blow to the gut. Quincy knew that their prayer partner relationship was a sham, but Jamal had felt that at least he could be someone Quincy could confide in. He'd guessed wrong. Now foolishness set in. With the exception of the matter between him and Chantel, Jamal had been an open book to Quincy.

"I really want you to go to the Men's Retreat. We always have a great time fellowshipping with one another," Jamal said.

Quincy nodded in agreement as he took another bite of his salmon. "I wish I could do it, but I just can't," Quincy said after he wiped his lips with a napkin.

His phone sounded and Quincy turned away to talk. Jamal did not know if it was Karen or someone else. Moments later, Quincy turned around and placed his napkin over his food to signify that he was finished eating.

"That's Karen. Listen, I have to go. Something has come up." Quincy seemed annoyed.

Jamal was very interested to know what was going on with his prayer partner.

Quincy paid for the dinner with his Black Card. Jamal only heard about the card from rap songs. He never saw anyone who could afford to own this aluminum card until now.

"Listen, I'll give you a call this weekend," Quincy said.

"If you change your mind about going to the Retreat, call me in the morning." Jamal gave Quincy a handshake.

Quincy left the table and Jamal continued to eat.

"Anything else I can get you?" Leslie, the bright Puerto Rican waitress, said to Jamal with a smile.

"No, I'm good," Jamal replied.

"Well, let me know if you need anything." Leslie left her phone number on the table. Even though she knew that Quincy had paid for the dinner, it was nice to see Jamal's good looks could get a girl's number at the Four Seasons.

Will was definitely losing his mind. The night was growing stranger by the minute. He was about to embark on a journey to a bizarre religious event with a stranger.

Will drove into his apartment complex. The Palms Apartments consisted of a two-story building designed in a U-shape. Will pulled into his neighbor's parking stall.

"Why are we here?" Chauncey asked.

"I have to make a stop for a minute. Let's go," Will said.

"I'm fine right here."

"I'm telling you right now, if you don't get out of this car, you're going to have problems," Will stressed.

Will got out of the car and Chauncey walked in front of him as they walked up the stairs toward Will's apartment. Will opened the door and the smell of sour milk arrested Will's nose. Will's little sister, Elisha, sat in her diaper on their chocolate brown carpet. His mother sat comatose on the couch.

"Hey, little momma." Will picked his little sister up and noticed the heaviness in her diaper. "Ma, how come you did not change her?" Will barked toward his mother. She was staring off into the TV with no regard to anyone else in the room.

Therein lay Will's sole frustration. He had to be the adult for everyone. If he did not go out and buy groceries, then the family did not eat. If he did not get up and walk Joshua to the bus stop every morning to make sure his brother got on the school bus safely, then his brother did not go to school. And, apparently, if he did not change Elisha's diapers, then Elisha would sit in the living room, soiled by her own feces.

"Who this?" Joshua asked, pointing to the man in their living room.

"He's a business associate." Will changed Elisha's diaper and maintained a visual of Chauncey.

"Hi, my name is Deacon Chauncey McClendon." Chauncey extended his hand, but Joshua was reluctant to shake it.

"He's cool." Will finished changing Elisha's diaper and, to her delight, began to smother her with kisses.

"Joshua's your name? You know, that's a name from the Bible. Joshua was chosen to be a leader after Moses had died, and to lead the children of Israel to the promised land," Chauncey said.

"Man, cut all that stuff out," Will said as he placed Elisha on the carpet.

Time was definitely of the essence. Will started to get calls from D-Loc, and he was afraid that soon he would come looking for him.

"Rent due," his mother muttered.

"I'm working on that. Don't worry; we ain't going to get put out."

In truth, Will had the money for the rent, but he got tired of his mother spending it on drugs. Will usually dropped rent off in a money order on the first.

"You ain't nothing like your father. Your father knew how to get money. You're just a sorry excuse for a man," his mother said without even looking in Will's direction.

Just like her, he thought. He was raised to expect something for nothing. She had nothing but contempt for those who longed to make something of themselves.

"Whatever, that's why I keep the lights on, right? That's why I keep a roof over our heads and food on the table?" Will reminded his mother. "Leave it up to you, you'll spend all our money getting high. But I ain't a man?"

"No, you're not! I wish your father was here instead of you. You too dumb to be the head of this family and you're too weak to be a man."

"May I say something?" Chauncey asked.

"Dude, if you knew what's best for you, you would pull your nose out of this business." Will held up his finger to Chauncey.

Will had endured his mother's abuse since childhood. When she grew tired of the physical abuse, his mother would then turn to the verbal abuse. In time, Will had come to see the physical abuse as helpful, a necessary attribute to survive in the merciless streets.

The verbal abuse, however, had a much more devastating effect. Will resolved that if he couldn't find peace in his own home, then peace was an elusive thing that he would never find. Oh well, he had to play the hand he was dealt, but Will refused to be degraded in front of a stranger.

"We wouldn't be in this mess if you weren't too busy getting high. You call yourself a mother, then be a mother to your kids. You got your kids starving and needing to be changed. You're a poor excuse for a mother," Will spat.

A tear emerge from the side of his mother's face. Some say heroin is the most addictive drug on the market; well, Will could attest to that. He never saw his mother take pleasure in anything other than her next fix. Even now, though she stared at the TV, he knew she was still thinking about her next fix.

Will also blamed himself. He did not help the situation by always catering to her needs. He resented her, and his father for making his mom so passive. She never left the house; she barely even left the couch. Her distaste for life caused her to be resigned to the couch and send her children out into the ruthless world to fend for themselves.

Will went into the bedroom without the need to turn on the light. What he needed from his room he could find in the pitch darkness. Underneath his bed was a plastic case. Will removed his keys from his pocket and unlocked the padlock around the handle of the case. He felt through the foam and removed his .357 Smith & Wesson. He loaded the gun with one clip and put the second clip in his front pocket. He wasn't the type who would leave his family unguarded. Will tucked the gun in the back of his pants as he left his bedroom. When he returned to the living room, the Jesus freak was nowhere in sight.

"Where's that guy I was with?" Will asked Joshua.

Joshua shrugged, and Will bolted out of the front door. Will was used to stealing cars, not people. As soon as he had taken his eyes off of his hostage, his hostage left. Chauncey had not gotten far down the stairs before Will was right behind him.

"Hold up!" Will stated.

Chauncey looked back and tried to move faster, but he tripped and stumbled down the last few steps. He rolled onto the ground, and when he saw Will, Chauncey put his hands up in a surrender position.

"I don't know how far you expected to get in some wingtips." Will pointed at Chauncey's shoes.

"I just want to go to church," Chauncey said, out of breath.

Will picked Chauncey up by his collar and stood him straight up. "You say you're a man of God, right?"

Chauncey responded with a nod.

"Well, I can't begin to explain how strange this night has been. It got me thinking about a lot of things. Then I meet you and I'm, like, trippin'. I mean, you might be the only one who could . . "

"Who could what?"

"Save my life."

"Only Jesus can do that," Chauncey replied.

"Well, we'll see about that, but if you try to run again"—Will flashed his gun—"then I'll have no choice but to use this."

"Will!" a familiar voice cried out.

Will turned around and saw his brother, Joshua, on top of the steps. "Come here, Josh."

Joshua ran down the stairs.

"Look, I got to go out of town for a couple of days and I need you to look after the family for me."

Will saw the weight of the world fill his twelve-year-old brother's eyes; Long Beach was not an easy place to live and there were always jackals waiting in the wings to pick off the weak.

"Don't leave me here, let me come with you." Tears filled Joshua's eyes.

"Stop crying. I need you to be strong for me. Be a man, all right?" Will dipped into his pockets and pulled out a roll of bills, which he handed to his brother.

"This is three hundred. That should tie you guys over until I get back. Don't leave this money lying around. You know how our mother is."

Will reached into the front part of his pants and pulled out the gun that D-Loc had given him and handed it to his brother, who placed the money in his front pocket and the gun in his back pocket.

"You know what to do if any trouble occurs. Just point and shoot." Joshua gave Will a nod as Will pointed to his brother to go into the house. "Be good. I got to go."

After Joshua ran up the stairs and closed both doors, Will took Chauncey by the arm and walked him to the car. Chauncey got into the passenger seat and Will made his way back to the driver's seat.

"Where are we headed?" Will asked.

"Monterey Bay."

Will had never even heard of Monterey Bay. The farthest he had been outside of Long Beach was Palmdale to visit family. He did not have a clue as to what was in store for him. All Will knew was that he had nothing to lose.

Chapter Eight

Quincy pulled up to his former two-story brick house. He paused for a minute, noticing that the lawn and the rosebushes were freshly trimmed. He remembered when he and Karen first bought the house and how they celebrated on the lawn, where Quincy picked her up and kissed her.

Quincy oversaw all of the details of the house. As an architect, he knew what enhanced the beauty of a home and what detracted. Quincy would have built their first home himself, like his original plan, but work on downtown lofts were too time consuming, so he settled for the home that he would have built if he'd had the time.

His father always told him that a man is not a man until he can walk on floors that he owns. One of Quincy's happiest moments was when he paid off the mortgage of their house and only had to worry about property taxes.

This was the first time Quincy had been to the house since he discovered that Karen was having an affair. He wondered if it was too soon to return home. God only knew what damage he might cause with his full set of golf clubs. He had to remind himself that he was Quincy Page, and Quincy Page did not lose control. No one was built like him, and for that, he could go into this house and face his unfaithful wife.

Quincy opened the car door against a heavy wind and let the car door close. He then followed the brick walkway to the

white door with the gold lantern positioned right above the
doorbell. Quincy pulled out his keys and was surprised that
she had not changed the locks. Karen stood in the entrance
dressed in a brown turtleneck and black slacks. That was sad
for eleven-thirty at night.

Karen was too attractive a woman to dress so conservative-
ly; this was another glaring example of why Quincy was not
necessarily fulfilled. That she dressed so seductive and sexy
around A-MOG burned him to the core.

Quincy noticed that she had gained some weight since the
last time he'd seen her. Maybe he was exaggerating, but maybe
she was going through a depression. Unfortunately, Quincy
could not feel too sorry for her. Karen had made her choice,
and now she had to live with it.

"You have any golf clubs with you?" Karen asked.

"I wouldn't crack jokes if I were you. You're lucky I'm even
here."

"Where have you been?" Karen folded her arms.

The audacity of this woman; she cheats on me with another
man and has the nerve to ask about my whereabouts. He was
raised to be a gentlemen and to never, under any circumstances, put his hands on a lady, but Karen was pushing it.

"Don't worry about where I've been. You weren't concerned about me when you were lying up with ol' boy."

"Look, you never gave me a chance to explain. That's why
I called you to come over. I wanted to talk to you about our
marriage."

"We don't have a marriage. You cheated on me, remember?
Our marriage exists only on paper, and come next week, that's
about to change."

"So you're going to file for divorce?" Karen asked.

"What do you think? There is nothing you can say or do
that will keep me from divorcing you."

"I've been praying that God will move your heart to try to work this out."

Quincy saw frustration emerge on Karen's face. He played coy because there was another issue to be resolved. Quincy had reclaimed his position of power in this marriage.

"I ain't trying to be funny or nothing, but how are you going to ask God to move my heart when you're the one who cheated on me, and you still haven't told me who it was you cheated on me with?"

"It's hard to talk to you when you have a golf club in your hands." Karen lowered her head.

"I ruined a perfectly good nine iron. But that's beside the point. The point is you can't even tell me who it is. Is it somebody I know?" Quincy waited a moment, but there was no response. "Here you go again with that silence. You care more about keeping your secrets than talking to your husband."

"It doesn't matter. You're still going to divorce me anyway."

"Why are you protecting this man, or is it a woman?"

"No! No! I ain't into women." Karen's face turned furious.

"I was about to say . . ." Quincy's words trailed off as his thoughts started to connect the dots. Quincy had been so blinded by inconsolable rage that he could not see that the person his wife was protecting was right in front of him.

"He's a minister at the church, isn't he? I know that the only men you seem to admire more than me are those ministers at the church."

Karen's eyes enlarged, and that admitted her guilt.

"He is. You're willing to let your marriage go up in smoke just to protect your pastor."

"It's not the pastor." Karen diverted her eyes.

"What does A-MOG mean? Can you at least tell me that?"

"I don't know what that means."

"Maybe that's because you're used to screaming it out in some Super 8 Motel."

"Don't talk to me like I'm some kind of whore. I made a mistake, and it's not like you're a perfect husband."

"So I got to be perfect in order for you to be faithful?"

"I'm not saying that, it's just that I wasn't getting what I needed from you." Karen pulled her hair back over her shoulders.

"Now if that would've been my reason, you would have called me a dog and thrown all of my clothes on the lawn."

This marked the longest conversation they'd had without resorting to throwing things. She was not getting what she needed? What kind of nonsense is that? Quincy had tried in every way to please her. He gave her everything, and to her that was not enough. Quincy had no reason to believe her. Karen used to run around with her girlfriends from church and they would talk about Pastor Dawkins as if he were their pimp. One girl even called Pastor "Daddy D."

Despite how inappropriate the comments and banter were, Quincy allowed them to slide because he did not suffer from insecurity, and he was confident in his relationship with Karen. Now he saw that he had been foolish. Karen was susceptible to strong men. He should have known, because that was how he won her over.

Karen placed her hand around her throat. That usually meant she felt a knot in her throat from being nervous. As a husband, Quincy would usually take advantage of this moment to reassure her that everything was going to be okay.

But as soon as he ceased to be her husband, something initiated by her infidelity, Quincy reveled in the fact that he could make Karen squirm.

"I wasn't thinking about saying anything. I was going to let it go, but at the same time I cannot imagine sitting there and allowing this A-MOG to continue to contradict himself in the pulpit. Isn't there a Men's Retreat this weekend?" Quincy said, knowing that there was.

Tears became visible in Karen's eyes. Quincy was convinced that she was reaching into her bag of tricks to manipulate him like she always did, but Quincy was not going for it.

"The Men's Retreat is not the place to air dirty laundry," Karen said.

"You know, that's the perfect place, since Greater Anointing likes to pride itself on having a strong men's ministry and a strong turnout of men." Quincy cleared his throat before he continued. "One thing I know about men is that they are not easily fooled. We're not like you women, who would just sit up there and worship the preacher. No, he needs to be brought to justice in front of other men, not women, who would only allow his actions to continue."

Karen's tears had become too much for her hand to handle. She reached into her pocket and removed tissues. Every time she wiped her eyes, more tears would emerge. This only added to her frustration.

"What happened to you? You didn't used be this vengeful," Karen said.

"I didn't know I would wake up one day to find that my wife of twenty years was having an affair, and the so-called God I pray to allowed it to happen. You would have a vendetta too."

Karen placed her hands together like a prayer. "Please, Quincy, I beg you, don't go to the Retreat to make a scene."

Quincy always got a rush from Karen's begging, whether it was a seductive plea during those romantic periods, or a pathetic plea like the one she was doing now.

"You forget I don't have to do what you say anymore. Divorce papers will be signed and on my lawyer's desk come Monday. You and I are done, and thank God for that."

It wasn't enough to humiliate Karen. Her lover needed to pay too, and the Retreat was a perfect opportunity. Of course, Quincy was too old to play high school games, but at the same time he had been bested by another man. His pride was damaged and his swagger was in jeopardy. Would he regret not confronting Mr. A-MOG?

Quincy had another big deal on the table, but his business partner was more than capable of being able to handle it. He wanted to confront this hypocrite who called himself a man of God.

Chapter Nine

For the first time in his Christian walk, Chauncey was unsure of God's will. He could not begin to put into words the events of tonight. Will coming along on this trip was either an act of God or the devil. There was also the story of Jonah; Chauncey likened himself to the prophet who spent three days in the belly of a whale because of his disobedience. He neither wanted to be disobedient nor did he want to miss out on a blessing. *What if God placed Will on my path to show Pastor that I am ready for ministry? Could this hoodlum be a sign of Chauncey's childhood prophecy being fulfilled? Only time would reveal.*

Chauncey expected to be bombarded with demonic rap music all along the Grapevine. The stretch along the 5 Freeway was dangerous without the accompaniment of Snoop Dogg and Dr. Dre. To his surprise, Will did not entertain the sounds of gangster rap; instead he entertained the smooth sounds of Miles Davis and jazz music.

"You listen to jazz?" Chauncey asked.

"What you think, I just listen to Lil Wayne and T.I.?"

Chauncey had no idea who those two hoodlums were. He assumed they were probably a bunch of young thugs with expensive chains and microphones.

Even though jazz was not as bad as rap music, Chauncey still felt like his car was being overrun by demonic forces.

He couldn't sit idly by and let the devil have a place in his sanctified Cadillac. He knew that Will had a gun on him. Maybe Jesus would give him the power to strip the gun away and seize control of his car.

"Do you think we could change the station?" Chauncey asked.

"Do you think you could walk to Monterey from here?"

Chauncey glanced out into the ominous darkness. In the midst of a mountain that looked like jagged teeth and open fields, Chauncey decided to remain silent.

The next two hours were spent in unbroken silence. The music must have worked a nerve with Will since he turned off the stereo. The Cadillac devoured the miles as Will sped along the 5 Freeway.

"What got you into jazz music?" Chauncey asked.

"It relaxes me. It's the kind of music you can take on a ride like this and cruise all along the coast without a worry in the world," Will replied.

Chauncey's mind went to the park. To him, jazz was like the rap music that had those thugs in a trance. It was demonic music to Chauncey. It was a form of music that promoted violence and greed. He did not understand how Will managed to escape its influence and how he found jazz music soothing.

"You ever listen to gospel?" Chauncey asked.

"No, not really. I mean, I heard a few songs from Kirk Franklin that were cool."

"Yeah, well, Kirk Franklin is a little out there. I'm talking about some James Cleveland, some, 'I don't feel no ways tired,'" Chauncey sang.

"That sounds like something the slaves sang on the ship," Will said.

"Boy, you don't know nothing about music. James Cleveland had a lot of jazz influence in his music."

"I just don't like being sold on some fantasy about a life that is better than this one."

"What's wrong with going to a better place?"

"Nothing, it just reminds me that not even God can provide you with a peaceful life in this world. He has to wait and promise you something when you die."

Chauncey had not encountered someone like Will. He seemed to be resigned to the idea that nothing good came out of life. That we live in a constant ebb and flow; one minute we are the victim, the next minute we are the assailant.

"I mean, you can't possibly think that all there is for you is robbing folks. Is that all you think you're meant to do with your life?"

"I don't know. I don't know what I'm meant to do. All I know is that this is what I'm good at and this is the hand that I was dealt, so I'm going to play it until it's time for me to leave the table."

It was absolute hopelessness that Chauncey heard in Will's voice. He did not know what to say. What could this young man have possibly experienced that would give him such a grim view of life? "Well, God is good, and you shouldn't let the devil make you think that there is nothing to live for."

"I believe that there is a God. I just don't think He's good, at least not in my neighborhood. As far as living, I'm only living for the moment."

"What about your family?"

"My mom is an addict. My dad is always in prison. If you add up the amount of time we have spent together outside of prison, I think it would total about six months. I got my brother and sister, but at the rate I'm going, who knows how long I'm going to be here."

Despite Chauncey's resentment toward his brother, he

knew that his brother did not want to die without making things right with his family.

He knew that right now Henry was in that hospital bed fighting with every ounce to live. The problem was that Chauncey believed that he would eventually return to his habit and betray those who believed in him. Henry had betrayed Chauncey too much for Chauncey to believe in him.

Will, on the other hand, did not seem to want to live. It was like he wanted to be released from this curse called life. Maybe that's why he spent his nights feasting off of the devil's pie. The God Chauncey served believed in giving people life, and life more abundantly. But, at the same time, the enemy's sole purpose was to steal, kill, and destroy. He thought that there were people who would find death a more compassionate act than life.

The car returned to silence and they merged onto Highway 101. They were now only a few hours outside of Asilomar Campgrounds and panic started to set in. If Will did not value his own life, then what made Chauncey think that Will wouldn't kill him as soon as this whole experiment did not seem worth it? There was a gun and a long stretch of highway where a body could get dropped off and no one would notice.

With that terrifying thought in mind, Chauncey bowed his head.

Lord, please protect and do not let this boy kill me!

Chapter Ten

Jamal tried to call Quincy after they'd met for dinner earlier, but all he got was Quincy's voice mail. The news of his separation from Karen and his abrupt departure from dinner were causes of concern for Jamal. After he hung up the phone, Jamal went back into Jamir's room.

Jamal had made sure to get a two-bedroom apartment. He guessed that in light of what had transpired thus far this week, he could move into a smaller apartment. He would save $300 a month on rent with a one-bedroom as opposed to a two-bedroom. He could stay with a two-bedroom and turn the second bedroom into his office, but that would require him to move Jamir's stuff out. That would be too much to do, but if he saved his money then maybe he could look into getting a house in a year or two.

Jamir was not his biological son and Jamal ached at the thought. Though he could have a close relationship with him, eventually, he and Chantel would have to tell Jamir the truth. Now, every time Jamir called him Daddy, Jamal felt like he was endorsing a lie. The Bible talks about the truth setting people free; but Jamal could not see it. The truth was that Jamir's real daddy died in cold blood and Jamal was responsible. The truth was that his mother and everyone involved in bringing him into the world were irresponsible little kids. How could that truth be anything but devastating to a young boy? This was the point when God's will was beyond Jamal's understanding. How come God could not let this boy be his son?

The situation was even more complicated by the fact that Jamal would give anything to be with Chantel. He noticed how neither he nor Chantel had engaged in a serious relationship since high school.

Deep down they were perfect for each other, but the last time they were together, a life had been destroyed. They'd made an unspoken vow not to go down the road of a serious relationship again. Instead, Jamal and Chantel chose to focus their attention on Jamir. And a love that powerful cannot be joined together, but must remain apart. Jamal turned on his flat-screen TV, set to engage in his latest conquest of Call of Duty. Jamal was very frugal, but he still had full indulgences, entertainment being one of them. The Bible warns about an idle mind, and usually this was the time of night when Jamal would be tempted to see what was on Cinemax. Around this time, the channel was notorious for showing soft-core porn. He loved God with all his heart, but the flesh craved satisfaction. Jamal's thoughts started to drift toward Mylessa and her proposal.

Since becoming a Christian, Jamal had been pretty good about abstaining from sex outside of marriage. In the beginning, Jamal still had a ferocious appetite that caused him to indulge in a few women a week, including several women at his job. One thing led to another, and word got around about his above-average performance in bed, because the next thing Jamal knew, a lot of women at the office began to take an interest in him. Jamal fasted and prayed until he nearly passed out, but eventually he was able to develop enough discipline to not give the devil even a foothold.

Jamal changed the channel, and as a result, he turned the TV off. He did not want his son to be exposed to pornography at a young age like he had been by his own father.

His son? Yes, Jamal had been there since his birth and had raised Jamir like a father would raise his son, but Jamir was not his son. Well, at least not biologically. Something about that revelation caused a disconnect with Jamal.

The news had brought a change. Jamal now had the freedom to leave Chantel and Jamir, and put the past behind him. Maybe this was God trying to signal to him that it was time to move on, and that maybe there was something better in store for him. Jamal never realized how strong a family tie was when the same blood flows through two people's veins, as opposed to just an emotional and psychological connection.

Jamir started not to feel like Jamal's own. He cringed at the thought that his separation was starting so soon. Jamal really needed answers. He did not know if he would get them during the Men's Retreat. God needed to intervene.

They arrived just after three in the morning. While Chauncey was exhausted, fear had made an impact on his sleep. Since Chauncey served on the Men's Retreat committee, he'd received his cabin key early, so he and Will were able to go straight to the room. But for most of the journey and since their arrival, Will had not said much. Even now, he just sat in the chair in the room, staring off into space, not even talking.

"You're not tired?" Chauncey asked Will.

"I don't sleep much. I'm always on the grind, and in my neighborhood, you go to sleep hearing sirens and helicopters. It's too quiet here. It makes me a little nervous."

"Trust in Jesus, He'll give you rest."

"Jesus never lived in the hood, so I doubt that!"

Maybe it had been a mistake for Chauncey to bring Will. He seemed to be diametrically opposed to the things of God. One could only hope that tomorrow the Retreat would start to work on his heart.

"You have to get at least eight hours of sleep. Your heart is working overtime. You could have a heart attack by the time you're thirty," Chauncey said.

"I might not even be around when I'm thirty. There's a lot more stuff for me to worry about than a heart attack."

"I'm going to pray for you. I'm going to bind that spirit in the name of Jesus!"

Will took out his gun and placed it in his lap. He gave Chauncey a smirk. "Just make sure you keep it down. Just because I don't sleep doesn't mean that I want to hear all of that praying stuff."

Chauncey figured he would exercise wisdom and pray silently. He'd never felt fear like he had felt today. God must have had something greater for him. That's why the devil was attacking him so hard. If this young man was an example, well, Chauncey refused to live in fear. Chauncey believed that he could save Will's life, and Chauncey needed to trust God in spite of his doubts.

"Why did you decide to come if you didn't want to have anything to do with Jesus?"Chauncey asked.

Chauncey's question caused Will to put his head down, like his only solace came from the floor. Finally, Chauncey may have said something that resonated with Will's conscience.

"It's like every day I get in a corner and I start swinging. But I learned a long time ago that I'm not fighting to get out; I'm just trying to keep the walls from closing in. You gave me a chance to get out, and maybe for once in my life it won't feel like a dogfight."

And like a gunslinger from a Western, Will stood up with his gun and walked over to his nightstand. Only he was not about to discharge his weapon, but laid it down on the shelf. Even Chauncey had to marvel at the display of a warrior surrendering his weapon, even if it was only for a weekend.

Chapter Eleven

A beautiful metallic '67 Chevy sat in a frail garage with the paint chipping away and the door off of its hinges. With the hood up, the car stood not in flawless shape, but anyone with a speck of knowledge about car history would know that this car was a classic. It took the smell of hazelnut to remind Jamal that his purpose was to drop off breakfast to his father before he headed to the retreat. He also had an ulterior motive and that was to get his advice on what to do about the situation with Chantel and Jamir. His father had forewarned him about fooling around with Chantel, and though he could predict how this conversation would play out, Jamal still had to try.

"She's a beauty!" Jamal said.

A burly man with a bald head emerged from under the hood. He closed the hood and wiped his hands off on an orange, dirty towel. "I just had its oil changed. I was thinking about taking it out for a drive along the coast."

Jamal scanned the wall at the pictures that had kept his father company since he was a child. He had pictures of naked women on top of cars, pictures of naked women with beer bottles in their hands, and just plain old pictures of naked women. Despite the collage of women, Jamal knew that the most beautiful thing in the garage was the '67 Chevy.

"Maybe we can hop in and head to the Men's Retreat," Jamal said as he handed his father his coffee.

"I don't know about that. All those men hugging and crying on each other . . . seems a little sweet to me," his father said sarcastically as he sipped his cup of joe.

"That's not what the Men's Retreat is about. It's about recognition of the broken areas in your life and letting God come in."

"A man ain't got no business crying in front of another man. That's why I'm concerned about you. I don't see you with no girlfriend. You still be running behind Clay's old chick."

"I'm about my B.I.," Jamal said.

"I was about my business too, but it didn't stop me from being a playa from the Himalayas."

"I know. I could hear my mother crying from the next room, because it was another night that you didn't come home."

Jamal knew he had crossed the line by bringing up his deceased mother. When she'd died two years ago, Jamal promised his father that he wouldn't talk about his mother around him. He regretted that promise, because all it did was allow his father to avoid talking about his shame. Jamal could not stand the sight of his father being proud of his actions.

"Son, there's some things in a marriage you can't understand that's only between a man and a woman."

"Well, Mother must not have gotten the memo, because she didn't understand either," Jamal said.

His father got up and raised his hand to smack him, but Jamal was not a little boy and his size and stature matched his father's. After a moment that bordered on eternity, his father lowered his hand. Jamal was convinced that his father might not fare well in the exchange.

"I'm trying to tell you something for your own good, but you go on and do what you want," his father snapped.

Wanting to switch subjects, Jamal tried to find something positive to talk about. "I got offered the promotion."

"Well, that's good. More money in your pocket never hurt nobody."

"I don't know if I'm going to take it."

"What you mean you don't know? Have I missed something here or aren't you a single father?"

"I found out the other day that I'm not."

Jamal's father's reaction was a shock to say the least. He flashed a smile and gave a reluctant Jamal a fist bump.

"Well, you're in the game then! What you tripping for?"

"For three years I treated Jamir as if he was my son. I can't just flick my feelings on and off like a light switch."

"I'm not saying you have to, but at least you don't have to worry about that broad trying to take advantage of you."

Jamal hated whenever his father talked about Chantel like she was a two-dollar hooker. His father couldn't handle a good woman, and that had been evident throughout his marriage.

"Don't disrespect Chantel like that. She's a good woman and a great mother."

"Is that why she let both you and your best friend hit that?"

"We were kids back then and we didn't know any better."

"Never trust a redbone! She proved that she's not above lying to you and now that you have an out, take it."

Jamal did not care for his father's archaic opinions. But, for once, he was making some sense. If there was one thing that his father was an expert on, it was scandalous women.

"I just don't know if I want to be a slave to a company. I mean, my purpose in life is not simply to work and cash a check."

"You have got to be the dumbest person I know. You're tripping over a kid who ain't yours and now you about to let that mess with your money." His father set the coffee down on the counter next to the radio. He then reopened the hood. "You can do what you want, but you can't say I didn't warn you."

Those was usually his father's last words after every visit. Of course, this Friday was different. Jamal was getting ready to head out of town and he was still no closer to an answer than before.

The sound of Jamal's phone signaled that he had a new text message. Jamal checked his phone, and he was elated that the message was from Quincy:

Going to the Retreat. I'll pick you up in an hour.

—Q

Chapter Twelve

Jamal was excited about being able to ride up to the Retreat with Quincy. Last night's dinner had not left Jamal with an optimistic view of Quincy and his relationship with God. In fact, Jamal really admired Quincy for wanting to go to the Retreat despite all that was going on at home. Jamal didn't know if he could attend a church event with his marriage being on the rocks. He had a lot of things to talk about, and did not necessarily want to sit in the car quietly and wait until they arrived at the Retreat.

"I'm sorry I cut out early the other night. I was finishing up some important business," Quincy said.

"Don't trip! Trust me, I know how it is. I'm just glad that you changed your mind about coming to the Retreat. Last I heard there was plenty of space available for last-minute registration," Jamal replied.

"Yeah, I haven't been to church in a minute, and I actually like the Men's Retreat. The church does a good job of picking out nice locations. I brought my golf clubs, so I can hit a few balls while I'm out there."

"I'm sorry to hear about you and Karen," Jamal said in a soft tone.

"What can you do? I mean, sometimes it's just not meant to work out. You have to move on. I still got a whole lot of living to do. So I'll just pick myself up and keep going."

"I know that things are rough for you, and I admire that you're still pressing forward. That's why I like to stay close to you. I figured, since you're in a place where I am trying to go, you could give me some great advice about my situation regarding my career and my son."

"So you're wondering which path to choose, career or fatherhood?"

Jamal did not see his situation as black or white. Yes, he was making a decision whether to advance his career or maintain the relationship he currently had with Jamir. The DNA test results made his situation even more difficult. However, Jamal considered whether the advancement of his career would provide a better situation. He no longer had any obligations to Jamir or Chantel. But the genetic separation and the emotional separation were of two different playing fields.

"I admire you," Quincy said.

"Why?" Jamal asked, taken aback.

"For most men it's not a choice. They would buy a Range Rover and wave to their kids in the distance. But you're a man of honor and integrity."

"So what do you think I should do?"

Quincy shrugged. "I think you should start your own business. I tell young guys like you all the time that now is the time, when you're young, to go into business for yourself. Don't depend on another man for your paycheck. As far as my situation goes, maybe I wouldn't be having the problems I am having now if I'd spent more time with my family, so go for it. Let your employer know that you cannot accept a promotion that would take time away from you and your son."

Jamal felt the need for full disclosure, but the mere thought cautioned him to fall back. He and Quincy had a decent relationship as prayer partners, but to disclose the truth about Jamir not being his real son would leave Jamal wide open.

At the same time, if Jamal expected to get sound advice from his prayer partner, then he would have to be honest.

"There is something that has come up that has complicated things a little bit," Jamal said.

Quincy motioned for Jamal to continue.

"Jamir is not my son."

The statement caused a minor swerve of Quincy's car as he looked at Jamal as if the Loch Ness Monster stood behind him.

"Whoa, whoa, whoa! You mean to tell me you're in limbo over a child who's not yours? How can that be?"

"It's a long story and it's not the point. For two years I have loved this boy like he's my own; I can't just up and disappear."

It was an understatement to say that Jamal regretted making his secret known to Quincy. His stomach turned into a pretzel as he zeroed in on the pine air freshener in Quincy's car. His skin rejected the nutmeg leather interior and started to itch.

"You've got to be kidding me. You're taking care of another man's kid?" Quincy said.

"It's a little more complicated than that."

"Obviously!" Quincy put both hands on the steering wheel and leaned forward as he shook his head. "J, you're too young to be worried about someone else's kid, especially since you're not with the mother."

"I've been around the kid his whole life. Like I said, I can't up and disappear."

"I ain't trying to be funny or nothing, but to commit career suicide is foolish. Now is not the time to be noble, now is the time to be practical. You're young, give yourself time to develop your career, then start a family. Take it from me with a daughter in college; it ain't easy being a family man."

Quincy had a tendency to be adamant, but Jamal was not use to seeing Quincy this adamant. He knew he meant the best, but he expected more optimism from someone who had been married for twenty years and had a daughter in college.

"I mean, you're young. You don't need to be weighed down with those types of responsibilities. If you learn nothing else from me, then at least learn that marriages don't last. Can you imagine where I would've been if I hadn't invested so much in my career? I would have really been messed up."

"I know, I know, but in my heart something is telling me to not abandon him. What if he turns out to be a menace to society?"

"I'm not saying not to help him, but how do you think you're helping him by lying?"

"Because the truth is whack!" Jamal shrugged.

"What is the truth?" Quincy asked.

He had said too much. He was embarrassed at how the conversation had unfolded, so, instead, he reclined his seat and folded his arms.

"Nothing, man, it's a long story."

Quincy could not believe his ears. He always saw Jamal as a sharp young man, a good father, and a hard worker. In so many ways Quincy admired Jamal because he lacked the discipline and focus that Jamal demonstrated in every aspect of his life. Quincy would not even dare say he was half the Christian Jamal was, and that was okay with him. Quincy fell into Christianity as a way to appease his sanctified wife. He had trouble being fully committed to the Christian doctrine. He desired to stay relevant. Jamal, on the other hand, seemed like someone who was fully immersed in scripture, and was willing to carry out his life according to biblical principles.

In light of recent events, Quincy had decided to be like God, and love from a distance. After this weekend, he did not even plan to step foot into God's house ever again. This Retreat would mark the end of Quincy's journey as a Christian.

He had one last task to do, and that was expose this phony A-MOG for the fraud he was. Quincy traveled and took bites into a once juicy red apple that had started to turn mushy during the course of the journey. In his periphery he saw the jagged mountains turn into tall redwood trees. The wide four-lane road that his Range Rover cruised upon turned into a narrow two-lane road.

This would also be the last time he and Jamal would get to spend together. Quincy planned to cut off all lines of communication from anyone who attended Greater Anointing. He never really saw himself as someone who needed to depend on another man anyway.

That was the great thing about being a man. Unlike women, men could stand alone if need be, and most obstacles in life required that a man do so.

Chapter Thirteen

Last night, Will had been a little spooked as his perilous little city evolved into a mountain range, and the mountain range evolved into a beach resort. Will had been to a beach before, but this beach was secluded, with no inner city nearby. When they arrived at a cabin that looked like something out of a Friday the 13th movie, now in the full radiance of the day, Will did feel more at ease.

The park just seemed to exist without any interruption from man. Even the buildings seemed to have evolved from nature itself. The main building was made out of stones that must've been collected from the beach.

Will started to consider that maybe he was attending some meeting by a cult, and really he was being led to a slaughter or a UFO probing. The birds chirped loudly and dominated the sound. Several men began on a slow ascent toward a solid oak building along a cobblestone road.

"This way." Chauncey took the lead toward the building. Intrigue led Will's steps along the path, as the auburn leaves cascaded down from the towering trees.

With each step, Will's kneecaps felt like they were made of jelly. Pockets of tension were released throughout Will's body.

They arrived at a double door entrance, where a man in a T-shirt two sizes too small stood guard. The guy had bugged eyes, and a receding hairline that withered into a widow's peak. Will hoped to spark a strong enough connection with the guy to tell him that he should have some dignity and cut all of his hair off.

There was a wooden table where the words WELCOME TO THE MEN'S RETREAT MIGHTY MEN OF VALOR were plastered on a banner.

Will did not have a clue what the words "Mighty Men of Valor" meant, but he assumed that it meant something good.

"Welcome, Deacon McClendon," one of the brothers said.

"Hey, Brother Richardson, how are you?" Chauncey asked.

Will realized that his companion carried a title with some influence. Will respected any man of power.

"Hey, young man. God bless you, and welcome to the Men's Retreat." The guy extended his hand.

Will shook his hand and surveyed the area. The room reminded him a lot of what he'd heard an AA meeting was: not a lot of decorations, just a bunch of chairs, and a podium toward the front that stood next to the chimney.

There was a small group of guys talking, but nothing was occurring that looked to be of any importance. Will wondered what had been so urgent about getting to this meeting that Chauncey would risk his life to attend.

"Is it too late to register?" Chauncey asked.

"Oh no, no, no, we still have room. We were prepared for last-minute registers," Mr. Richardson said.

Will watched as Chauncey peeled off two one hundred dollar bills and handed them over to the man. The man put the two hundred dollars in a metal lockbox and handed Will a brochure.

"Thanks!" Chauncey looked at Will. "I am going to go say hello to a few people."

Will followed suit and stood next to Chauncey.

"Hey, Deacon McClendon," a muscular guy greeted Chauncey.

"Gentlemen, this is Will. I met him last night and I convinced him to come and join us."

"Praise the Lord!" one man said.

"We were just talking about Michael Vick and his return to football," the muscular guy said.

"Yeah, that man messed up by having a bunch of snitches in his camp," Will said, taking comfort in the fact that their conversation revolved around something other than church.

"The lesson is to watch the company you keep. Because God blessed that boy with a gift worth millions of dollars and he threw it away betting on dogfights. Not everyone is meant to go with you to the top," one guy said.

"He should be all right. He got Tony Dungy helping him get his life straight with the Lord," the muscular guy commented.

That's when the conversation derailed for Will. He did not think that Vick's redemption lay in his spiritual relationship with an ex-football coach. Vick just needed to be more wise about who he kept in his camp.

Will zoned out of the conversation and wondered what he was doing at the church event. He was certain that he would die of boredom.

"How did you meet Deacon McClendon?" one man asked Will. The question snapped Will out of a daze.

"Oh, I had some car troubles last night and Will was kind enough to assist me," Chauncey said.

The statement started a chain of curious looks from the brethren.

"I don't understand how this could happen." Will turned around to see a tall man with a gray beard. This guy looked

like he could have started on the Lakers back when they had
Jerry West and Wilt Chamberlain. The man was talking to a
much smaller white man. He followed Chauncey, who obviously knew the man, as he headed toward him.

"Pastor Dawkins, what's wrong?" Chauncey asked.

This guy had to be the biggest pastor Will had ever seen. He
always saw pastors who were either fat and bald or skinny and
bald. This pastor's voracity was somewhat intimidating. For a
moment, Will almost did not want Chauncey to bother him.
The guy seemed visibly upset.

"The enemy seems to be up to his old tricks," the pastor
replied.

"Is there something wrong?" Chauncey asked again.

"I'm truly sorry, Pastor, for this mix-up," an employee said.

"He doubled booked us with a woman's book club," Pastor
Dawkins said to Chauncey.

"Lord Jesus, have mercy! The devil is a liar," Chauncey shouted out.

Will could have sworn he missed something. He was in the
middle of nowhere with a bunch of strange men, the person
who'd invited him being the strangest of them all. He could
not understand why a group of women being at the same lo-
cation was a problem; unless these men were gay. Will vowed
that if he somehow stumbled upon a gay religious event, then
he would never tell a soul.

"Listen, you still have all of your conference rooms available, but to be honest with you, we could use the extra guests,"
the ground's rep said.

"You don't understand. The whole purpose of why these
men travel all this way is to be free from the distractions of
women and the things of the world," Pastor Dawkins ham-
mered.

At this point, Will had concluded to leave this place just as soon as he robbed Chauncey of all of his money. He hadn't come all this way for nothing.

"We'll try not to let our other guests be a distraction," the employee replied.

This pastor sucked in so much air that Will thought he was about to sock this dude, which would have been pretty cool.

"Lord have mercy, I guess we are going to have to figure out a way to work things out," Pastor Dawkins replied.

"Thank you, Pastor, for your understanding. We'll make sure that you will still have a pleasant stay."

The pastor shook the guy's hand and rubbed his own head after the man left.

"Boy, the devil is working overtime, but he won't get the glory. This weekend was ordained by God," Chauncey declared.

"You're right about that," the pastor said, and then turned toward Will. "I don't believe we've met. I'm Pastor Dawkins." The pastor held out his fist.

Will smiled and bumped the pastor's fist back. "Will."

"Welcome to the Men's Retreat. How do you know Deacon McClendon?"

"He had a little car trouble last night. I had to help him out."

Will chuckled at the inside joke, but Chauncey did not. Will found last night's events both strange and hysterical.

"Well, I'll see you at tonight's events." The pastor moved swiftly away, like he was in a hurry or something.

A few moments later, Chauncey turned to Will. "Let us go and get freshened up for the afternoon sessions. This way, Will," Chauncey said as Will followed him along the boardwalk back toward the cabins. Chauncey opened the door and

Will immediately noticed something that was insignificant to him before. There were four beds, which meant that Will could expect to share this room with two more Jesus freaks.

Jamal felt like he had been to a party and finally got the joke being passed around. Sadly, the joke was about him. Jamal had been convinced that he was the father of Jamir.

He disregarded his father's comments as the opinion of a player who refused to let people get caught up, but Quincy's words penetrated Jamal's security wall and brought everything crashing down.

Now in the midst of an already tough decision, Jamal had to come to grips with reality. The reality was that he was seriously considering putting his career on hold for a child who was not his own. Jamal feared that so much attention on what to do about Jamir could cause him to miss the real message God was trying to convey to him.

His train of thought led him on such a journey into self-reflection. He was only conscious of the fact that he and Quincy arrived at their destination when the car came to a stop and Quincy's car door slammed.

Quincy ascended some cobblestone steps, and Jamal wrestled with the thought that he no longer wanted to be at the Men's Retreat. He'd come to the Retreat with a sea of questions and he got his answer. He was a fool, now he had to figure out what to do, and the Men's Retreat did not seem like the place. The door closed and snapped him out of his consciousness.

"I just registered and got our room keys," Quincy said. Jamal did not even look at Quincy. "Listen, man, I don't know what to tell you. It's tough enough being a single parent, but

I don't understand you putting your life on hold for a kid who's not even yours."

Quincy's words had done enough damage. Jamal barely paid attention to what Quincy said. Instead, he observed a tree a few yards ahead. The branch had money green leaves on it. The wind tossed the leaves to and fro as they cascaded down to the ground. Jamal felt very vulnerable at this point. However, he did not want Quincy to think that his words shattered Jamal's confidence, so Jamal took in a fist full of air and exhaled a deep sigh as he leaned his head back against the headrest.

"I'm tired," Jamal said.

"Come on, let's get to our rooms. Maybe you can get a power nap in before the first session," Quincy said.

A chill penetrated Jamal's bloodstream as he got out of the car and threw on his black cowhide-leather jacket. He balled both of his hands up and blew into them to create instant warmth. Quincy popped open the trunk and handed Jamal his black duffle bag. Jamal felt like he had bricks inside of his bag. Quincy closed the trunk and pressed a button on his chain to trigger the lock.

Jamal followed Quincy's lead as they walked along a boardwalk toward the room.

He took time to admire the scenery, despite the pale sky that hung over the campgrounds. Jamal watched as a squirrel ran in front of him. The squirrel stopped midway and stood up in front of them before dashing off into the woods. Jamal adjusted the position of his duffle bag to avoid back pain. They arrived at their room and Quincy opened the door. Jamal stepped in front of Quincy and used his shoulder to open the door all the way. He examined that Chauncey was neatly moving his folded clothes into a drawer, while an unknown young man lay on the edge of the bed with his feet planted on the floor while text messaging on his cell phone.

"What's going on, fam?" Jamal asked.

The young man diverted his eyes from his phone long enough to give a nod. Chauncey stopped putting away clothes long enough to extend his hand to Jamal.

"Brother Jamal, praise God. How's it going?" Chauncey asked.

Jamal bogarted his way into the room and dropped his overnight bag on the first available bed, which just so happened to be positioned right next to the window. It gave a nice view of the beach. Jamal figured a good view of the ocean and the rising sun would make getting up early more bearable.

Jamal extended his hand to the new guy. "What up, fam? I'm Jamal."

The new guy smacked Jamal's hand three times before snapping his fingers to signal that the handshake was over. Then he stated his name, "Will," as he diverted his eyes back to his cell phone.

Jamal laughed at the new way to greet someone.

"I haven't seen you before. You must be a new member at church?" Quincy asked.

"We met last night. Will was kind enough to help me with car troubles, so I invited him to come," Chauncey answered.

Jamal had never known Chauncey to be the type to travel in areas where he might encounter a young man like Will.

"Well, praise God. So you came to the Retreat to get closer to God?" Jamal asked.

"Whatever that means," Will said, not taking his eyes off of his cell phone.

There was a certain aura about Will. His nonchalance stood out in a room full of egos. Only, Will's nonchalance was not of someone who freed himself of worry, but of someone who just did not care to begin with. Jamal was a pretty good judge of character, and he could tell when he was looking at his former self in the mirror. Jamal, too, had been in that place until he had what he called a Damascus moment. Will may have needed a Damascus, and Jamal's purpose at the Retreat may have been to assist Will in his Damascus moment.

Chapter Fourteen

There was only one reason why Quincy was at the Retreat: to confront his wife's lover. He figured the best way to figure out who he was was to interrogate the people who Karen associated with at church. A stroll along the boardwalk led him to spot Douglas, the choir director, aka minister of music. Karen sang in the alto section of the choir and she spent many late nights at choir rehearsal. Douglas stood along the shore with headphones in his ears. He gestured as if he were conducting the waves.

The misconception that most male choir directors were gay did not deter Quincy's suspicion. He approached Douglas and got his attention.

"What's going on, Brother Page?" Douglas removed his headphones.

"Nothing much, just trying to get ready before everything starts."

"I know, I know, I know! We're going to be on fire this weekend. Are you going to join the male choir on Sunday?"

There was only two occasions when Quincy sang: in the shower and right before he made love to his wife. The latter was inspired by the soulful sounds of Teddy Pendergrass.

"No, not me. Well, you know, that's the wifey's thang, not mine. She looks forward to singing every Sunday. Just this last Sunday I saw her shoot out of the house wearing nothing but sweats and a T-shirt."

"Sister Page did not have on any sweats. She wore a skirt."
Douglas seemed confused.

Now right there, he messed up. "How do you know what
she had on?" Quincy was curious.

"All the girls were talking about it." Douglas was skeptical.

"What were they saying?"

"They were saying, 'Look at Sister Page trying to look
young.' I'm surprised you didn't know what she had on."

Douglas came off as very obnoxious, and if it weren't for
the fact that Quincy needed answers from him, Quincy might
have punched him in the face. However, Quincy could con-
clude that the choir director and his wife were not engaged in
any hootie-hoo-Timbuktu.

"Listen, Douglas, if there was something going on that I
needed to know about, would you tell me?"

"Yes, of course, Brother Page, I would."

"Thanks, man, I appreciate that." Quincy patted Douglas
on the back and headed toward the boardwalk. The introduction ceremony was not for another ten minutes, but with
nothing else to do, Quincy decided to head over to the conference room.

He looked forward to locking eyes with Minister Hypocrite.
He looked even more forward to confronting him in front of
his fellow brethren. Quincy bit into a pear he'd bought at a
rest stop. He found momentary sweetness on the other side of
the coarse texture of the pear skin.

Arriving at the empty conference room and taking a seat
near the podium, Quincy had one purpose in mind and that
was to get to the truth. Quincy wished he could confront him
the second he walked through the door.

He was certain that A-MOG was a minister. Next to a pimp
or politician, ministers were some of the most smooth-talking,

charismatic people he knew. Maybe Quincy would wait until he got the chance to speak before he confronted him. Maybe he'd wait until the good old minister got into a deep, passionate sermon, and then expose him with the truth. He knew that the timing had to be perfect, and, at this moment, he was certain that today might be the day. This weekend was supposed to be about the men confronting who they were in the empty moments when no one was around except God. The minister needed to remove his facade and confront his hypocrisy.

Jamal soon joined Quincy, along with Chauncey and his new friend, Will. Quincy wished he had time to dissect the mystery surrounding Will, but that was neither here nor there. Quincy's mission was clear, and, more importantly, it was free from any distractions.

More men started to pour into the conference room. Judging by the foul odor, it was clear that they had been playing on the basketball court. Over sixty men had made an arrangement to be here over the course of the next two days in Monterey with fellow Christian men. For a moment, Quincy reconsidered his actions.

He found it narcissistic of himself to crush these guys' hopes of turning their lives around, only to have another glaring example of how leadership fails to uphold the standard it preaches. Brother Evans was both a minister and a high school football coach. He had hands that could punch a hole in a tank. He used those hands to begin a loud clap, and soon the majority of the men joined in. Quincy did not join in the clap.

Unlike his brothers, he was not caught up in the emotions of the moment. If the devil existed, he sure was in the midst of this gathering.

"Hallelujah. I've been waiting all week to come here and be

with my brothers," Brother Evans said. "I couldn't wait to get together with my brothers and fellowship. I told my wife when she kissed me good-bye that the man who's leaving would not be the same man who returns."

Brother Evans's words were greeted with mighty "Amen's" and claps. Quincy wondered if Evans's joyful act was just that—an act—or genuine. Maybe Quincy had been a fool this whole time, thinking that this weekend was a holy event. Maybe it was an actors' workshop, and maybe the men here only pretended to be religious.

"Now, I'm going to turn the podium over to the angel of this house, Pastor Dawkins."

Brother Evans led the ovation that carried Pastor Dawkins to the front of the podium. Pastor Dawkins had yet to enter a room without ducking down. In his early days, he'd started as a small forward for UCLA. A torn meniscus ended his professional career.

Pastor Dawkins pulled the microphone toward him and adjusted his square glasses. "Oh, how marvelous it is when brothers can dwell together. Yes, yes, my heart is heavy."

Those words caused the men to settle down. He removed his glasses, and with his massive hands he wiped the tears from his eyes before putting his glasses back on.

"Fierce warriors of God surround me and I know that the battle is intense. I can see it in your eyes. The wounds are visible. The burden of being the head of your household is heavy, especially in these uncertain times."

Though the "Amen's" returned in low tones, the nods symbolized that Pastor Dawkins did not lose his audience. The religious stuff aside, Quincy had always been a big fan of Pastor Dawkins and his eloquence.

"That's why this time is so necessary, so that we can remove our armor and be able to show God that He is still head of the throne. You guys are in for a treat this weekend. I know we've traveled a long way, but it was worth it. God has a transformation waiting for us." Pastor Dawkins waited until the "Amen's" settled down. "Now, as always, I would like to go around the room and ask each man what he is expecting this weekend."

One guy—who Quincy saw at church from time to time, but whose acquaintance he'd never had reason to make—stood up, eager to be the first one to speak.

"Praise the Lord, brothers," the gentlemen greeted. "It's great to be here with you."

He received a well return of "Praise the Lord" from his brethren.

"As some of you know, I got laid off from my job about three months ago and I've been trying to find a job. It's been hard trying to put food on the table with a wife, two kids, a mortgage, and two car notes. But I come hoping that God has a word and a job for me. So that's what I'm hoping for this weekend."

The brother sat down on cue, and Quincy thought the guy's entire reason for being at the Retreat was a waste of time and money. This was not a job fair, and he could not expect to provide for his family while shelling out $200 for a Men's Retreat. On second thought, maybe Pastor Dawkins assisted the guy with paying for the Retreat.

Regardless of which, Quincy saw the man's reasons as naive. Several men had gone up and given less dramatic reasons for attending the Retreat. Jamal had turned quiet as a result of his and Quincy's conversation in the car, but Jamal had decided to stand up anyway. "Praise the Lord. I am excited to be here with my brothers. I have a tough decision to make that will have a huge impact on my family. I'm hoping that God can help me make the right decision."

Of course, Quincy knew that Jamal's reasons for going to the Men's Retreat were not as noble as they sounded. He was a fool and really there was no choice. He needed to cut his losses and spare himself future disappointment.

Ministers Perkins and Jacobs entered the room. Quincy was certain that one of the men in that room had slept with Karen. She'd never said who, but Quincy knew that, based on Karen's after-service interactions, it had to be one of them, namely a leader. Karen was always full of praise regarding Minister Perkins and his Bible Studies. Karen and Minister Jacobs served together on the feed the homeless ministry.

Coincidentally, Quincy was prepared to stand, and he stood up right as another brother stood up. Quincy's desire to speak outlasted the awkwardness of the moment until finally the other brother sat down.

"Praise the Lord," Quincy said to a warm welcome. "The scripture says that He is the way, the truth, and the light. Well, I'm hoping that God will bring some things out of darkness and into light."

Will watched as, one by one, each man stood up and stated why he was there. Will did not have a clue why he was there. He felt peace in the midst of an otherwise hostile lifestyle.

Soon there were only a few people left who had not gone up and spoken. A sweet tobacco scent brought Will's attention to the Black & Mild he had in his pocket. Tonight would be a good night to smoke; of course, he would have to wait for the church boys to go to sleep before he did so. Lost in his train of thought, Will realized that he was now the last person who had not spoken. The tall pastor extended his hand to Will. All the air left the room, and Will's body temperature increased as he stood.

"Um, I'm here to get closer to God," Will said, and sat back down.

It seemed like a legitimate thing to say. The question was whether Will really meant it. The vibration from his cell phone caught his attention. D-Loc must've called him about nineteen times. His mother had called just as many. Will dreaded going back home, but he could not leave his brother and sister at home with the wolves. He wondered when he would get a chance to think about himself and what he wanted.

What did Will want? For starters, he wanted this feeling he'd had since arriving at this place to never leave. He wanted to actually own a car instead of steal one. He wanted to not feel invisible. The world he knew buried his kind without any remorse. With billions of people in the world, how could he possibly matter? Just him thinking of life as something to live and not merely exist in was taking away his only edge. He did not want to go back, but he could not stay. And there existed Will's paradox.

Chapter Fifteen

Chauncey's brother had called twice while he was enjoying dinner. He was annoyed as the caller ID on his cell showed St. Mary's Hospital, so he made the decision to send all of his brother's and sister's calls to voice mail. Chauncey was constantly confronted with his brother's plight, and disgusted that his brother always reached out to him more than he would reach out to his Lord and Savior.

"How's your brother, Deacon McClendon?" Jamal asked.

"He's fine." Chauncey put his phone away. He did not feel the need to explain himself to a neophyte like Jamal. Instead, Chauncey turned his attentions to his guest, Will. At first, Chauncey had been certain that God was interceding on Will's behalf. He seemed to be in deep thought at the introduction meeting, and he'd seemed compelled to come here to the Retreat. But something seeped into Chauncey's consciousness during the introduction ceremony.

He became aware that maybe Will was not here to get closer to God. Maybe Will was a Trojan horse and he was here to do the devil's work. A chill scattered throughout his body at the thought that he may have been a vehicle that allowed the enemy to penetrate the camp.

A sly smile emerged from Chauncey's face at the thought that he had uncovered the devil's plot. At the same time, terror reemerged at the thought that it might be too late. Chauncey closed his eyes and began to pray with both hands interlocked and his head bowed, to the point where they were touching his forehead.

"Lord, give me the strength to do what is right in the face of evil," Chauncey prayed.

"Amen," Brother Evans said from across the table.

Chauncey realized his prayer may have been a little louder than he planned, because it caught the attention of Will, the one person he did not want to become antsy.

"You can get service all the way out here?" Chauncey asked Quincy, who was text messaging.

"I can get service on Mars with this phone," Quincy replied.

Chauncey found Quincy's texting rude, considering they were at a church event where the emphasis was on fellowship between men. Quincy disengaged and preoccupied himself with his cell phone.

"What you do for a living, fam?" Will asked Quincy.

"I'm an architect. Any of the new buildings you see in downtown Long Beach were either designed by me, or I gave very critical advice on the project," Quincy replied.

Humility was not one of Quincy's strong suits, which was why Chauncey and he often avoided each other as much as possible. Besides, Chauncey seriously doubted if Quincy was even saved. He barely attended church and he seemed more concerned with worldly things than the things of God. Of course, Chauncey did not want to judge him . . . out loud anyway.

"So you're the man at your job? Huh?" Will asked.

Quincy smiled and put away his cell phone. "Let me tell you, doc. Aspire to be your own boss. Times are hard, man, and I would be going crazy right now if I were in a position where my paycheck rested in another man's hand. I got tired of seeing my supervisor take credit for my ideas and take the spoils as well. I started my own firm with my best friend and have not looked back since."

"Real talk," Will said with a nod.

Quincy's words only reaffirmed the street logic Will already possessed. Chauncey had to steer Will away and make allowances for the fact that the pompous Quincy did not know the true nature of Will's attendance at this Retreat.

"You mean it is because of your faith in Jesus. God is the supplier of all our needs," Chauncey replied.

Quincy responded to Chauncey's statement with a short chuckle. "Yeah, that's true too."

"Looks like I've seen you around the hood before," Will said to Jamal.

"Possibly. You went to Poly?" Jamal asked.

"Naw, I went to Jordan," Will answered. He snapped his fingers with a big smile and pointed. "Jamal Bryant. You played running back."

Jamal smiled and nodded as a confirmation.

"I saw you rush for five TDs against Wilson."

"I remember that game too."

"So what happened? You was the truth back in high school," Will stated.

"I went to Cal State Long Beach and got my degree. I wasn't good enough to go pro, but I turned out all right," Jamal replied.

"Didn't you have a friend name Clay?"

Will noticed a change in Jamal's demeanor. Jamal shrugged and put his head down.

"Yeah, I did."

"Gentlemen." Pastor Dawkins walked up and put his hands on both Chauncey's and Will's shoulders.

"Pastor!" Chauncey said.

"I hope you're not too full from this meal. Definitely make sure you make room for the Word. Pastor Watson is going to bring it tonight. The service tonight is going to be off the chain."

"What you know about that?" Will interjected.

"I know what's up!" Pastor Dawkins gave Will a fist bump.

"All right! All right! I see you." Will smiled.

"Finish up your meal and I'll see you guys tonight." Pastor Dawkins walked away with the same stride as Denzel Washington.

Chauncey was relieved to see that Will made a connection with Pastor. His only hope was that the connection was strong enough for Will to want to change.

As a kid, Will had watched a movie called *Cadence*, where the soldiers in the movie marched, clapped, and sang songs of praise. Their voices were masculine, and they sounded like an old chain gang or field workers. Will got that same feeling tonight as the men sang.

"I don't know what you came to do," Douglas said.

"I don't know what you came to do," the brothers said in perfect sequence.

"But I come to praise the Lord. I came to jump for joy," Douglas shouted back.

And like puppets, men began to jump up in the air. When the song was over, the men went into a clapping fit of celebration, as if their favorite team had just scored. Will was skeptical at first, but he kind of liked the camaraderie among the men. Chauncey seemed to be really enjoying himself because he was crying and sniffling and mumbling gibberish under his breath. The man who had been leading the group in song had one hand on the mic and another hand in the air. His eyes were closed and tears ran down his face as if he had just viewed the most beautiful picture in the world. Will wondered what he'd seen that would bring a grown man to tears. He could barely recall the last time he cried. All the years of seeing his friends killed in cold blood had sapped his ability to feel emotions.

Emotions led to a woman crying over her baby's body while the coroner put the white sheet over her body. Will had passed by countless crime scenes where he did not feel any emotions. Before last night, Will did not see God in the midst of this life. He never contemplated how life began; to him, that was irrelevant. Will saw no rhyme or reason to life. We live, we suffer, we die. If a person was lucky, he found happiness in this life, but even that was a fool's hope at best.

But at this moment, as the men started another song, Will was overpowered by the pain and emotions in these men's voices. Something inside of Will started to stir. He felt an emotion that was as sweet as nectar. When the song concluded, Pastor Dawkins took center stage and took the microphone from the song leader.

"We are in for a treat tonight. A very good friend of mine, Dr. Watson from Abundant Fellowship, is here and he has brought a word for us here tonight. Let us stand and receive him."

All the men stood for a man who looked like he was chiseled out of bronze. Will hesitated, but decided to stand in order to avoid the awkwardness of being the only person not standing. Dr. Watson took the mic and gave Pastor Dawkins a hug.

Dr. Watson started to rub his bald head as if he had a scratch that he couldn't get to. "Uh, I don't know about you, but I came to praise the Lord. Amen," Dr. Watson said.

"Amen!" the group said.

Dr. Watson waited until men were in their seats and the only noise was the sound of the speakers buzzing. "I only have one question to ask you tonight. Where are you?"

Everyone perceived the question to be rhetorical in nature. Dr. Watson went on to read a passage in the Bible from the book of Genesis.

Will did not have a Bible, but that did not deter Chauncey from sharing his Bible with Will. Chauncey's Bible looked like a coloring book, with yellow, green, and orange highlighter marks throughout the majority of the pages. The highlighter marks were the only thing that Will could understood. The words could have been gibberish for all Will cared. It was amazing how one could run the streets and neglect the need to be able to read. He was confronted with the shame of being a high school dropout, a shame that he buried under the responsibility to his family; the need to hustle to provide for his young siblings and strung-out mother had caused Will to abandon his education. The preacher asked where he was: he was lost between ignorance and hopelessness.

"Where are you? It's important to know exactly where you are. God knew where Adam was to draw his attention to a disconnect in his relationship with God. When there is a disconnect with God, you have to correct it. Now, instead of mannin' up to his responsibilities, Adam launched into a series of excuses," Dr. Watson said.

Will noticed that this preacher had a raspy voice and sounded as if it pained him to talk.

"I ask you right now, where are you? Some of your minds are on your women. And some of your minds are, as Snoop says, on your money."

Will chuckled at the fact that this old preacher could recall a popular song by Snoop.

"Let me tell you something, God has placed too much inside of you for you to have less than your capabilities. You are meant to have power and dominion. You're not supposed to kill yourself working three jobs. You're not supposed to think that the only thing you can achieve is by shady means. No! Don't let the devil push your back against the wall. You push back."

The preacher had the men in an uproar.

"Why would you go anywhere else but to God? If God created me, then God has the best plan for my life. It's time to stand up and take our rightful place. It's time! It's time to stop tucking our tails between our legs and running every time we are in trouble. No more excuses. It's time to declare that for God I live and for God I'll die."

The preacher's words hit Will like a Mack truck. It rocked his beliefs to the core. He always thought that he was being a man by taking whatever he wanted from people.

His mentor had taught him that the weak were not meant to have and only the strong survived.

Will had buried these thoughts deep into his psyche, and that made him a predator of the weak. As he watched the pastor take brief moments to wipe the sweat from his face, Will recalled a time when he'd stuck a gun in an elderly lady's face. At the time, Will found the story to be amusing, but now he became aware of how heinous his actions were. He also thought about the time he beat this sixteen-year-old boy senseless to take his car. Maybe that was his parents' only car. Maybe that old lady went into cardiac arrest after she got jacked. In either case, Will doubted that there was a redeemable quality in his entire body.

"Where are you? If I were to ask, some of you would say that you're still at your job trying to get your next promotion. Some of you would say that you're at home with your family trying to squeeze in some quality time. Some of you will keep it real and say that your mind is on the football games, but none of those things can tell you where you are in relation to God."

Out of the corner of his eye, Will saw something wrestling in the bushes outside of the conference room. He did not know if it was a raccoon or a mountain lion. All he knew was that he was glad that he was on the inside and not outside.

"It takes courage to be a father when you had no father to serve as an example to you. It takes courage to stay faithful to a woman when the spark of romance is long gone. It takes courage to be a man when it's so much easier to be a boy. It's time to put away childish things. It's time to stand up and be accounted for." The preacher pointed to the floor. "It's time to come down to this altar and vow not to leave until there is a change. Come on right now. We ain't got time to waste."

Men rushed to the altar as if they were giving away free beer. Will sat in his seat, frozen, torn between the life he had always known and the possibilities of a new life being born at this moment. He could not move; he could not see himself kneeling to a God that, up until this point, he had never thought twice about.

As a child, he was taught that he should never kneel. Life would constantly deal him hard blows, even death blows, but he was never to allow his knee to touch the earth. His back would touch the earth when he laid his body down for good, but his knee? Never! There was more wrestling in the bushes, but this time it caught the attention of the few men who were not whipped up in a euphoric state. All of a sudden, two women emerged from the bushes, trying to spy on the Retreat.

One of them tried to run away, but got tripped up by the bush in the process and fell. Will could not help but laugh. The entire event was hysterical, and now he understood why women being at this event was a distraction.

Chapter Sixteen

Whenever Pastor Dawkins heard a great word like the one that Dr. Watson gave, he would usually go for a walk along the beach. On the beach he came into contact with the omnipotent presence of God. At night the sand looked like ash, and he allowed his feet to sink into the cool sand and enjoy a barefoot night stroll.

While the guys retired to their rooms to shoot the breeze and indulge in whatever entertainment they brought for the trip, Pastor Dawkins walked. He found the night to be a great time to commune with God. Though Pastor Dawkins enjoyed the fellowship of his brothers, he also longed for moments when he could be alone with his thoughts.

As a pastor, he was amazed at how much time was devoted to counseling and ministering to others. He could not imagine having to work a full-time job and minister at the same time. There was just not enough time, which was why Pastor Dawkins clung to the Apostle Paul's advice that it is better to not marry. How could he put a wife through his hectic schedule?

Pastor Dawkins found it peculiar that off in a distance was a woman in an olive green blouse. She seemed to have had the same idea that Pastor Dawkins had, and he was drawn to her.

"Breathtaking, isn't it?" The woman pointed toward the ocean as Pastor Dawkins approached her.

The moon lay suspended over the ocean. The waves crashed

along the rocks. For Pastor Dawkins, the ripples in the ocean were the only distinction between the ocean and the sky. It was a special moment that Pastor Dawkins would normally spend in tranquility or in prayer.

"You're here with the book club?" Pastor Dawkins asked.

"Yes, Pastor Dawkins," the woman said with a smile.

"How do you know who I am?"

"I attend Bethany. I know the mighty Pastor Dawkins very well."

Her blouse may have been olive green, but her eyes were emerald. She was enchanting as she stood along the shores. One would have thought that she was waiting for her lover to return.

"Well, you know my name, but I didn't—"

"Grace." Her smile would make any sanctified man bow and repent.

"I thank God for you every day," Pastor Dawkins said.

The two enjoyed a laugh at Pastor Dawkins's play on her name, and, for a fraction of a second, Pastor forgot the reason why he was there.

"Some of your girlfriends were spying on us," Pastor Dawkins said.

"I can't speak for myself, but when some of our members see a gathering of good-looking Christian men, they have to take a peek. I'm sure you can understand. I mean, y'all are almost an endangered species."

"Which is why I didn't want anybody else to be booked here during our Retreat. These brothers don't need any distractions this weekend," Pastor Dawkins said.

He noticed his comment was a little coarse, but it was too late in the evening for the Pastor to be eloquent.

"This place is big enough for the two of us. What's wrong

with us girls getting together to talk about books and enjoy the quality of sisterhood?"

"The problem is that you guys have no problems getting together. There are about forty women here just to talk about books. My ministry has labored tirelessly for months to get sixty men here. We made constant phone calls and announcements just for men to put aside one weekend to do something spiritual. We can't even get brothers to read. We tried to have them read *He-Motions* and most of them only read a few chapters before they put the book down."

Pastor Dawkins was surprised to find that Grace was not in combative mode.

She was not quick to trade blows with him, but she stared off into space and pursed her lips. "You seem like a man consumed with his ministry."

"Which is why I'm not married." Pastor Dawkins followed his statement with a laugh.

"Oh yes, I know." Grace laughed as well.

"What's that supposed to mean?" Pastor Dawkins asked.

"Your single status is notorious throughout the metropolitan area. I'm surprised you haven't met your future wife."

"I meet a different one every Sunday." Pastor Dawkins could not help but laugh again. He always believed that pride goes before a fall. He stayed humbled and focused on the cross.

"Is there a reason why you never got married?"

"I wanted to, but then I thought about it and realized that if I got married, it would no longer be my money, it would be our money. When I'd travel, I wouldn't be able to stay over for a couple of extra days and take in the city; I would have to come straight home. Lord have mercy!"

Grace laughed so hard that she let out a snort. Even this noise was attractive to the Pastor.

"I don't think that's it. I think it's that you're afraid."

Pastor Dawkins was a firm believer that faith and fear could not coexist within the same person. He was both taken aback and a little offended by her claim. "Afraid of what?"

"Afraid to be vulnerable," Grace said.

Grace had made a point that Pastor Dawkins could not shrug off as a nebulous comment. "Maybe you're right. A man is at his most vulnerable point when he is married. If you're unwilling to be vulnerable, then that leaves the door open for manipulation."

"And from my experience, marriage and manipulation go hand in hand," Grace said.

Pastor Dawkins was a third-generation preacher. Though neither his parents nor grandparents had divorced, Pastor Dawkins knew that his mother and grandmother often struggled with the dual personalities that accompanied their men. He could not afford to put a woman through that kind of ordeal, but as he stared at Grace, he could not deny his attraction for her.

Chapter Seventeen

Jamal had heard Dr. Watson speak on many occasions, so unfortunately his message did not carry the same effect it might have with someone who was hearing him speak for the first time. He walked along the trail that led back to his room.

Despite the inner turmoil regarding little man, Jamal still took the time to appreciate the stars that lined the sky. The world was a symphony and God was its great composer. He allowed the sun to rise and set, and the moon to take its place. If it were not for the sound of waves crashing together, Jamal would have thought that he had just gazed into infinite darkness instead of the ocean.

Will stood afar. Jamal did not want to approach him for fear that he was deep in thought, but an unsettling feeling came over Jamal and he knew that was the Holy Spirit at work within him. Jamal, under the direction of the Holy Spirit, headed over to strike up a conversation.

When he arrived at the beach, he saw Will with his feet sinking in the sand, splitting a cigar with his fingers. He did not know where Chauncey had met this man or how he managed to convince Will to come to this Men's Retreat. There was one thing Jamal was sure of: Will was fresh off the streets and this whole experience was overwhelming for someone like Will.

"What's going on, man?" Jamal asked.

Will was just about to light up a blunt when the sound of Jamal's voice startled him. "Man, you scared the mess out of me." Will had his fist up with his blunt in one hand.

"Man, I didn't mean to bother you, I just saw you here by yourself."

Will's eyes seemed to be watery, and when he locked eyes with Jamal, he did not look like a man being disturbed, but someone who needed a listening ear.

"What's up with you?" Will said with a nod.

"Nothing. Just saw you out here by yourself and thought you could use the company."

"This is bugged out right here." Will turned his blunt to the side and pointed toward the ocean.

"Yeah, the ocean is a trip," Jamal agreed.

"I'm terrified of the ocean," Will admitted.

Jamal was shocked to hear an admission of fear. "What did you think of the service tonight?" Jamal asked.

"It was cool." Will took a drag of his blunt and exhaled. "Dude was deep."

"Yeah, Pastor Watson always brings a good word."

The conversation fell silent, though it seemed unfinished. Jamal and Will gazed out at the ocean. "Let me ask you something," Will said.

"Sure, go ahead."

"Do you think God can forgive you no matter what you do?"

A chill swept through Jamal's entire body. It was like he was talking to a younger version of himself. He remembered asking Pastor Dawkins that same question years ago.

He also remembered Pastor Dawkins's answer. "I believe that God forgives you no matter what you've done, but you have to be sincere and genuinely want to have a relationship with God."

Jamal saw that the young man was taken aback by his words and that his brain began to spin with new possibilities.

"I've seen and done some foul things in the hood. Things that I felt like I had to do to survive. You know what I'm saying?" Will confessed.

Jamal knew exactly what Will was saying. He used to carry that same mentality.

"But even in the direst of situations, you still have a choice. I was like you at one time. I was on the block getting it in. Then I came to the crossroads and I chose life over death. You know your path leads to destruction and it's on shaky ground," Jamal concluded.

The vast darkness that was night could not conceal Will's eyes nor his heart. He wanted to change, but he grappled with what type of realistic change he could make.

"I just don't know about bowing down and praying to some Jesus that I can't see." Will shrugged.

"My brother, I learned something a long time ago. It is better to bow down to Jesus, who is the answer to all your problems, than to bow down to the circumstances of life and let life dictate for you how far you can go."

Jamal just did not know how much he should push. He knew that the slightest increase in Jamal's appeal for Will to change his life could lead to Will rejecting the entire process.

"It's cool talking to you, because you know what it's like out there," Will told Jamal.

"Man, I have done and seen some things that I'm not proud of, but through it all, God has been there. He teaches me how to leave my past where it belongs: behind me." Jamal paused before asking, "Do you believe in God?"

"Sometimes. But all I see is evidence that there is either no God or there is a lesser God. I can't see myself bowing to a God like that."

"We all have free will and that gives us either the choice to do tremendous good or great evil."

Will only responded with a nod. In truth, Jamal still wrestled with some of the things that plagued Will. He'd seen kids born in some of the most destitute of situations, kids with the odds already stacked against them; they had no choice but to accept the lot afforded them. On the flip side, he had seen kids reject their lots in life and aspire to accomplish great things. Jamal chose to focus on the positive and not the negative. He left questions like, "Why is there suffering?" to the experts.

"You've walked some of the streets I've walked. How could you expect God to take care of you?" Will asked.

"I stay focused on God and I allow Him to order my steps. If I stay in God's will, then I don't have to worry about what's to the left or right of me. Everything that comes against me has to fall. "

It was Jamal's hope and prayer that he did not come off preachy to Will. He knew the young man was not looking to be sold a bill of goods. He wanted to give the young man something real to grasp.

"Look, Will, where do you see yourself five years from now?"

"I don't know."

Jamal got chills from that statement. Will had to be at least eighteen or nineteen years old. To be in a mental place where he had no idea where he was headed with his life was beyond belief. "That's the thing; when you're out there running the streets, you can't see the future because there is no future. You owe it to yourself to at least give yourself a chance to see if life can turn out for the better with God. Because with God, the possibilities are endless."

Everything Jamal said seemed to go over Will's head. He seemed to be overwhelmed, and Jamal could understand. Sometimes an encounter with God could be terrifying.

Jamal's attention was turned toward the stars. The moon seemed to have plenty of company tonight. Out of his peripheral vision, Jamal could see that Will was also enjoying His goodness tonight. A peaceful night was another example that God could show something better than words could describe. At this moment, Jamal could pull all of the words from the dictionary, and none of them would satisfy what his eyes were beholding.

Quincy admitted this: Dr. Watson could still put on a good show. He was thoroughly entertained by Pastor Watson's sermon. For a spell, Quincy allowed himself to be caught up in the emotions of the event, and neglected his original purpose: to destroy one of the ministers. He strolled along the rocky path and considered the question posed tonight. Where are you?

The question brought him to a complete stop just short of his room, where several of the men had begun to congregate. Where are you? Quincy was a middle-aged man with the arms of a twenty-year-old and a mouth that could sell snow to an Eskimo. He was at the pinnacle of his career, and he was about to release his soul from his biggest mistake: his wife Karen. So why did something feel out of joint? He was never someone who was afraid to reach up and grab the brass ring, but the thought that he had cleared every hurdle and had nothing else to claim frightened him. There were no more mountaintops, just conquered territory.

Yet, something eluded him. He felt kind of silly for just

standing in the road. So he walked slowly toward the group of men and considered what was missing. He pulled out his cell phone and was about to call Karen, until he realized that the nature of their relationship had changed.

Usually he would give her a call after the service and let her hear the excitement in his voice and how jubilant he was about getting closer to God. Quincy had also made vows to be a better husband. Most of his attendance at church was to appease Karen, but the Retreat was one event that brought forth an earnest desire to get closer to God. Vows that he would disregard no sooner than his return home.

Quincy reminisced about previous Retreats, and how Karen would stand outside of church on Sunday and wait for him to return in the caravan with the rest of the guys. She would then flash a big smile and run down the church steps to wrap her arms around him and plant a big, fat, juicy kiss on Quincy's lips.

It was a tradition at Greater Anointing that the men lead the service in praise and worship upon their return from the Retreat. Karen would sit in the pews with a glow on her face as she watched her husband give praise unto God. After church, Karen would cook Quincy his favorite dish: catfish and greens. She would let him watch the football games uninterrupted, and at night she would give him good loving by the fire.

None of those things would await Quincy when he got home this weekend. He imagined he would down a bottle of brandy and maybe watch an adult movie. He might even go back to Vegas. A marriage needed more than just a few days out of the year to go the distance. Twenty years of marriage were marked by different checkpoints and several crossroads where the marriage might meet its demise. But Quincy never questioned Karen's loyalty, and had been blindsided by her affair. The affair had rocked him, and to this day he could not see a foregone conclusion.

Until a few days ago, he upheld the vows of his marriage, though for years it felt like a slow strangle. His rendezvous with Candy the call girl did not make him feel any better. He did not feel like he evened up the score. Candy was a girl who Quincy had to pay for her time. She gave him pleasure and left Quincy with shame; the kind of shame that does not wash off easily. Karen, on the other hand, had formed a bond with another man. That was a microcosm of how distant their marriage had grown.

Yes, he could, at times, be difficult to be with, but none of Quincy's offenses could warrant his wife to cheat.

"Hey, Quincy, what you doing just standing there?" Jonathon, a member of the church, said.

Quincy became embarrassingly aware that he had just been standing in the same spot, allowing his thoughts to impede his steps.

"Oh, I was about to give the wife a call, but I keep forgetting that she's probably asleep by now," Quincy lied.

"Not mine. My wife has trouble sleeping if big daddy is not there to hold her," Jonathon said.

Quincy forced a smile. He was not up for a sword-measuring contest at this hour. Besides, if the challenge involved comparing wives, then this would be a challenge he would automatically lose. Quincy walked over and put his hands on top of the extending doorway. He leaned forward as if he was about to do pull-ups. He observed the men standing around, shooting the breeze.

"It's good to see you, Q," Jonathon said. "I haven't really seen you at church lately."

"Work has consumed all my time. What do you do when

you're the best at what you do and people cannot seem to work without you?"

Quincy could tell that he was talking to a sheep rather than a shepherd: a man who followed orders rather than gave them. Fear and mediocrity permeated these men. Quincy couldn't wait to free himself from men who used their faith as a justification for a lesser life. From a distance, the sound of chatter caught Quincy's attention, and he saw two figures move through the concealment of night. Jamal and the new guy, Will, soon emerged.

"What's up, guys?" Jamal greeted them.

"Nothing, just shooting the breeze," Jonathon replied.

"So, Will, what do you do for a living?" Jonathon asked.

"I'm into exporting cars," Will said.

"How old are you?" Quincy asked.

"Nineteen," Will replied.

His age went over everyone's head except for Quincy's. "Exporting cars" for someone Will's age meant "stealing cars." He now had a clear question mark over his head regarding Will and his place of employment. He wondered if Will was involved in shady dealings.

"Look at that!" Jonathon pointed into the darkness.

Several creatures moved throughout the darkness, and Quincy became aware of how loud his heart was beating.

"What is that?" Jamal asked.

Just then the creatures took off running and revealed themselves to be raccoons heading toward the men. The guys scattered like buckshots, some running into their rooms and others toward their cars. They were soon outnumbered by the small fleet of raccoons. Quincy didn't believe himself to be in any real danger, and he could not tear himself away from the scene unfolding. Grown men were running from raccoons.

"I'll handle this!" Quincy headed toward his vehicle. He opened up the trunk, removed a new 9 iron, and started to stomp toward the raccoons.

"Fore!" Quincy swung at the raccoon like an opening drive. He not only missed, but slipped and fell on the ground. "Aw, get away from me!" Quincy got up and took off running toward the corner of the cabin with everyone else.

He heard the sound of his room door open and checked to make sure a raccoon had not ran in. Moments later, Will emerged with a gun in his hands, and fired shots into the ground.

The men stopped running and noticed that Will had a gun in his hands. The raccoons scattered into the bushes.

"What? I go hunting," Will said.

"You go hunting with a handgun?" Quincy asked.

"Yeah, I hunt bears."

All the men began to laugh at the surreality of the moment. Quincy did not laugh, but became certain that Will was not all that he said he was.

Chapter Eighteen

Quincy could not remember the last time he laughed so hard. For that matter, he could not even remember Chauncey ever laughing. He did not know that laughter could exist in such a stiff-neck.

"Man, I need to put that on YouTube, you and that golf club!" Jamal laughed while lying down.

"You can't make money off of YouTube, but America's Funniest Home Videos is a different story." Quincy continued to laugh, then pointed toward Will. "And Wesley Snipes over here came out of nowhere shooting. Talking about you go hunting. And where you from again?"

"Long Beach!" Will said.

"What are you hunting in the middle of Long Beach?"

There was another round of laughter, and then Quincy lay down on his bed and played with his BlackBerry. Jamal sat at the edge of his bed and started to do arm stretches. Chauncey lay next to his nightstand, thumbing through his Bible, while Will sat in a chair next to a table.

"This has made the whole weekend worth it to me," Jamal said.

"As funny as the whole raccoon thing is, it's nothing in comparison to Dr. Watson's sermon. That man was on fire tonight," Chauncey said.

"Whatever." Quincy rolled his eyes and continued to play with his BlackBerry.

"That man was deep. I can't lie," Will said.

"Is this your first time at a Retreat?" Quincy asked Will.

"Yeah. I used to go to church with my moms, but I wasn't feeling it. I mean, they made Jesus seem like a punk!" Will said.

"Oh, my Lord. That's not true!" Chauncey popped up.

"Is he always like this?" Will asked Jamal, referring to Chauncey.

"Pretty much," Quincy interjected.

"Why do you feel that way about Jesus?" Chauncey asked.

Will shrugged. "I don't know all this stuff about turning the other cheek, loving your enemies, and Him being spit on and not doing nothing. That's weak to me. There's no way I could survive in this world if I thought and acted that way. There is no way Jesus could survive in my world."

"That's where you're wrong. The scripture says that he was wounded for our transgression and condemned for our iniquities." Chauncey started to spank his Bible.

"I ain't trying to be funny or nothing, but I just got out of church. I mean, you didn't even listen to the man before, now you're spitting out scriptures at him," Quincy said.

"I have to combat such nonsense with the Word. I'm serious about this Christian walk. I've memorized over six hundred verses."

"So what? You're at a cocktail party and all of a sudden you just start spitting out scriptures?" Quincy asked.

"I don't go to cocktail parties." Chauncey sounded accosted by Quincy's statement.

"I'm not surprised. I couldn't imagine you going, or anyone inviting you for that matter," Quincy replied.

"Hold on, hold on. Will brought up a real serious issue." Jamal turned to Will. "Jesus was not a punk. He chose to be a powerful example instead of an example of his power. It's easy to disrespect people when they disrespect you. The real power comes when you choose to go against the grain and not react.'"

"Amen!" Chauncey said.

"And it's offering time," Quincy said as he sat up.

Will and Quincy enjoyed a good laugh.

"I also can't get into the whole sex thing. I mean, my father raised me that a man don't turn down nothing unless the girl is fat, ugly, fertile, or has an STD," Will remarked.

"Your father sounds like my father. Otis Bryant?" Jamal asked.

Quincy could see the Christians closing in on the new guy, and though Quincy understood that Chauncey and Jamal were only trying to help Will, he could not stand to see anyone get double-teamed.

"I can kind of see where he's coming from," Quincy said.

"No, Q, that's horrible. That's why so many men have problems now," Jamal said.

"I'm not saying that I totally agree, but look at him." Quincy pointed at Will. "What are you, eighteen, nineteen?"

"I'm nineteen," Will answered.

"See, when I was his age, you wouldn't find me at no church event. I'd be in a car, cruising the boulevard. I had to go see those honey dips, why you playing?"

"You're just corrupting his mind. The Bible is clear on sex outside of marriage. It's a sin," Chauncey said.

"C-man, you can't tell me you ain't slipped up and got a piece," Quincy said with a smile.

"Actually, I haven't." Chauncey was nonchalant in his remark.

"You're a virgin?" Will asked.

"Yes, I'm a virgin. I am waiting for the right woman. God's best!"

"What about when you weren't saved?" Jamal asked.

"I got saved when I was eight years old. God's way is the only way I've known."

Will let out a long whistle and Quincy nodded in agreement to Will. Quincy could not wrap his head around what Chauncey had just said. If it weren't Chauncey spilling this ridiculous story, he would not believe it.

"C, you're older than me. If you're still a virgin, that's a sin! And waiting for the right woman, she's going to be eligible for social security by the time you get ready."

"I'm only thirty-seven," Chauncey replied.

"Keeping it one hundred. I respect you, Chauncey, for waiting that long. I wish I was that strong," Jamal said.

"You are—we all are—and we all got the light of God flowing inside of us." Chauncey made eye contact with everyone.

"Speaking of light, I'm about to hit the lights. I'm tired and I know we got a big day ahead of us tomorrow."

Will took off his shirt and started to flex his muscles in his white tank top. Jamal also had on a white tank top, and he too started to flex his muscles. Not to be outdone, Quincy took his shirt off and started to flex his muscles. Of course, his flabby stomach was evident through his white T-shirt.

Quincy vowed to join a gym as soon he returned home. Quincy did not notice that Chauncey had gone into the bathroom until he heard the sound of a flush. The door opened, and Chauncey emerged in a blue nightgown. Now Quincy was convinced that Chauncey was a virgin.

"I will say one thing though, Will. I'm not a virgin, but I wish I would have waited. There is something special about waiting until you find your wife," Jamal said.

"I don't, playboy. What if I waited and she turns out to be horrible at sex?" Will asked.

"You're a guy; she would have to be darn near a corpse for that to happen," Quincy said as he lay back down in the bed.

All the men laughed, and Quincy even caught a laugh from Chauncey. For the first night, Quincy would have to admit that it was eventful. One could only wonder what was in store for tomorrow.

Chapter Nineteen

The alarm woke Chauncey up and seemed to only cause a minor disruption in the sleep of his roommates. He avoided hitting the snooze button and switched the alarm off. The paleness of dawn peeked through a small curtain opening. Chauncey got up, put on a black sweat suit, and grabbed his Bible as he exited the door.

The ocean water was gray and choppy. Seagulls had already started their routine of flying about. Chauncey found a spot on the beach next to the rocks where he planned on having a morning devotional. He brushed some of the sand off the rocks and sat on one of the smooth stones.

He saw all the endless footprints in the sand and thought about the poem "Footprints." He loved the last line of the poem, where the author sees a single set of footprints, and how that was when God carried him.

"Lord, I'm looking for you to carry me today." Chauncey lifted his hands up in praise.

While his eyes were closed, Chauncey imagined his brother lying in his hospital bed. In the midst of crashing waves and the smell of seaweed, Chauncey contemplated how sin was completing its work with Henry. The scary thing was that Chauncey did not feel anything for his brother. He was not even concerned with his brother's soul burning in eternal fire. In Chauncey's mind, he had done all and sacrificed all for his brother. The turning point came a year ago when Henry barged into Chauncey's home uninvited.

"Get out of here, Henry." Chauncey pointed at the door.

Henry continued to ravage through the living room of Chauncey's home, breaking anything that was not of value.

"I need the money." Henry smashed a porcelain vase. "They going to kill me unless I have it."

Chauncey was petrified with anger and fear. His baby brother was possessed. He seemed demonic and hell-bent on destroying himself and anyone who stood in his way. "You need Jesus. The devil's got a hold on you."

"I need the money! I promise I'll get help afterward."

"That's what you always say, but it's all lies."

Henry began to rub his head as if voices in his head were getting louder and louder.

"You know it would break Momma's heart to see you like this. Let me help you," Chauncey pleaded.

Henry stopped his pacing and then locked eyes with the gold necklace around Chauncey's neck. The chain was a gift from Chauncey's mother. It did not carry much value in Henry's case, but, nevertheless, it was priceless to Chauncey. A chill crept along Chauncey's spine. He recognized the look on Henry's face. It was the same look his father used to get whenever he craved something to support his heroin addiction. That same looked caused Chauncey's father to beat his mother's head into a kitchen counter until she gave him all of her valuable jewelry. All except the cross that she gave to a twelve-year-old Chauncey, who was too badly beaten to protect his mother.

Twenty years ago, their father ran up a debt with a drug dealer that he couldn't pay, so he took his own life and his wife's life as well. A fit of rage left the children without any parents. It had been twenty years since Chauncey's melancholic ascension to patriarch of his family; he now confronted his brother, who had the same demonic look.

"Don't you even think about it," Chauncey said as he tucked his chain into his shirt.

Henry rushed over to Chauncey as he retreated into a corner. Henry reached for Chauncey's chain and Chauncey tried as best he could to keep Henry from getting it. But he felt the chain break apart, and despite how hard he fought, Henry was the stronger of the two.

"Let go, Henry," Chauncey pleaded.

Henry responded to Chauncey's pleas with his fist. Chauncey felt his nose fracture and his air disrupt. Before he could recover, Chauncey received a punch in the stomach and he fell to the floor. Henry took the chain, along with a couple of other valuables.

Chauncey made a vow that he would not ever allow his brother to get within arm's reach again. He no longer trusted him and would not stick his neck out for him. The thought of the vow filled Chauncey with so much rage that he closed his Bible and bent it until it resembled a scroll.

He placed the Bible to his lips and tears streamed down his face. He had been kicking his brother out for his entire life and always opening the door for Henry to come back in.

Now he found himself in a position where he did not want to open the door for his own brother. In his heart, he kind of enjoyed his brother's suffering, because he'd lost so much behind Henry and it was time for his brother to feel the consequences for his actions. Chauncey knew that this was not a way for a Christian to feel. Only God could change both his mind and his heart.

Jamal was too active to sit still and pray. He arose Saturday morning to find that Chauncey had already gotten up and left. Jamal threw on his gray sweats and white cut-off shirt as he headed out the door. He started jogging along the shore.

The icy air gave him the confidence that his body temperature would balance out with the strong wind. He passed by
Chauncey, who sat along the rocks with his Bible rolled up
in his hands. His lungs started to burn as he remembered to
breathe in and out. He could not shake the advice that Quincy
had given him in the car; it bothered him like a hangnail. He
thought about how he got mixed up in the situation. He only
put together partial images of what had happened that night.

"It's cracking at this club tonight," Clay said while he danced to
the music.

"Yeah, it's full of dime pieces." Jamal surveyed the landscape of
the club.

Everyone on the dance floor was coated in candy apple red neon
lights as they danced to Dr. Dre's "The Next Episode." Jamal and
Clay made their way to the bar. They squeezed their way through
tight, curvaceous women, and once they arrived at the bar, they
nudged each other to notice that the bartender was cute.

She had a face too young to be a bartender and hair that was wild
and curly. "What can I get you gentlemen?"

"Coke and Hen," Clay said.

"A screwdriver," Jamal said.

"Drinks are on me, Jamal," Clay said.

"Good looking!" Jamal replied.

Moments later, the bartender returned with the drinks. She took
Clay's one hundred dollar bill and examined it in the light. After
Clay got back his change, he and Jamal held up the glasses.

"Live like a man," Clay said.

"Or die like a coward," Jamal replied.

Jamal made Clay think that they were at the club to celebrate life.
True, he and his best friend were living the life that people would not
expect two kids from Long Beach to live. Jamal had just landed a
good-paying job, and Clay was preparing to become a dad to the child
of his longtime girlfriend, Chantel.

Truth be told, Jamal was not sure if the club would be the best place to confess to Clay that he'd slept with Chantel. It had only been one time and he had vowed not to tell Clay. In fact, it was possible that Jamal may have been the father of Chantel's baby.

His conscience convicted him day and night until he had to confess to his friend.

"You ever think about getting married?" Jamal asked his best friend.

"Never! Pimps don't get married, they just change up."

A sable-complexioned woman, wearing a purple dress that hugged her frame, passed by. Jamal's and Clay's eyes followed her.

"You better handle that," Clay said.

Jamal had just started to reconnect with his faith. As a kid, he used to go to church with his grandmother. He stopped going to church after high school. He never stopped believing in God, he just believed that he did not have to go to church to experience God. After having attended a three-on-three basketball tournament at Greater Anointing, he reconsidered growing closer to God.

"Let me ask you something," Jamal said to Clay.

"Man, not now, I'm trying to rub on something." Clay started dancing.

"That's what I wanted to ask you. What's up with you and Chantel?"

Clay stopped dancing. "What you mean?"

"Are y'all together or what?"

"Why, you trying to take her from me? I'm letting you know right now, you ain't got the heart to pull her from me. You never had it in you."

Jamal's pride was under attack. His best friend since the fourth grade was questioning his manhood. He was supposed to be a Christian, but right now he did not feel like turning the other cheek.

"Oh, I'm man enough!" Jamal snapped back.

"Please! You wouldn't know what to do with her. You can't handle a woman like her," Clay said.

"Apparently I can, since I've been hitting that while you're at work. And from what she tells me, you often come up Mugsey Booges."

The Mugsey Booges was an indication that Clay came up short in the sexual department. It took a moment for Clay to register Jamal's words. He pushed Jamal and Jamal pushed Clay into a short guy with braids.

When Jamal and Clay turned around they saw that the guy was wobbly.

"Say 'excuse me,' fam," the guy ordered.

"What you mean excuse me?" Clay snapped back.

Clay was notorious for his anger, so Jamal grabbed him by the arm. For a brief moment, Jamal knew he had control of his friend. But Clay fought his arm away from Jamal and the little guy pushed Clay.

"What up now?" the guy asked.

Clay wasted no time and threw a haymaker that connected with the guy's jaw. The guy fell back like bowling pins. Jamal lurched forward and punched the guy, who tried to take a swing at Clay.

The entire crowd constricted; guys and girls tried to make their way outside. Jamal's sole focus was on leaving the club in one piece. They at least accomplished that, and made their way to the parking lot where Clay's Camry sat.

"Give me the keys," Jamal demanded.

"Don't say nothing to me, just get in," Clay replied.

"We ain't got time for this. Give me the keys!"

Clay did not usually let anyone drive his car. Jamal knew it was not smart to drive in the car with someone who had drunk as much as Clay. For whatever reason, Clay handed over his keys to him. Maybe it was Clay's anger or the alcohol that made him realize that he was in no condition to drive. Whatever the reason, Jamal was grateful. He just continued to pray that everyone in the car would make it home in one piece. They were posted at the light for a minute. Awkward silence dominated the moment.

"How long?" Clay asked.

How long? That was all he asked, and from Clay's body language, Jamal was sure that the light could go from red to green several times before Clay would utter another word.

"It's been a minute. It just happened."

"Just happened!" Clay punched the window twice. "You're supposed to be my boy. Bros before hoes. Remember?"

"I love her," Jamal said somberly.

"You love her? That's my girl! That's the mother of my child. I trusted you. I loved you, man."

Jamal knew his best friend was hurt. He and Clay were both secure in their masculinity, so it did not bother them to verbally express their love for one another. But they chose to reserve the expression for pivotal moments. This occasion reminded Jamal that in being with the woman he loved, he had hurt the friend he loved as well.

Just then, a car came up alongside the passenger side of the Camry. The windows rolled down and guns emerged from the vehicle. The assailants shot up the Camry. Blood splattered on Jamal's face like someone had just shaken a can of soda and opened it. Clay absorbed all of the shots as the car sped away. This was not happening. Jamal's best friend was breathing one moment, and now he lay lifeless, covered in blood.

Jamal sped away with his vision clouded by red: the red of his best friend's blood and the red for the rage he felt.

The nearest hospital was less than a block away, but it seemed like a thousand miles. Jamal hit the accelerator until it reached the floor. He had to make it, even though he knew that his friend probably would not make it. An hour later, the blood on Jamal's shirt had dried. His best friend was gone and had left his bullet-riddled shell behind.

Jamal's mind never gave him a reprieve from that moment. He knew his friend's death was the result of retaliation, the code of the streets. But Jamal questioned whether he could respect a code that would leave an unborn child without his father. Jamal's decision to become a dedicated Christian was birthed out of his desire to live at a higher code.

Chapter Twenty

By the time Will woke up, his room was empty. He'd had trouble sleeping last night, so he was not surprised that he was up earlier than normal. At 8:45 A.M., Will assumed the push-up position and formed his hands like triangles, and began a set of thirty push-ups. By the time he finished his third set, the muscles in his shoulders and chest had tightened and were burning.

Will took a shower with hot pressure to relax his muscles. While in the shower, he tried to figure out what was going on in his life. For the first time he was not burdened with a sense of having to look over his shoulder. He had no other life than a life of crime. Stealing cars was his one and only skill. He had been baptized in it and it was the only thing his father had taught him.

Will could count on one hand how many times he'd cried. One of them had been when his father was sentenced to ten years. The toothpaste fell from Will's lips and he snapped out of his daydream. In the last ten years he'd looked up to his father and loved him deeply. His father taught Will how to think ahead, see the angles of a situation, and how to stack his money. In regard to money, his father taught him that it rained more than it was sunny for a black man. So he'd taught him to put money away for a rainy day. His father proved to be a better teacher. Will had yet to see the inside of a prison cell.

However, the feelings that Will had been in touch with

lately were dangerous, because they made him feel vulnerable. In fact, this whole trip was dangerous, because it was opening him up to a new world. Still, Will figured that it was better to quit while he was ahead.

Will spotted the belongings of the gullible Chauncey, who had left his wallet and car keys in plain sight. He did not want to steal from a man who would rather take him to a church event than jail; but it was innate in Will's nature to exploit any kind of generosity. Will grabbed the keys from the nightstand and removed $300 from his wallet.

He threw on a puffy coat and exited the cabin. Will was greeted by a powerful sun that pushed through the clouds.

The warmth of the sun levitated his soul as he inhaled the seaweed from the beach and listened to birds. Even the tall green grass acknowledged the sun's presence and waved to it. Will closed his eyes and took a deep breath.

"Young man?"

Will opened his eyes and saw it was Pastor Dawkins. He was with two guys, who he assumed were his bodyguards.

"What up, Pastor?" Will said.

"Nothing much." Pastor Dawkins held out his fist and Will bumped it. "I was wondering if you wouldn't mind joining us for breakfast; I hear the pancakes are off the hook."

Will and Pastor both shared a laugh at such a lame effort on Pastor's part to sound cool, but Will needed to get out of town before Chauncey came back.

"I'm not really a morning person, Pastor," Will replied.

Pastor Dawkins's countenance changed. He wasn't angry; he was more disappointed than anything else. It was like he looked forward to spending time with Will.

"Not even waffles?" Pastor Dawkins asked.

Will could not hold back the laughter. Maybe he could

get one more meal in before he left. It wasn't like his family missed him. He knew Joshua did, but it was important that Joshua learn how to stand on his own when he was not around. His mother couldn't care less, and his sister was too young to understand anything. Will also knew that he would have to answer to D-Loc after flaking on him the other night. Despite everything that told him not to stay too long in this place, Will could not leave.

"That's what's up! Let me just drop something off in the room right quick." Will did not even wait for Pastor Dawkins's response. He entered his room and made a beeline toward Chauncey's nightstand.

He could not believe that he was actually about to return something that he stole. He removed the money from his pocket and placed it back into Chauncey's wallet. After Will set the keys down next to the wallet, he headed out the door and locked it.

"Sorry about that, Pastor Dawkins." Will began to walk alongside Pastor Dawkins.

"Now, tell me, Will, where are you from?" Pastor Dawkins asked.

"Long Beach, by Jordan High School."

"Oh yes, I'm very familiar with that area. It can, at times, be very difficult for a young man such as yourself to grow up."

Will found Pastor Dawkins's voice very soothing. He treaded through a sandy sidewalk, but was not in a rush to go anywhere.

"Where I'm from cats do what they have to do. It's hard out there, Pastor."

"Indeed it is. That's why we must rely on the scripture that says we are more than conquerors. That means that we do not have to be dictated by our circumstances, but with God we can overcome any circumstances."

Will had never heard anyone talk with such conviction. Pastor Dawkins seemed like a man empowered by his faith and not weakened.

"Is there anything that you desire to do with your life?" Pastor Dawkins stopped and asked.

No one had asked Will a question like that since his high school guidance counselor. There was a period of time when Will gave school a chance, and he would have graduated from high school with a 3.0, but his father went away to prison again and Will could not stand to see his family struggle. He thought about going to Long Beach City College, but the needs of his family were too great for him to waste time with school.

"I mean, I love to cut hair, and I thought about maybe one day owning my own barber shop. I don't know," Will stated.

"Are you any good?" Pastor Dawkins asked while rubbing his head.

"Oh, for sure!" Will agreed. "I cut my brother's and homies' hair all the time."

"Then maybe later tonight before the main service we can put those skills to use," Pastor Dawkins said.

"All right, bet," Will said with exuberance.

Will was honored that this pastor was willing to give him that one thing he rarely had: a chance. More than a conquer. He liked that! Maybe there was something to being a Christian after all.

Chapter Twenty-one

Quincy took a bite of his grain muffin and one gulp of his orange juice. He was not much of a breakfast person, but the cafeteria gave him ample opportunity to study the interactions of his brethren. Today would be a day full of workshops and interactions with the ministers. This was his best chance to expose Minister Hypocrite.

As fate would have it, Quincy would get an opportunity to talk with Pastor Dawkins face-to-face. Pastor Dawkins entered the room with his entourage and Will. The group made their way through the breakfast station.

"They have a much better selection this year than the year before." Jamal had just returned from grabbing his breakfast, and took a seat next to Quincy.

"What do you think is the story with Will?" Quincy asked.

Jamal shrugged. "I know too many people like Will in the hood. They consider making it to twenty-one an achievement. I just hope that this weekend sinks in for him and he makes a change for the better."

"Do you buy the story that he helped Chauncey with car troubles?" Quincy asked.

"Who knows? I wouldn't put it past Chauncey to invite the Easter Bunny to church." Jamal's statement caused both men to laugh.

"Good morning, brethren." Chauncey arrived at the table with a plate of food.

"Speaking of the devil," Quincy said.

Chauncey sat down and began to add salt and pepper to his scrambled eggs. He barely got two bites in before his cell phone rang. After a brief pause, Chauncey pressed a button before turning his cell phone off and putting it back in his pocket.

"Who was that?" Jamal asked.

"My brother," Chauncey replied before scooping some eggs into his mouth.

"I didn't know you had a brother," Jamal said.

"That's because he ain't saved and I would rather not talk about him."

"But he's your brother. It shouldn't matter if he's saved or not," Quincy replied.

"Gentlemen, do you mind if I sit with you?" Pastor Dawkins arrived with his armor bearers and Will.

"Oh, of course we don't mind, Pastor." Chauncey got up and started to pull chairs from a nearby empty table. Pastor Dawkins took a seat along with Will and the entourage.

After a brief prayer, everyone resumed eating. Quincy could not have set up this situation any better. He had the pastor sitting across from him at the breakfast table.

"Let me ask you something, Pastor." Quincy waited for Pastor Dawkins to give him the nod to proceed. "Why do you think Christianity is on such a decline?"

"I don't." Pastor Dawkins put his fist over his mouth to cough. "I just think more people desire Christ and less religion."

"You don't think the hypocrisy in the church has anything to do with it?" Quincy asked.

"Give an example?" Pastor Dawkins asked.

Quincy thought Pastor Dawkins would never ask. "Well,

the Bible talks about the husband being the head, but when you go to church it seems like more emphasis is put on the pastor being the head."

"The pastor is the spiritual head of the church," Chauncey said as he gave Pastor Dawkins a wink.

"I know that, but the pastor is projected as the perfect man, and women feel utter contempt to have to go home with their less-than-perfect husbands."

Quincy generated a bunch of stares from around the table, particularly from Jamal. Of everyone at the table, Jamal was the only one who knew that Quincy's questions were related to his current situation with Karen.

"I agree with you, Brother Page, and that's why I've never tried to project myself as perfect. That is also why I've encouraged women who are having problems with their marriages to try to use more love and less judgment."

"Yeah, but, Pastor, you have a bunch of women lined up outside your office on Sunday mornings. I mean, that is some influence; you must be tempted."

"No, because it would cost too much for me to take advantage of the sisters at the church."

"Brother Page, you have to let Pastor eat so he can be ready for the workshops today," one of Pastor Dawkins's armor bearers said.

Quincy was not satisfied with Pastor Dawkins's answers. The pastor still could be Karen's lover. The thought alone made Quincy lose his appetite.

"I'll see you guys at the workshop." Quincy placed his napkin over his food and left the table.

He did not even bother to respond to the farewells from the table. Quincy made his way up the walkway toward the conference room. He felt the sun pierce through the sliding glass windows and the sun's rays heat his legs. This workshop would be pointless if Quincy did not get answers.

Minister Perkins walked into the conference room with his hands full of copies. He also had a Bible in his hands.

"Good morning, Brother Page," Minister Perkins greeted him.

"Good morning, Minister Perkins."

Minster Perkins had a smug look on his face that made Quincy want to break his nose just for the sport of it. The dark-skinned brother with the fake green eyes had on a Lord's Gym shirt with Samson pushing away from the pillars.

"How's your wife?" Minister Perkins asked.

That was a dead giveaway.

"She's fine. She told me to tell you hello."

Quincy noticed the awkward look on his face, which was a telltale sign.

He scrambled for an appropriate response. "Well, tell her I said hello."

"Why don't you tell her yourself?" Quincy got up and walked toward Minister Perkins. "By the way, do you know what A-MOG stands for?"

"I don't," Minister Perkins said curiously.

"Of course you don't. You're just an innocent little church boy," Quincy said.

Quincy got within striking distance. He was one word away from unleashing a merciless assault on the good minister. He just needed a little bit more confirmation. "You know, don't you?"

"I know about what?" Minister Perkins replied, confused.

"My wife."

Several of the brothers interrupted the standoff by entering the room with laughter and meaningless chatter. Quincy embraced the missed opportunity and backed away from Minister Perkins. He savored the awkward look on the minister's face.

"Praise the Lord," Minister Perkins said, relieved to see the brothers.

Quincy took a seat as Minster Perkins handed out copies of a workshop pamphlet called "Fight for Your Marriage." Minister Perkins always bragged about being successfully married. That all could have been just a front; Quincy found it hard to believe anyone was that happy in his marriage. Quincy did not see a reason to continue to fight for something that was already dead. The problem with most marriages was that either people married for superficial reasons or they married out of convenience. In essence, Quincy had more respect for two adults who had come to grips with the fact that their love had had a good run, but it was time to go their separate ways.

"When you think about marriage, you have to be honest here. Marriage is a lot of hard work," Minister Perkins said.

The men started to agree.

"We are constantly at battle. We're constantly at war. Our flesh craves attention and, honestly, our wives are not always willing to satisfy our cravings." Minister Perkins started to bounce around like he normally did when he got excited.

Quincy could not believe that he would have the nerve to talk so boldly about his lustful desires and dissatisfaction in a marriage.

Minister Perkins pointed down toward his private. "This piece right here; the Bible is clear that there can be no perversion of this piece right here."

Minister Perkins paused to let the shock from the guys in the room disappear.

"That's why when the scripture talks about putting on the whole armor of God, the first thing you are to put on is a belt to hold your pants up. Christian men should never be caught with their pants down. We have to cut off the door of infidelity and fornication."

Quincy got a kick out of Christians who talked big, but failed to live up to their own standards. This added to the list of reasons why Quincy was not as committed to church as he used to be.

"If we can be honest with ourselves, then we would admit that sometimes our coworkers make us feel more appreciated than our wives do."

Minster Perkins had everyone's attention except for Quincy's. Despite all of Karen's faults, Quincy never felt unappreciated by her.

"How do we fight for something when we are constantly questioning our value and worth?"

Most of the men, now, had quizzical looks on their faces.

"The answer is that we remember the sacrifices our wives made to be with us."

Minister Perkins's question prompted a brother to raise his hand. Quincy remembered seeing the guy at a Super Bowl gathering at the church. He believed his name was Theo, Theo Garrett, and he usually had a joyful disposition, but not today. Today he seemed perplexed.

"Brother Garrett, you do not have to raise your hand. Go ahead and say what's on your mind," Minister Perkins said.

"I hear what you're saying, but what do you do when you feel like you're getting abused at home? Now see, my wife, she ain't giving me no loving at home. She talks about me like a dog. What should I do?"

Quincy thought the prescription required him to develop a backbone. He refused to let a woman talk to him any old kind of way when he paid the bills.

"Brother Garrett, may I ask, how do you treat your wife?" Minister Perkins asked.

"I treat her according to the Bible. I remind her that I'm the head, and she went along with it until I lost my job. Now she talks to me like I'm a joke."

Brother Garrett's comments seemed to strike a chord with the married men. When a man hits rock bottom is when he can no longer walk with his head held high in his own home. Quincy understood this concept too well. A man could take on the world so long as he felt like a champion in his own home. When a woman takes that away, she's dealt a deadly blow to his manhood.

"Brother Garrett brings up an issue that a lot of men struggle with. How do we maintain being the head of our home when our circumstances change, like losing a job? Losing a job is devastating for a man because we take pride in our work."

James stood up. Quincy barely knew James, but what he did know, he liked. He was a little bit lighter than Quincy, with a similar build.

"Brother Garrett, I just want to say that I feel you," James stated. "I know what you're going through. I've been there and I'm telling you that no matter how frustrating it may be at home, don't lose faith. You can call me up anytime, because unlike you, I didn't have a brother to call on for help. My wife used to say a lot of negative things, and I got so mad at her one time that I hit her, and I continued to hit her until I lost feeling in my arms." James paused for a moment to regain control of his emotions. His eyes were closed and one could only speculate that the images of his actions were more horrific than what he described. Tears escaped his eyes. "I nearly killed her, man. I nearly killed her. I swore to her that I would never hurt her and here I was praying that she would die. I just didn't feel like a man, and I wanted to get my manhood back even if I had to take it by force."

The room was silent and the air was thick. Even Brother Garrett was sitting down.

"I had to pay for what I'd done. I spent three years in prison, but when I got out, God was waiting for me to restore my life, and my wife was waiting for me to restore our marriage."

"That's a powerful testimony, Brother James." Minister Perkins paused long enough the let the claps and praises reign. "It's important to know that there is no such thing as a Lone Ranger Christian. We're all battling just to keep from losing our minds. What is also important to remember is what our wives gave up to be with us."

That statement penetrated the fortress that surrounded Quincy's heart. Karen had been halfway through an art degree when she'd met Quincy. He convinced her that an art degree was a waste of both time and money.

Quincy vowed to take care of Karen and build her an art studio if she desired. Her parents were furious that she was both quitting school and getting married. Quincy knew that she took solace in the fact that she was marrying the love of her life, and Quincy knew that there was no other woman for him. Those sacrifices seemed like they occurred a lifetime ago, and, over the years, Quincy had tried to be a good man to her.

"Joseph refused to let his fleshly desire prevent him from becoming all that God wanted him to be. We must be the same way. I know that there are some fine sistas at your church and job, but guess what? God isn't going to stop making them, so we have to learn to master our fleshly desires," Minister Perkins said.

Lately, Quincy believed that the best way to resist temptation was to yield to it. He did not deny himself any pleasure.

Why should he? In fact, from now until they buried him, Quincy was going to live it up like his idol, Sammy Davis Jr.

"I love my wife, but if I'm not careful with my words and my thoughts, I could find myself going down a road that I had never intended going down. Honor your commitment. Keep God first and remember her sacrifice," Minister Perkins concluded.

Quincy was skeptical about whether Minister Perkins was the actual person who'd had an affair with his wife. He seemed genuine at this moment. His feelings could be a front, but at the same time, admitting that Minster Perkins may not be the one placed him back at square one. Quincy felt his phone vibrate. He removed his BlackBerry from his pocket. There was a text message from his business partner Gregg. The text read:

Call me ASAP. We have a problem.

Quincy stepped outside of the conference room, and upon being greeted by the cool air, he called his partner.

"Gregg, what's up?" Quincy asked.

"Where are you? We're on the verge of losing the deal." Gregg was beyond frantic.

"What do you mean we're about to lose the deal? It was airtight. We just needed to sign the papers," Quincy said.

"We've been lowballed," Gregg informed his partner.

Quincy had been afraid that they might be lowballed. Quincy loved money, but he never got greedy. The deal was worth a lot of money, but Quincy believed that if a person wanted the best, then he had to pay for the best.

"I'm on my way; call an emergency meeting." Quincy hung up the phone and made his way toward his truck.

He would call Jamal later and explain his abrupt departure. Quincy was certain that one of the brothers would offer Jamal a ride home. Quincy did not even bother to grab any clothes.

Quincy pushed the Range Rover over eighty-five miles per hour. The leaves on the ground swung wildly in the air as he crushed the open road. He saw a red and blue flash as a police officer on a motorcycle pulled him over.

"Are you kidding me?" Quincy said to himself.

Quincy pulled over his Range Rover and rested his head against the headrest. He was not worried about the ticket, but every second counted. After the officer gave him his ticket for speeding, Quincy received a text message that they had lost the deal.

To lose both his wife and a big business deal all in the same week was inexplicable. $15 million was gone in an instant. Quincy was trying to find out what he had done to put himself on a war path against God.

Jamal always looked forward to the workshops for single men. He knew that there was no stronger battle than the one a single Christian man faced. When Will entered the conference room, it was a pleasant surprise.

"What up, fam?" Will greeted him.

"What up?" Jamal said as he gave Will a pat on the shoulders.

Minister Jacobs walked in with his packets and his black Bible. "Oh, how good it is for men to dwell together."

All the men stood up and gave a clap for the lecturer.

"Joseph is my hero, because I don't know about you, but if I stood before a woman naked, the last thing that would go through my mind is my covenant with God."

The men laughed, and, with a smile on his face, Minister Jacobs started to pass out copies of his packet.

Jamal admired and respected Minister Jacobs. He was youthful and practical in his approach. Jamal had learned a lot under Minister Jacobs's teachings. He taught Jamal how to walk out the principles of the Bible.

"You have to know that you're the baddest brothers on the planet. You're strong, good-looking, athletic, and well-educated Christian men. There is no more powerful force on God's green earth."

Out of the corner of his eyes, Jamal saw Will nodding in agreement.

"Before we go any further into the lecture, let's start off with a word of prayer," Minister Jacobs said as he bowed his head and prayed. "Heavenly Father, bless each and every brother in this room. Look past our faults and see our hearts as we gather together to draw closer to you. Amen."

Minister Jacobs concluded his prayer and waited until he'd made eye contact with every man before he continued. "Joseph was in our league, and when you're powerful and have the light of God inside of you, you are a target. What do you do when your light draws a fine sister close to you and she pushes up on you?"

"You hit that!" Will said.

The room went silent before it exploded with laughter.

"Naw, brother, we can't hit that. That's for when you're married," Minister Jacobs said.

Jamal knew that the phrase "waiting until marriage" was foreign to Will.

"The world teaches us that when you're a man, you don't turn nothing down, but we live by the principles of God, and God says that sex is reserved for marriage," Minister Jacobs continued.

Jamal struggled in this area. He knew what the Bible taught about this subject matter. For the most part he avoided placing himself in compromising situations, but there had been a few times when Jamal slipped up with random women. He prayed for forgiveness and asked God to reveal the strength within him that could cause him to be victorious the next time around.

"You want God's best for your life and a random girl at the club may not be God's best. If you allow your animal desires to control you, then you will find yourself in a mess."

Jamal thought about that night at the club, and how if he and Clay had never gone to that club, his best friend would have still been here. Chantel had been a good girl, perhaps better than any other girl you would find in the hood. She had her head on straight and she handled her business. Jamal had thought about hollering at her back in the day, but he felt she deserved better than him and his best friend.

"If we can walk the way Joseph walked, then God will elevate us to places that we never dreamed of achieving," Minister Jacobs said.

Jamal looked over to Will and saw that Will hung on to Jacobs's every word. He thought about Chantel, and how he let so much time pass without letting her know how he felt.

"Oh, one last thing . . ." Minister Jacobs let out a sadistic smile. "No messing around with 'Palm-olina.' Masturbation is a sin. If you're fantasizing about Rhianna while doing it, you're lusting after another woman. Second Corinthians tenth chaper, fifth verse tells us to cast down vain imaginations and anything that seeks to exalt itself. Jesus said that if you even look at a woman lustfully, you've committed a sin. Bottom line, your mind is too precious to God to waste on fruitless images."

The room exploded with laughter, and Jamal struggled to regain his breath as a result.

"The point of this whole lesson is that we have to be men of integrity, and the Bible calls for us to present ourselves as a living sacrifice. That means that we have to put to death the things that our flesh craves, such as pornography and fornication. These things are in direct conflict to the things of God."

After a moment, Minister Jacobs continued. "We need to be a generation of young men who take a stand for the things of God."

Jamal was reminded why he admired Minister Jacobs so much. If God asked him to, Jamal would follow Minister Jacobs to the gates of hell, but hopefully it wouldn't take that for him to be all that God desired him to be.

Chapter Twenty-two

Will was starting to appreciate all of this church stuff, and when the guys decided to go out and play football before lunch, Will decided without any hesitation to play. Whenever Will played football back home, his games were interrupted by the oncoming traffic of cars that cruised down his neighborhood. Out here, Will only worried about the traction from the sand slowing him down. That and being hit by golf balls from Quincy.

Quincy had disappeared for a little bit, but he came back and seemed a little irritated. Will assumed that hitting balls from the top of the hill into the ocean was Quincy's way of relaxing. Even though Will had a lot of respect and admiration for Quincy, if he hit Will with one of his golf balls, Quincy was going to be wearing one of his golf clubs.

"Down, hut, hut!" Jamal said.

Jamal drew back with the football cocked back in throwing position. Will scrambled to beat his bigger, slower opponent. Despite the resistance brought by the hard sand, Will blew by his opponent rather easily.

Will was wide open, and turned around to see the football spiraling against a gray sky. The football was just outside of his reach and began its descent toward the ground. Will dove for the ball and caught it as he slid into the sand.

"Yeah!" Jamal yelled as Will jogged back with the football

in his hands. He dusted off some of the sand from his arms. He scored the game-winning touchdown, and with that, he had worked up an appetite.

Updates came in frequently on Quincy's BlackBerry from his business partner as Quincy sat in the dining room with his roommates. He was no longer upset about losing the deal. He'd overreacted at first, but since deciding to return to Asilomar to settle some unfinished business, Quincy had returned to his calm state. He had lost multimillion-dollar deals before. That was a part of business, but the succession of events that had unfolded this week was what had Quincy perplexed.

"That phone never leaves your sight," Chauncey said to Quincy.

Quincy wondered if Chauncey had a problem with him or if he was against technology. "I missed a big-time deal to be here," Quincy said. He looked around the table and made eye contact with everyone. Jamal seemed transfixed on his napkin.

"Well, it doesn't seem like you're here. Every time I look up, you're fooling around with that thing." Chauncey pointed at Quincy's BlackBerry.

"Brother McClendon, I could've sworn that I left my wife at home," Quincy said as he put his BlackBerry away.

Will and Jamal let out a laugh while Chauncey shook his head in disapproval.

"Let me ask you guys something. What does A-MOG mean?" Quincy asked.

"Almighty, magnificent, omnipotent God!" Chauncey guessed.

Quincy was sure that A-MOG did not mean that.

"Advice: money over God!" Will said.

Quincy knew that was not it either.

"Anointed Master of Godliness," Jamal guessed.

Quincy was certain he was wasting his time with this question. He was in the company of gullible church boys. He would have to dig deep if he was to uncover the truth. A-MOG was here at the Retreat. In such a tight-knit group, it might be hard to spot him, but Quincy was confident that if he looked hard enough, he would find answers.

A waitress in tan shorts delivered their food. Usually whenever a meal was brought, Chauncey would engage in a short prayer before diving in. The mushy vegetables and the dry baked chicken were what caused the men at Quincy's table to pause.

"Lord Jesus, bless this food. Bless this food from the top of your head to the crown of your feet, Jesus. Don't let this harm us in any shape, way, or form, Jesus. Amen, Amen, Amen!"

"I'm not sure about this food," Jamal said.

"I know; they serve better food than this in the county. I'm thinking about going to get some food from Fast Burgers," Will said.

"They got a Fast Burgers out here?" Jamal asked.

"We passed one a few miles back," Will replied.

"I don't know about going to some fast food joint. I prefer to be served and waited on," Chauncey said.

Some of the ladies from the book club came in to eat, and Quincy observed how some of the married men eyed them in their short jean shorts. Some had to pull out pictures of their wives and kids to keep from lusting.

Quincy studied the baked chicken in front of him. He took a bite of chicken and had difficulty chewing the dry texture. There was a distinct difference between their top-notch breakfast and their subpar lunch.

"This chicken is about as dry as the Mojave Desert," Jamal said.

Quincy looked up and recognized the look of disdain on Jamal's face, as well as the other gentlemen's faces. Will coughed up into his napkin a piece of chicken that was still considerably dry, and set the balled-up napkin on top of his plate.

"I'll drive," Quincy said.

Quincy's lunchtime annoyance did not cease when they arrived at Fast Burgers.

"I'm sorry, sir, but we don't take bills over a twenty," the short Asian cashier said.

Quincy looked at Jamal and Will with a stunned look on his face. He never thought that he would be denied spending cash in a restaurant. "Are you kidding me? How do you actually expect to run a successful business when you can't even break a hundred dollar bill? That says a lot about your infrastructure," Quincy said.

The girl just gave Quincy a shrugged shoulder, and adjusted her burgundy and gold visor.

"Look, I'll get lunch." Jamal pulled out a twenty dollar bill.

Quincy shot a look at the $19.64 total on the register, but he was not deterred.

"No, I got lunch. I don't have time to argue with seven-dollar-an-hour people." Quincy put the hundred dollar bill back in his wallet and pulled out a gold American Express card.

"We only take Visa or MasterCard," the cashier said.

Quincy shoved the American Express back into its slot in his wallet, pulled out a Visa card, and handed it to the cashier.

"Your entire establishment is going to crumble unless you change your ways," Quincy said as he took both his card and receipt from the cashier after the cashier rang up the order.

Once the battle between Quincy and the cashier had concluded, the food was ready. With pursed lips, Quincy picked
up his tray and joined Jamal and Will at the booth they were
already seated in.

"Man, this is good." Quincy savored the seasoned, salted
French fries.

"That's a nice Rover you got," Will said.

Quincy took a huge chunk out of his double cheeseburger
and left tomato and mayonnaise in its wake. "Yeah, it cost a
pretty penny too." Quincy scratched his ear with his pinky.
"I'm a firm believer that if you work hard, then you deserve
to play hard."

"This man has also got a Bentley," Jamal added.

Will sucked out the last bit of cola from his medium-sized
drink. He then lifted his eyes up in awe at Quincy.

"Those cars cost an arm and a leg, but they're worth it. I've
always had a fascination with cars, which was inspired by a
fascination with girls. When I was fourteen I was driving; I
had to go see them. I couldn't be on no bus trying to get at a
cutie pie." Quincy let out a laugh.

"I'm trying to get it like you. You doing your thing." Will
wiped his lips with his napkin.

Quincy saw an opportunity with Will. Some of the prestige
that came with being a black architect involved speaking en-
gagements. Quincy reveled in the chance to talk with people
about their potential, especially youths.

"I've been blessed, I can't deny that," Quincy told Will.
"I've had a lot of opportunities to go down the wrong path. I
had friends who got off into drugs, but I could never see the
long-term benefit of that occupation."

"Sometimes that's the only choice you have," Will replied.

"I've come to realize that you cannot surround yourself with
people with limited thinking. It takes time to build something

that will endure. It takes time to make money. Do you have any goals or skills?" Quincy asked Will.

"I mean, nothing other than cutting hair," Will said.

"What's stopping you from doing that?" Jamal finally spoke after inhaling his food.

"The truth is, I didn't finish school," Will finally said after a brief pause. "Pops went to jail and I had to be the one to go out and get it. So that left no room for school."

Will's story reminded Quincy of the narrow road one has when one does not get an education. If it weren't for his father being such a disciplinarian, Quincy might have found himself in the same situation that Will was currently in.

"Well, you got to finish your education first before you can do anything," Jamal said.

"I know, but it's hard because right now I'm caught up. I mean, I can't just drop everything and go and do me." Will scooped a handful of fries and ate them.

"What is it that you're good at?" Quincy asked.

"Well, what I'm good at isn't really on the up-and-up. I can cut hair, but that would require me going to school on top of school."

Quincy saw Will as someone who had drive, but very few opportunities. It did not surprise him that Will was not engaged in honest labor, but it seemed like Will's hand had been forced into that lifestyle. Quincy always looked for a project to work on. It was his nature to build something, whether buildings or people.

"If you're serious about cutting hair, I would be willing to invest in you," Quincy said.

"You don't even know me," Will fired back curiously.

Perhaps there was some part of Christianity that had rubbed off on Quincy. He had no logical reason why he was willing to help this young man, who had been a stranger to him just twenty-four hours ago. To say he was compelled to help him was an understatement.

"In life you take risks for opportunities. I'm willing to take a risk. Are you willing to take the opportunity?" Quincy asked.

That was a question that resonated within Quincy's spirit. So much of life came down to risks and opportunities. Even in his beliefs, God was willing to take a risk on man. Was man willing to take the opportunity?

Quincy received a text message that he could not ignore. It was from his business partner and it seemed vital that he reply. "Excuse me one moment," he said as he got up and left the restaurant.

"What's going on?" Quincy decided to call Gregg when he got outside.

"Man, where have you been? I'm going crazy right now," Gregg said.

"You can't even close a simple deal? Do I have to do everything myself?" Quincy asked.

"We got lowballed again, Q. This time it was the Century City deal, and with the way the economy is looking, I think this is going to continue."

Quincy was not somebody who bucked at the first sign of danger. He held firm and did not worry about things out of his control. He knew that he was the best when it came to architecture, and that, in the end, quality would win out.

"When are you coming back?" Gregg asked.

Quincy surveyed his surroundings. In the midst of redwood trees, small-town stores, and biker gangs, one could get lost.

Quincy was not too sure if he wanted to be found.

"Look, man, I got some personal issues I got to handle. You're just going to have to man up and hold it down until I get back. I can't hold your hand through this." Quincy hung up the phone.

Quincy's world was folding, and with the week he'd had, Quincy wondered if he was cursed.

Chapter Twenty-three

Pastor Dawkins was actually happy to see Grace on the beach reading with a group of girls. The sun stood over them as it held its heat so that the girls could enjoy a day at the beach.

"Hello, Pastor Dawkins," Grace said with a smile on her face. The rest of the women in her group snickered like school girls.

"You ladies enjoying yourselves?" Pastor Dawkins asked.

The wind from the ocean was so strong that it blew back the brim of Grace's straw hat. She used her hand to keep her hat from flying off.

"Oh, we're having a great conversation about this book." Grace held up a copy of Steve Harvey's, *Act Like A Lady, Think Like A Man.*

If Pastor Dawkins had a dollar for every woman he saw with a copy of that book in her hands, he would have Will Smith's type of money.

"Well, I hope you find it insightful." Pastor Dawkins started to walk away, wanting to avoid an awkward moment.

"What do you think is the problem in most relationships?" Grace asked.

Her question stopped Pastor Dawkins dead in his tracks, which is what he felt Grace wanted to do anyway. He thought for a moment. "Lack of a father in both a young boy's and young girl's lives." Pastor Dawkins paused a moment to let his statement sink in. "You see, a young boy needs a father to show him how to navigate through the different stages of manhood. A young girl needs a father to model an example of what a man is. Too many times you have guys who don't know how to be a man and you have women who don't know what a man looks like."

He could tell that his point hit home with the group. Some of the women looked at each other and blushed, while others looked at Pastor Dawkins as if he had just stepped out of a cave.

"Do you think part of the problem is how we set our expectations?" Grace asked.

"No doubt! No doubt, but part of the problem is that we are not real with ourselves when it comes to the expectation we set. If you set a standard for excellence, then you can not waver in that standard even if that means that you are alone. There is a difference between being alone and lonely."

Grace flashed another award-winning smile. Every time she smiled, Pastor Dawkin's resolve began to weaken. He had thought about her a lot since last night. Thank God that she was not a mind reader; otherwise Pastor Dawkins would have been embarrassed if his private thoughts of Grace were exposed. His thoughts of Grace were innocent if there was such a thing. But in all honesty, Pastor Dawkins hadn't interrupted the girls gathering at the beach in order to teach, he just wanted to see Grace. He wanted to see if her radiance still held up in the daylight as much as it had last night. He was pleased to find that she was every bit as breathtaking as he thought.

"So how are things on your end, Pastor Dawkins?' Grace asked.

"We're having an awesome time in the Lord, and thanking God that we are not being distracted." Pastor Dawkins looked at each girl as if he were a disappointed father. Every girl looked ashamed except for Grace, who flashed another girly smile. She was going to ruin him with that smile, which only made her high-yellow cheekbones glow.

What was God doing? Was it possible that Grace could be a trick from the enemy? But he doubted that such beauty could exist in an evil plot.

Chapter Twenty-four

The Circle of Power was a highlight of the Men's Retreat. For Quincy, the Circle of Power carried an even more special touch to it. This would be his opportunity to pinpoint the man responsible for sleeping with his wife and breaking up his marriage. It almost seemed like divine intervention that in front of Christian men he would confront his wife's lover.

Quincy beat the crowd coming in and had a seat next to the front door. He tried to replay in his mind a scenario where he had failed Karen as a husband. When that moment had occurred, what did she do? Did she run to the church and confess her sins to the minister? Maybe they met at a hotel or a movie theater and carried on like two young lovers.

Karen had been too ashamed to talk about it. She had to take responsibility for her actions. Quincy was not to blame for shutting down and proceeding with the divorce. She knew not to suggest marriage counseling; as far as Quincy was concerned, Greater Anointing was a house full of hypocrites.

Brother Thomas entered with a group of brothers and began clapping. "Hallelujah!"

The men clapped and Quincy joined in. Soon all the men, including Jamal, Will, and Chauncey, took a seat in a big circle. Pastor Dawkins came into the middle of the circle and all the men clapped.

"Be seated, please be seated," Pastor Dawkins ordered.

All the men took their seats, and Pastor Dawkins did a slow spin and made eye contact with every man. "What's wrong?" Pastor Dawkins asked. Pastor Dawkins let the question sink into the hearts of the men, but Quincy did not internalize it.

"Whatever is wrong, now is the time and this is the place where you can leave it on the floor. Confess to God and to your brothers, and let's become advocates for change. It's time to be men." Just like that, Pastor Dawkins took a seat on the opposite side of the circle from Quincy.

A middle-aged man walked to the middle of the circle with one hand covering his mouth. "I'm so glad to be here with my brothers. I almost didn't make it here. On Thursday night I was in a crack house when someone walked in and started shooting up the place. A bullet just missed my head." The guy paused to clear his throat. "I crawled into a corner and prayed that if the Lord got me out of this one, I would never be the same again."

Quincy was as terrified as anyone else in the room. To come so close to death would turn anybody religious.

"I'm here because I need my brothers' help. I can't make it without you, and I need you guys to hold me accountable," this man confessed.

He received a score of "Amen's" and he took each one as a sign of encouragement as he sat down. No sooner had the man sat down than Chauncey followed and stood in the middle. Quincy rolled his eyes because he knew—and everyone in the room knew—that Chauncey talked too much.

"Praise the Lord, brother!" Chauncey pointed to the man who had just sat down.

"Brother Edwards, you don't hesitate to call me, you hear? I'm going to lift you up in prayer." Chauncey then looked around the room. "I just wanted to encourage you all to put

God first and keep Him first in your life. Be blessed, brothers." He sat down in his chair.

To Quincy's surprise, Chauncey had been brief. The next man was someone who Quincy had not seen in a long time: Clarence Reeves. He was one of the few men who attended Greater Anointing who Quincy liked. He liked Clarence because he was white and was not at all fazed by skin color. He just loved church. Clarence looked frail, like he had not been eating. Quincy could not blame him; the food at that place was terrible.

"Brothers, I'm here because I'm tired of running. I thought I was running from God when really I was running from who I am. For the last two years I've tried to hate God, because I can't understand why God would make something that He hates."

Quincy's heart went out more to Clarence, because he did not think anybody was ready for what Clarence was about to admit.

"I've been living on the down-low for five years now. I used to come to church on Sunday mornings and dance and shout. Then I would spend Sunday night in the arms of another man," Clarence confessed.

Everything went silent, including the crickets. Men were able to understand and relate to a lot of things: drugs, alcohol, abuse, pornography, and adultery, among other things. Homosexuality was the one thing that a lot of straight men could not wrap their heads around. If Quincy were to conduct a survey at this Retreat of fantasy threesomes, he would get a whole bunch of participants. The hypocrisy lay in what was acceptable to the softer gender and what was unacceptable for men.

"I didn't want to come here. I swear to you I didn't, but I

missed being in His presence." Clarence started to choke on his words. "Despite the fact that most of you will look at me differently, I missed being around you guys. I want to be able to come to church and not feel guilty. I believe I can overcome this, but I need God and my brother's help to do so."

It was rare to find someone who was gay and wanted to choose against what seemed like his human nature. Pastor Dawkins proved why he was so celebrated as a pastor. He walked up and gave Clarence a hug as Clarence sobbed onto the pastor's shirt.

"It's going to be okay. You can't run far enough to get away from God's loving arms," Chauncey remarked.

Clarence received claps as he returned to his chair. Will was the next to get up.

"Um, I wasn't sure about coming here, and, to tell the truth, I hadn't really given God that much thought before this weekend. I mean, where I'm from we see the devil more at work than anything else.

"The one thing I can say about this weekend is that for once in my life, I got a chance to be at peace. But if I don't see you guys again, I just wanted to tell you thanks for showing me love. I'm so used to seeing life one way, and you guys have turned me on to another way I can live my life."

Will gracefully sat down as another brother got up and gave a detailed account of his addiction to Internet pornography. After that Jamal stood up.

"Praise the Lord. It's good to be in the house of the Lord, especially with my brothers." Jamal paused to allow the praises to cease.

"I came here thinking that I needed to hear a word from God regarding my job situation. I realize that I needed to confront my past." Jamal locked eyes with Will. "It wasn't until I met you this weekend that I realized that." Jamal took a step toward Will. "You remind me of my best friend, who died. This whole time I've felt guilty for his death and I realize that I have to let it go. I've allowed pride to stop me from being forgiven."

Jamal could not even say anymore. Quincy imagined that he was so overwhelmed with grief that he could not bear to say another word.

Minister Jacobs got up with tears in his eyes, unable to clearly get his words out. "I'm sorry, brothers, I can't just sit here and act like everything is okay. I'm a hypocrite. A back-slider. How can I sit and tell y'all how to live your lives when I can't even live up to the standard myself?" Minister Jacobs wiped his face dry.

Quincy leaned forward with his hands folded on top of each other, and concentrated on being able to catch every single word from Minister Jacobs. He, too, was a suspect, since Karen assisted Minister Jacobs with feeding the homeless.

"I have lust in my heart and I've allowed the desire to grow so strong that I slept with another man's wife. I mean, I'm supposed to be an anointed man of God," Minister Jacobs confessed.

It took Quincy a moment to realize what Minister Jacobs just said. Anointed man of God. A-MOG. "You son of a . . ." Quincy jumped up and threw his chair at Minster Jacobs before running toward him. The chair caught Minister Jacobs in his back after it bounced off the wall. Quincy wrapped his hands around Minister Jacobs's shirt and tried to choke the life out of him.

Other men, despite their confusion, rushed to the aid of Minister Jacobs.

"You slept with my wife and had the nerve to talk about it without first coming to me like a man," Quincy shouted.

"I'm sorry." Minister Jacobs swallowed hard.

"Too late!" Quincy snapped back. Quincy was finally separated from him. "I filed for divorce. You better be glad God is forgiving, because I'm not!"

"She was miserable," Minister Jacobs said.

"So was I, but I didn't cheat."

Quincy felt a hand on his shoulder that calmed him down. He saw that it was Pastor Dawkins. "We all need to settle down and calm ourselves."

Everyone except Quincy calmed down. It was all out in the open. There were no more shadows in the lives of Quincy and Minister Jacobs. He sized up Minister Jacobs in an effort to understand what Karen could possibly see in him.

Yes, he was good-looking, but he carried with him a disposition of a guy fresh out of college with a mountain of student loan debt. That reason alone put Minister Jacobs out of Quincy's league. Jacobs had to be in his mid-twenties, and, at forty-three, Quincy was not as physically fit as Minister Jacobs, but he had an obese bank account.

"I'm so sorry, Brother Page," Minster Jacobs said through a veil of tears.

"I'm not interested in your apology. In so many ways I blame you." Quincy pointed at Pastor Dawkins. "Women talk about you like you're their pimp. My wife was more loyal to one of your ministers than she was to me." Quincy took a moment to catch his breath. "So let's just get this out in the open right here, because after this weekend, I'm gone and y'all are not going to ever see me again."

"This is the best place to deal with this issue. What do you want to know?" Pastor Dawkins asked calmly.

"I want to know why." Quincy took a look at Pastor Dawkins. "And I want to know what you're going to do about this situation."

"Perhaps we can go somewhere and talk," Minister Jacobs suggested.

"Aw naw," Quincy said, shaking both his head and hands. "We're going to settle this right here and now, because, to tell you the truth, I'm afraid that if we go somewhere to talk, then one of us is not going to come back."

Pastor Dawkins outstretched his hands to signal to both Quincy and Minister Jacobs to settle down. Quincy sat down, not out of respect to Pastor Dawkins and his position, but because his adrenaline had come down and he was starting to feel lightheaded.

Pastor Dawkins continued. "Let's allow both the Holy Spirit and cooler heads to prevail. Now, Brother Page, you have every right to be upset. And, Minister Jacobs, you are responsible to tell Brother Page what's going on. I don't think that I have to remind all of you that we are covered with a vow of confidentiality. We're not like little school kids who run around here gossiping and carrying on. We are men, and a man can look to his brother and tell him what's going on."

"How can you let someone like him minister from the pulpit?" Quincy pointed toward Minister Jacobs.

"I'm in no way excusing his actions, but he is human. He could be the greatest human being walking the earth and still be susceptible to folly," Pastor Dawkins reasoned. "That's why we need grace and mercy to live in this fallen world."

Pastor Dawkins took a moment to clear his throat. "Furthermore, you know that I preach against the sisters of the church having unhealthy relationships with their pastors. I've seen too many scandals unfold and I refuse to be a part of it. You are the head of your household and no man should come before you." Pastor Dawkins locked eyes with Quincy.

"Reverend Pimp Daddy must've been asleep when you taught ethics in ministry class," Quincy replied.

"You're hurt, and as a man you're taught that to show emotions is to show weakness, but it's okay. You have the right to feel hurt and betrayed. What happened should not have happened, but it did and I'm sorry. But don't let what happened to you cause you to give up on God and the purpose He has for you."

What purpose could God have for Quincy? The weight of the whole situation collapsed onto his shoulders. Quincy's knees buckled and he fell to the ground. Tears followed without restraint. Quincy did not know why he was crying. Maybe he was embarrassed; maybe he was sad that his and Karen's marriage was on the verge of divorce; maybe he realized that he still did love Karen.

Only a man in love would risk his entire existence to destroy another man for the sake of regaining his lost honor and his love. God was suppose to be resolving matters, but all Quincy felt was more confusion then before.

Chapter Twenty-five

Jamal did not know what to think after that Circle of Power. It seemed more like something out of The Jerry Springer Show than a Christian retreat. With each passing moment, Jamal's reason for being here became more unclear. This weekend was not bringing him closer to a higher truth. There were no revelations that he could take back to his life and declare victory. He could have spent the weekend with Jamir and Chantel.

"Brother Bryant?"

Jamal turned around and saw Pastor Dawkins emerge from the shadows. As always, Pastor Dawkins was in the company of two men.

"Good evening, Pastor," Jamal greeted him.

"I would say that this has been an eventful weekend so far." Pastor Dawkins let out a smile.

"I guess." Jamal did not see anything amusing about the situation.

"Are you okay? You seem weighed down."

"Honestly, Pastor, I can't lie. I am, and I'm not sure why I'm even here."

Pastor Dawkins signaled for his armor bearers to leave. "Let's go have a talk in my room, shall we?"

Pastor Dawkins led Jamal down a trail that led to his room. Upon opening the door, he found that the room was filled with up-tempo jazz music that had been left playing on a radio.

"Go ahead and have a seat." Pastor Dawkins pointed toward a coffee table with a stack of books. After Jamal sat down, Pastor Dawkins walked over to his nightstand and grabbed a bag of trail mix. "Would you like some?"

"No, thank you, Pastor."

After Pastor devoured a handful of trail mix, he sat down on the edge of his bed. He took off his glasses and placed them behind him. "So you're wondering what are you doing here?"

"I came here with such high expectations, and I can't help but wonder if I am wasting my time. I need God right now to show me the way; otherwise, I'm going to be lost."

Pastor Dawkins rubbed his head. "I know. After tonight, I wonder if we are doing enough. Is a Super Bowl fellowship and a prayer breakfast enough? Can one weekend out of the year make a lasting change in the life of a man?"

"I don't know. I don't know, Pastor," Jamal stated.

"In any case, we have to press on. And with good men like yourself, we can build a strong ministry."

"I'm not good. I slept with my best friend's girl, and, up until this week, I thought that her child was mine."

"Wow, that truly is what I call 'strama': stress induced by drama!"

The laughter from both Jamal and Pastor Dawkins eased the tension.

"Tell me about it. I'm waiting for Maury Povich to show up," Jamal said.

"Well, Jamal, you got caught up in the same set of circumstances a lot of men your age find themselves in. You were too busy thinking with your manhood and not your head. So, I take it that you and your best friend are no longer on speaking terms."

"Something like that; he was murdered the night I told him about me and her."

Jamal had always admired his pastor for his quick wit and ability to handle some of the most jaw-dropping circumstances with panache, but not even he could handle with ease Jamal's revelations about his fallen comrade.

"Wow, so you've been guilt ridden this entire time?"

Jamal's mind raced back to that night at the club. Maybe, just maybe, if he would have waited to tell Clay, maybe his friend would still be here. Maybe they would have reconciled.

"I mean, I've got a chance to advance my career. To make some real money and set up a better life for myself, but I wonder if I should sacrifice all of that for a kid who's not even my responsibility."

"Biologically that child may not be yours, but he is your responsibility. He's my responsibility as well. His life will be shaped and molded by the people he encounters. If his only examples of men in his life are a father who was killed in a senseless violent act, and his father's best friend who up and disappeared, then what does that tell him about being a man?"

Pastor Dawkins's words were as heavy as an anvil. Pastor Dawkins leveled Jamal with his moral imperative. "I think that's what the problem is in our community. We have forgotten that our success is intertwined and God will not bless you with a great job just for the sole benefit of you, but for the benefit of the community."

"I've always been taught that a man takes care of his own."

"If you look at the Bible, there is a stark contrast between how the world defines a man and how God defines man. I would put my money on God's definition, since God declares that He knew you before you were even formed in your mother's womb."

Pastor's words lit a fire inside of Jamal. He knew that he had to be responsible and do what was right from God's standpoint.

"Listen, I would love to continue this conversation, but I have a hair appointment." Pastor Dawkins brushed his hair with his hand.

"Thanks, Pastor." Jamal left the room and found a reason to go and rescue his prayer partner.

After the explosive Circle of Power, Chauncey decided to go for a stroll. He skipped dinner and walked toward the beach. He thought about brother Edwards, and he wished that his brother Henry had been there to hear his testimony. He loved his brother and felt that tough love was a requisite for change, but even Chauncey could not continue to be callous toward Henry. Chauncey pulled out his phone and decided to check his messages.

Chauncey, why aren't you answering your phone? I'm here at the hospital and the doctors wanted me to alert any family members to come and visit him. Henry's not in good shape and I just wanted to let you know before it was too late.

It seemed automatic for Chauncey to delete not only this message from his sister, but the several subsequent messages that followed from her. He was in the midst of a revival.

Pastor Hughes would be preaching tonight and he did not want to miss a chance to hear him speak. He also wanted to have time to talk to Pastor Dawkins about his selection for the minster's class. Chauncey did not feel like sacrificing anything for his brother at this juncture.

Besides, the doctors were often wrong, and chances were that Henry would still be alive on Sunday when Chauncey got back into town. Instead, Chauncey wanted to go by Pastor Dawkins's room before the evening service. He looked forward to the meeting. To his surprise, Pastor Dawkins was not alone. Will was in the room, cutting Pastor Dawkins's hair.

"Hello, Pastor." Chauncey closed the door and absorbed the vanilla incense.

Will gave Chauncey a nod as he continued to cut Pastor Dawkins's hair. Pastor Dawkins's room was decked out in maroon drapes and bedspreads. Maroon just so happened to be Chauncey's favorite color. Chauncey did not know whether Will should be present in this meeting.

"How's your brother?" Pastor Dawkins asked Chauncey.

"He's not good. He's dying and unrepentant."

Pastor Dawkins gave Chauncey an awkward look. His sister made Chauncey feel guilty, but he knew Pastor Dawkins sided with him.

"Why are you here?" Pastor Dawkins asked.

"To get closer to God," Chauncey said with a nervous laugh.

"I appreciate your desire to get closer to God, but Christianity is about being there for the sick and being your brother's keeper. Your brother needs you more now. You have a strong relationship with the Lord. I know the Lord would understand if you missed the Men's Retreat to be by your brother's side to pray for him."

Chauncey could not believe the words that came out of Pastor Dawkins's mouth. "With all due respect, I don't want to be there with my brother, Pastor. He has been selfish all his life. He has taken advantage of everyone in his path and now I just can't find a way to be there for him," Chauncey concluded.

Pastor Dawkins let out a smile that did not ease the tension. "You find a way, the same way God finds a way to forgive you. You have to be willing to forgive, and you do not want the regret of not being there for your brother in the final moments." Pastor Dawkins paused. "What if your prayer was the one that turned your brother's life around?"

"Pastor, I can't afford to be distracted."

"Distracted from what?"

"I know God has a calling on my life and that is to preach His word."

"God has a calling on all of our lives and that is to minister to his people. We accomplish this by showing compassion to those who are in need of the gospel. Until you learn that, I cannot accept you into my minister's class."

The bottom fell out for Chauncey. The only thing that Chauncey regretted was this moment. He felt like no one was on his side, not even the man who he admired the most. "With all due respect, Pastor, I think you may have been distracted yourself."

Pastor Dawkins reached his hand up and blocked Will's clippers from continuing to cut his hair. He stood up to allow his massive size to fill the room and dwarf Chauncey. "Distracted? What do you mean I've been distracted?"

Chauncey now felt incredibly foolish for overstepping his bounds, but maybe God was using him to convey a message to his shepherd.

"I'm just saying that we knew that having women here at this event was a distraction. I never thought that you would be caught up in this distraction with that young lady I've seen you with."

Chauncey's statement provoked Pastor Dawkins to walk toward Chauncey with his eyebrows pointed in an arch. "Make no mistake about it. I have not been distracted this weekend and I've not engaged in any inappropriate conduct. Before you take the speck out my eye you need to remove the beam from yours."

Pastor Dawkins's words were sharp and they cut to the core of Chauncey's being. It was not possible that Chauncey could feel any lower than he did at that moment. His spine had been ripped out and all he could do was escort himself out of the room.

"I apologize for my words," Chauncey said before he left the room.

He greeted the cool air and exhaled, hoping to restore some of his decency. He could not believe the betrayal that had just taken place. He knew that God had spoken a destiny in his life. For Pastor Dawkins to deny him God's will made Chauncey question whether he could serve a man who refused to follow God's will.

"Hold up, Chauncey!"

Chauncey turned around and saw Will closing the door behind him.

"Hey, Will, what's up?"

"I just wanted to say thank you for bringing me here this weekend. It takes lots of guts to take a complete stranger and offer him a chance to change his life."

Chauncey realized that the circumstances surrounding Will's attendance at the Retreat were peculiar at best. The truth was that Chauncey's reason for attending was more self-centered than anything else.

"Don't thank me; thank the Lord that He put me in your path."

"I don't know how many times I came close to giving up this weekend. Thanks to you and the guys I managed to hang in there. I at least got some kind of peace before I head back."

"Do me a favor, Will." Chauncey waited for Will to give him the signal to proceed. "Don't bow down to the circumstances of life. If you think that all you have is what waits for you back at home, then you have surrendered to a mediocre existence. You were meant for more than that."

Chauncey did not know if the words he spoke were from the spirit or from disgust. All the work he had poured into the ministry, all the devotion Chauncey had shown Pastor Dawkins, only for Chauncey to get rejected in the end.

Quincy had seen Will checking his gun earlier. He's lucky everyone agreed not to say anything to anyone about the gun shots. He knew that Will was not straight up and that Chauncey probably found him in the gutter. He opened the drawer where the gun was hidden, underneath a Bible, of all things. A beautiful chrome 9 mm. He occasionally went to the gun range. Firing a couple of rounds felt more therapeutic than prayer.

He placed the barrel of the gun underneath his chin. One bullet and it's lights out. One bullet could send him to heaven, which would make him the envy of every brother at this Retreat. One bullet could also send him to hell. It was a moment that he could never get back.

Quincy closed his eyes, and a tear snuck out of his closed lids. He had made a mess. A collapsed deal and a failed marriage not even a great architect like Quincy could rebuild.

"You've got to face it," Jamal said from the doorway.

Quincy should have known that God would not have allowed a suicide to occur on His turf.

"I know you think you made a mess of things and that it would be easy to just end it here." Jamal closed the door and walked toward Quincy, who had turned around with the gun in his hand.

Quincy sat on the bed, and a cold chill enveloped his body. "I wanted revenge, that's why I came here. I couldn't care less about getting closer to God. Now I have my answer. What else is there?" Quincy put the gun on the nightstand and started to pack up his clothes.

"You can't leave," Jamal said.

"There's no sense in staying. I would offer you a ride, but I get the feeling that you would probably stay," Quincy said as he removed the clothes from hangers.

"How come you didn't tell me about Karen?"

"That's none of your concern."

"I'm your prayer partner. I'm supposed to be the one person you can go to about anything, but you didn't want me to think that you didn't have everything together."

"I did have everything together until God came into the mix."

The front door sort of hit Jamal in the back. He looked through the crack and saw that it was Will on the other side. Jamal opened the door and let him in.

"On the real, what happened to you was fowl. What you going to do?" Will asked Quincy.

"I'm going home," Quincy barked.

"Home? So you're going to let him get away with it?"

"A disgraced minister is hardly getting away with anything," Quincy replied.

"Don't leave," Jamal said.

"There's no reason for staying." Quincy shrugged.

"Stay for me, because I need you here and I've been a true friend to you."

"I can't believe what you're asking me."

"I'm asking you to give God a chance to work things out."

"I know God is in the miracle business, but not even He can work this out."

"Please give it a chance."

Quincy did not even say anything; he just dropped his bags and considered his prayer partner's request. He would even consider that his life was starting to return to its normal pattern, until a knock on the door produced Minister Jacobs. Quincy's heartbeat nearly broke his ribs.

"Can we talk?" Minister Jacobs's voice trembled under his words.

Quincy had something else in mind that he and the minister could do, but, instead, he gave a nod to Jamal and Will. The two men left the room.

This was the moment that Quincy had waited for: he was alone with the man who had been sleeping with his wife. The culprit was within five feet of him with nothing but space and opportunity separating them. He could break his nose or choke him to death. For a millisecond he thought about the gun on the nightstand. He wished he could say that God was responsible for preventing him from reaching for it. The truth was, Quincy knew that by the time he reached for that gun and pointed to shoot, Jacobs would be halfway to Carmel.

"I bet you want to punch me," Minister Jacobs said apprehensively.

Quincy leaped up, ready to pounce on Minister Jacobs. He had to remind himself that Quincy Page did not lose his cool. Quincy Page did not get into fights like some street thug. "I ought to break your jaw. You don't take something that belongs to me."

"It was a moment of weakness."

"I love how you Christians like to downplay your actions! 'It was a moment of weakness'! You slept with my wife! You used your title to seduce her, and ruined a marriage." Quincy gave Minister Jacobs the thumbs-up.

"Have you ever considered how unhappy Karen was?"

"Excuse me, but you don't get to psychoanalyze my wife's and my marriage to make it seem like your affair is really therapy."

"I came here to ask for your forgiveness."

"You don't need my forgiveness. Ask God, He seems to have plenty for you."

Minster Jacobs started to cry. Quincy could not believe what was going on. He would have much rather had a fight than see a grown man standing in front of him, boo-hooing. At least then he would know that he was engaged in an intense battle with another man. He did not know if he could really call Minister Jacobs a man. He was a punk, if anything.

"I don't want to forgive you. I really don't. You get to destroy my marriage and get redeemed?" Quincy spat.

"I'm not getting away scot-free. My ministry is ruined. My integrity has been compromised. Yes, I believe God will restore me, but I have to first seek forgiveness, and I don't want to go on without making things right with you first."

In the end, Quincy could not fault Minister Jacobs for desiring his wife. It wasn't like Karen was some postmenopausal widow. She was a fox, beautiful, with a fat bank account provided courtesy of her husband. She was the real offender. Karen was the one who'd made a vow before God and Quincy to forsake all others. There was nothing to be gained by holding a grudge against a minister.

"Whatever. You're forgiven," Quincy mumbled.

"Thank you, thank you," Minister Jacobs said, like he had just been granted a stay of execution.

Minister Jacobs would be redeemed. Quincy was sure of that. God always redeemed His children, while he himself was still looking for a chance to be avenged.

Chapter Twenty-six

If a bull wore glasses, he would look just like Pastor Hughes. He was a robust man with pepper black skin. "You think you're a real man, what, because of the size of your manhood? Because you can go out and make money?" There was no response from the crowd, so the question came off as rhetorical. "That don't make you a man. A real man is a man after God's heart. David was a real man. Sure he had slipups, but that didn't stop him from being all that God would have him be."

Will was moved by the story of David. He was a man most people could relate to and admire. He was flawed, but he was not a punk. He got down when he needed to, and with everything, he trusted God.

"We have a great example in David. We have to put aside the petty competition, because we rob ourselves of a great brotherhood that could be formed, like David's and Jonathon's relationship. You see, the devil knows that, and he appeals to our competitive nature. That's why we have to have the prettiest wife, and if that doesn't work, we go out and get someone else's wife."

Pastor Hughes took off his glasses, then placed them on the podium as he stepped away and stood in front of the men.

"The scripture says that a friend loves at all times, but a brother is born for adversity. How many of you can honestly say that you have a brother you can call in times of adversity?"

Pastor Hughes's question sparked the brothers throughout the room to look at each other.

"I know I have one in Pastor Dawkins. I called him the other day when someone stole our church van and roughed up Deacon Porter."

The statement caused Will to look the other way out of guilt. The name Celebration Christian Center had sounded familiar, but what were the odds that the church that Will had stolen a van from earlier was the same church in attendance tonight?

"Get this: David was a king before he ruled over Israel. He was a king because God had already set him apart. You are all kings because God has already set you apart. The lion is known as the king of the jungle. We know that there is more than one lion, so there can be more than one king of the jungle. We can all exist and occupy the same space without sacrificing our God-given destiny."

Will had considered himself a lot of things over the years: a thief, a hustler, a gangster, and a menace. But he'd never possessed enough self-worth to consider himself royalty. Could God have gone through such great lengths to reach him? Was Will caught up in an intricate plot by God?

"There's someone here who can't believe that God loves him so much that he would go through such great lengths for him. If that's you, friend, I want you to come up here."

Will was spooked by how well the pastor read his thoughts. Despite his reservations, Will got up and walked toward the preacher. Pastor Hughes put one hand on Will's shoulders and gave him a look like he was going to punch him in the stomach. Then Pastor Hughes put the mic to his lips.

"Young man, everything that society has said about you is a lie. You've been told that you're worthless and that you won't amount to nothing, but God wanted me to tell you that He loves you and he has a great work in store for you to accomplish."

Tears burst from Will's eyes, and the large pastor gave him a big hug. All of his life he'd felt invisible. His gang was an invisible army that just wanted its existence to be known; even if their existence was more of a deficit than a benefit. They rained shots in the air, tagged on walls, and wreaked all kinds of havoc just so that the world would recognize that they were here. That they mattered.

Now Will had a new understanding. He had always mattered to God and he was not here to simply exist. He had a purpose, and while that purpose was at the moment obscure to him, he knew it existed.

"Is there something you want to say?" Pastor Hughes put the mic to Will's lips.

"I want to get my life right with God," Will said.

Every man in the room jumped out of his seat and started dancing and shouting. Will sat down and buried his face into his hands. Jamal and Chauncey surrounded Will and prayed for him.

Every tear was purifying and an ache followed every beat of Will's heart. The emotions ran so rampant inside of Will that sitting in the chair was no longer a desirable position. Will fell to his knees and surrendered.

Chapter Twenty-seven

Quincy needed some fresh air, and the smell of seaweed was, at this point, alluring. He embarked on his journey toward the ocean with a question in mind. Would he stop at the shore or would he keep walking?

While listening to the minister speak and watching his brethren receive their breakthroughs, Quincy came to the realization that everything he had done had been for Karen and his daughter. What was the point of conquest if there was no one to share the spoils with? There were plenty of moments when Quincy could not stand Karen. There was also no shortage of moments when he wished he and Karen had decided not to have a child. But, even still, Quincy would trade all of his bellyaches with a wife and kid than the emptiness that accompanied his current state.

"Q, wait up."

Quincy turned around and saw Jamal jogging toward him.

"Where you going?" Jamal asked.

"For a walk. Care to join me?"

Jamal simply gave Quincy a nod and walked alongside him. At night, the boardwalk that led to the beach seemed to fade into darkness. Quincy could barely make out his feet in front of him. In fear that he might misstep and injure himself, Quincy walked slowly and made calculated steps. He could hear the rumblings of nature's wildlife, which only made the walk more eerie. Heavy footsteps started to close in, and both Quincy and Jamal turned around to see Will jogging toward them.

"What y'all up to?" Will asked as he approached the two men.

"Just going for a walk," Jamal answered.

With Super Dad and O-Dog accompanying him, Quincy knew that he was not about to commit suicide. The sound of the waves crashing was an indicator that they were getting close to the water, and the sand looked more smoking gray at night. The wind started to pick up, and Quincy noticed that there was a pile of wood sitting on the sand.

"We can build a fire," Quincy suggested.

Will and Jamal walked ahead of Quincy. When they arrived at the pile of wood, Quincy stood back and watched as Jamal and Will piled the wood together to create a bonfire. Will ignited the wood with a lighter from his pocket. When the orange-red flames became emboldened, Quincy sat in silence and listened to the ocean. Jamal and Will stared at the flames, waiting for Quincy to say a word.

"I was wondering where you guys went off to." Chauncey emerged from the darkness and sat between Quincy and Jamal.

"Look, man, don't come over here with no sermons. I ain't in the mood," Quincy said.

"Brother Page, I'm really sorry to hear about you and Karen. The way she used to talk about you around the church, she made it seem like you had stopped coming to church for no reason."

"What do you know, C? You're not even married," Quincy said.

"There's a reason I'm not married."

"I already know," Quincy said. "It's obvious you're gay. I see the way you hover around Pastor. I don't know if our pastor is like that, but it's obvious that you got a thing for men. I don't judge you, if that's your thing," Quincy said.

"I am not gay!" Chauncey jumped up and scanned his brethren.

"I don't know, playboy. I can tell by your hands that you get manicures, and you dress a little too feminine for me," Will added.

"It's called grooming, you idiots. I'm not gay. I'm just a deacon with a sense of style."

"Deacon McClendon, I've never seen you really interact with women at the church. At least not in that way," Jamal said.

"That's because my father used to beat my mother's head in whenever she did not give him money for his drug addiction. My brother inherited the drug addiction and I inherited my father's temper. I wouldn't be able to live with myself if I beat on a woman. I don't hate women, but I just don't trust myself around them." Chauncey paused to clear his throat. "Pastor Dawkins is the father I wish I had, but we don't get a choice in that matter."

Quincy was pleased to discover that Chauncey had not been born in a manger. He did not walk on water, but he walked on earth with the rest of the common folks.

"I can't even stand my father," Jamal said, scratching his chin. "He has taken better care of his cars than he did my mother. It was like my mother was his mistress. He would run around on her all hours of the night, and then come home and go straight to the garage to work on his car. He didn't even respect my mother enough to tell her where he had been."

"You see, this is why I don't too much care for Father's

Day." Quincy stood up and dusted the sand off his butt. "It's more of an indictment of fathers than a celebration. I'm fortunate. I saw my daddy slave at a factory plant for twenty years before he decided that he would no longer take any orders from a white man. He struck out on his own and started his own business. Though he struggled for the rest of his life, I'd never seen my father prouder. I know he would be proud to see his son become a great architect," Quincy stated.

"Let me just say this." Chauncey put his hands up. "If you don't have God as your foundation, then nothing you build will last."

Quincy took Chauncey's words to heart and knew that there was truth within them. Though he couldn't care less about the messenger, Quincy did get the message.

"Q, God is not asking you to forgive Karen and Minister Jacobs for their sake. He's asking you to forgive them for your sake. Because the pain doesn't go away the longer you hold on to it," Jamal replied.

"Man, don't give me no sermons," Quincy spat. "I just want somebody to be real with me and feel where I'm coming from. You don't know what it's like to be betrayed by the one person you love and trusted."

"I know, because I've been on both sides of that equation. Have you ever stopped to think what you might have done in the process?" Jamal asked.

Even now, Quincy could not see the error in his actions. He had done everything he was supposed to do as a husband, and what Karen did in appreciation for that was reprehensible.

"Think about it, Q. Neither you nor Karen got into this thing planning to mess up. So how did you guys end up here?" Jamal asked.

"I paid the mortgage, I paid the light bill. Cars, vacations, and shopping sprees. What more could she want a brother to do?" Quincy wondered out loud.

The bonfire transformed into a pulpit and Quincy was about to educate his young, single brethren about what it took to be a man. "You see, part of the problem with women is that they don't know what they want. They say they want a man like their father, who is strong, works hard, believes in God, and takes care of his family. That man could be staring them right in the face and you know who they would pick over him? Soulja Boy!"

The last statement conjured up some laughs from all the men. Quincy was surprised that even a stiff-neck like Chauncey knew who Soulja Boy was!

"Man, you were doing extras. I don't know if I could do all that for a female," Will said.

"But keep it one hundred, Q. I may not be married, but I know that it takes a lot more than that to be a man. I mean, real talk, you might as well have been a Visa card and not her husband," Jamal said.

Quincy felt the sting of Jamal's comments. He had never heard anyone challenge his philosophy before. He did the same thing that he'd watched his father and grandfather do, and that was to take care of their women. What more could Karen expect from him?

"I did more; I even went to church with her on Sunday. Y'all saw me." Quincy looked for confirmation among his brethren but did not find anything.

"Um, I don't know about that. I mean, yes, you were physically present at church, but mentally and spiritually you were somewhere else," Chauncey added.

Quincy could not believe this; he was having his entire manhood tested. He did not like being questioned, and if this kept up, a fist fight was about to break out.

"Q, what happened to you was cold, and whatever you decide to do with your marriage is up to you and Karen, but at least give God the chance to try to work it out," Jamal said.

"I don't have anything to say to God." Quincy turned away as if he were turning his back to God.

"But God got plenty to say to you. If you would put your pride down and listen, you might get the answers you need," Chauncey said.

"I thought I was in a hopeless situation, and if God didn't give up on me, then I know He hasn't given up on you," Will added.

Quincy was overwhelmed with emotions. All he'd wanted to do was to confront the man responsible for all that he had lost. He did not expect to gain a brotherhood. And in his darkest hour, he never expected to find comfort. Quincy had an epiphany, that there was no hole he could fall into that God could not pull him out of. And, in the meantime, God would send His saints to comfort him. That was what had transpired this weekend, and Quincy could no longer dwell in God's presence and with God's people and be resentful. His will had finally decided to bow along with his head. *Lord Jesus. Forgive me of my sins and forgive me for trying to do it on my own. I have made a mess of things and only you can fix it.*

Tonight Pastor Dawkins walked along the beach without his swagger. He did not even dare venture to where some of the brothers had gathered around for a bonfire.

Normally he would be walking on a natural high. Tonight, however, he was confused, to say the least, about how this weekend had unfolded. Pastor Hughes was awesome, there was no doubt about it, but was he enough to cause a breakthrough? Will had dedicated his life to the Lord and all of heaven would rejoice, but how long would it be before the streets became too much for him to resist? How does a man let go of what the world says he needs and lay hold of what God know he needs? That question perplexed him beyond anything that could possibly transpire this weekend.

"Hey, you."

Pastor Dawkins turned around and saw Grace walking along the beach. She carried with her an aura that could pull anyone from the depths of melancholy. And melancholy had been keeping Pastor Dawkins company this night.

"Hey. How's things with your book club?" he asked her.

"We concluded our meeting hours ago and all the girls packed into their cars and left. I drove up by myself and I wanted to stay back and enjoy this evening some more."

Pastor Dawkins would have loved for her to say that she stayed back for him; his ego could enjoy a boost. They looked out to the ocean, and the moon's reflection made a white puddle in the mist. It was not like Pastor Dawkins could not see a beach where he lived, it was just that he spent most of his time in the broken neighborhoods of Long Beach, trying to keep people from falling through the cracks.

"How did everything turn out? I mean, if you're at liberty to talk about it. I know that everything that goes on at a Men's Retreat is hush-hush," Grace stated.

He laughed because, in truth, most women could not handle the flaws and the struggles that their men encountered on a daily basis.

The Men's Retreat was an outlet for men to vent their frustrations.

"Some men received their breakthroughs, while others are still waiting for their time."

"You're doing an awesome work with these men. I can see it." Grace patted Pastor Dawkins on the shoulder.

"Right now it feels like I'm trying to skate up a mountain during a blizzard."

"Sarcasm doesn't suit you." Grace flashed him a smile.

Pastor Dawkins surveyed her hands and did not see any rings on any important fingers. "Let me ask you something. How come you're not married?"

"I was married, but I got too old for my husband, so he decided to go and get a woman twenty years younger."

Her husband was a fool. Grace was not only beautiful; she carried a beautiful aura and had more class than most women.

"Now, I ask you, why hasn't the great Pastor Dawkins gotten married? And be honest."

"To tell you the truth, I never wanted to bring shame to the cross. So I hid behind it and thought that I was being super spiritual. The truth is, I'm afraid of being vulnerable to anybody but God."

A weight lifted off his shoulders. He was naked, not in a literal sense, but on a deeper level that only someone who was ready to entrust his heart to a person could possibly understand.

"You don't have to be afraid to be vulnerable. That's where your strength comes from. Jesus was perfect so you don't have to be."

What irony it was that Grace was the one teaching Pastor Dawkins a lesson about grace.

Chapter Twenty-eight

When Will awoke the next morning, he was free from the burden of his previous life. He ignored all the calls from home and from his boys. He was not sure what to do next, but this overwhelming feeling made him believe that nothing was out of the realm of possibility.

He went into the conference room where all the men had assembled. Will could not believe that all of these men had gotten up and gathered at five in the morning. The plan was to meet and then head back to Long Beach in an effort to make the eleven-thirty service at Greater Anointing.

"What size?" Brother Evans asked.

Brother Evans held up a black and gold T-shirt of two men side by side holding up the cross. Will pointed to a XXXL and threw the shirt over his shoulders as he had a seat. The men formed a circle around Pastor Dawkins, who paced around the circle in his T-shirt.

"God has certainly revealed a lot about who we are and where we are in relationship to Him. Now, this is usually the part where we go home and make vows to be better men. But I'm wondering, what can we do to sustain that transformation?" Pastor Dawkins asked rhetorically.

Will had learned that Pastor Dawkins liked to ask a lot of rhetorical questions.

"It is crucial that we make a long-term commitment to

change. I am going to encourage you to form a bond with the men in this room because we are going to need each other and God in order to get to the next level."

All the men clapped, and Will clapped with pride for Pastor Dawkins and for his new God.

Jamal always looked forward to returning to church on the Sunday of the Men's Retreat. As a tradition, the men who attended the Retreat would lead the congregation into praise and worship.

Sixty men of different walks of life filled the choir stand, and they shouted and praised God with their hands lifted and smiles on their faces. It was truly remarkable. The women certainly enjoyed watching their husbands, sons, relatives, and prospective suitors praise God.

"Oh, what a sight to behold. Men coming together to praise God," Pastor Dawkins said as he approached the podium in his black and gold T-shirt.

His words were greeted with shouts and aggressive claps. Pastor Dawkins set his Bible and notes down on the podium. He looked back and saw the men in the choir stand still praising God.

"You don't have to stop on my account." Pastor Dawkins walked away and the musicians revved up the music, allowing men to dance in their seats. Some started to dance on the floor right in front of the pulpit. Even the women in the congregation joined in on the praise as they started to fill the aisles and dance.

Pastor Dawkins then returned to the podium with a smile on his face, and leaned against the pulpit with the microphone in his hand. "All right now, I've got to eat at some point today." Pastor Dawkins paused for a moment to laugh. He then turned to the men in the choir, who stood tall and proud. "You can be seated." Pastor Dawkins turned back to face the congregation.

"As you can see, we had a marvelous time in the Lord this weekend, and He revealed some things in us that we needed to change. What's important to know is that God is always in the business of changing us. There is no condemnation for those who are in the Lord, what there is is an opportunity to become better and serve as a better example to others."

Jamal scanned the congregation, and, to his surprise, Chantel was in the pews with Jamir sitting next to her. Chantel was not much of a churchgoer, but she did believe that religion was vital in a child's formative years, so she allowed Jamal to take Jamir every Sunday. Seeing Chantel in church without an invitation was a minor miracle.

"I would submit to you that the choice to become men or women of God lies ultimately in you," Pastor Dawkins continued.

The congregation started to holler and shout. At the end of service, when altar call was announced, even Chantel and Jamir went down to the altar. Jamal went to stand beside Chantel and Jamir. He heard the prayer that he had wanted to hear for quite some time: the prayer of Chantel giving her life over to God.

When the prayer concluded, Chantel and Jamir both embraced Jamal. They felt like a family. This should've been Jamal's family, but maybe this was part of his punishment for betraying his best friend, to be close but to never actually be a family. Jamal recalled reading about this in Dante's Inferno. Though he could not remember the circle, he did remember reading about two lovers who could never be together. They were like tornadoes that bounced off each other. Jamal would not consider his situation hell, but he could empathize with the analogy.

"It's a blessing to see you here," Jamal said to Chantel as they walked out of the church with a sleepy Jamir draped over his shoulders.

"Jamir and I missed you this weekend and we wanted to see you." This was the first time that Chantel had ever included herself in the mix of Jamir and his longing to be with Jamal.

"My father is having a cookout today. I was wondering if you'd want to go."

"I don't know. I might pass."

Even before this week, Chantel and Jamal's father's relationship was so-so. Jamal could understand why Chantel would be apprehensive around his father, especially given the recent revelations.

"Come on, you know my pops can throw down on the barbeque. It will be fun, I promise."

Chantel fidgeted for a moment, but a smile emerged. "Okay, let's go, but I don't want to stay long."

On Sunday mornings, Otis could not be found in any church, but he could be found in front of his flat-screen TV, and if it was a beautiful, clear day, then he could be found in front of his barbeque pit. Otis would sacrifice slabs of ribs to the gods of good food. With a football game, good food, and friends from his job at Hudson Automotive, Jamal knew that his father felt like a king. The whole crowd gathered around the grill. Of course, Otis also took pleasure in poking fun at his Christian son.

"Go ahead and bless the food," Otis said once most of the food had been prepared.

Jamal bowed his head and closed his eyes. "Father, in the name of Jesus—"

"Jesus weep, let's eat!" Otis started to hand his friends pieces of ribs from his tinfoil pan.

"Dad, don't disrespect God like that!" Jamal hissed.

"Ain't nobody disrespecting God. We just know that you pray long and we need to be considerate of the fact that people are hungry."

By the time three pieces of ribs with hickory barbeque sauce were placed alongside Jamal's plate of potato salad and baked beans, Jamal had forgiven his father's offense. There was no sense in starting a fight. Jamal had had a great time at the Men's Retreat, and he had come to a decision that it would be in his best interest to accept the promotion. There were some positives to more money. Jamal maneuvered his second plate, and instead of his father putting on ribs, he glanced over Jamal's shoulder to where Chantel sat.

"So what? You done put an apron on my son now? What's wrong with your legs?" Otis asked.

"Dad, don't even start," Jamal said.

"What you mean don't start? This is my house."

"It's okay, Jamal, I'm not even hungry." Chantel helped Jamir wipe his face as he devoured corn on the cob.

"See? She's not hungry." Otis turned around and continued to pull meat from the flame and put it in the pan.

"What's wrong with you?" Jamal snapped ferociously.

"I should be asking you the same thing. Why are you still messing around with this slut?"

"Excuse me, I heard that!" Chantel replied.

"I wanted you to hear it!" Otis turned back and said.

"Hold on, hold on! Pops, you are crossing the line. She's a guest of mine." Jamal was seething with anger at this point.

Otis tossed a towel over his shoulder and placed his hands on his hips. "You know, sometimes I wonder about you. I don't know about your religion or this silly little girl over here, but you're acting like a little girl. Man up!"

Rage flowed through Jamal's veins and his fist balled up. Jamal was at a crossroads between what his two fathers had taught him. His biological father taught him not to ever let another man disrespect him and to never run away from a fight. His Heavenly Father taught him to turn the other cheek. It was clear which ideology was winning out at the moment.

"What, you want to do something?" Otis turned off his grill and took off his towel with his fists balled. The standoff caught the attention of the other partygoers.

The tension drowned out the music and all the witty banter.

"Come on, Jamal, let's go." Chantel took Jamal by the arm, and being aware of his frailty, Jamal decided to follow along.

"That's right, follow your little slut like the broad you are." Otis waved Jamal on toward the direction of Chantel.

With all his fury, Jamal swung, vowing to hit anything on the other end of his fist. His fist found his father's rock-hard jaw, but even his jaw nearly shattered upon impact with Jamal's fist. Otis fell back and landed on his butt next to his barbeque pit. Otis was on the ground rubbing his jaw, shocked from what had just happened.

All Jamal could think of was how his father had better not get up, because all of those years of his father beating him over the head with his male propaganda had boiled over.

"You've lost your mind!" Otis jumped up and ran and tackled Jamal.

The wind got knocked out of Jamal as he wrestled to get distance between himself and his father. Several of his father's friends managed to separate Jamal and his father.

"Get out my house!" Otis said while being restrained.

"Gladly! Let me give you what you deserve. Because all you've ever done is hurt the people closest to you. You ain't no man, you're a fifty-year-old boy!"

"Daddy!"

Jamal turned around and saw Jamir with tears in his eyes. He became aware that his actions were reprehensible for his son to witness. He still had difficulties seeing Jamir as anyone other than his son.

"He ain't your daddy. Your mother was running around loose," Otis yelled.

"Shut up!" both Jamal and Chantel said.

Jamal and Otis had calmed down enough for Otis to grant them safe passage out of his home. But the damage was done, and though Jamir was too young to understand, his ex-grandfather had just exposed him to the truth.

Chapter Twenty-nine

It was a typical Sunday after the Retreat. Quincy felt like the moment was on borrowed time. In his black and gold T-shirt, he sat at the dinner table as Karen cooked him a good meal. The salmon had been marinated and grilled. Karen looked really good, and he knew that she was going to put on a full-court press to win him back.

"You know, I used to love whenever you came home from the Retreat. You always had a glow and a swagger," Karen complimented him.

"I always have swagger, ever since I first saw Sammy Davis Jr. perform," Quincy said.

"Yeah, but the swagger God gives not even Sammy can match."

He did not want to ruin the meal Karen had offered to cook him after church, but he did not feel the need to delay in getting to the real reason he'd accepted Karen's offer.

"I found out that it was Minister Jacobs," Quincy said.

Karen put her head down in shame. "So that's it?"

"Karen, I forgive you for what you've done. I wasn't the best husband. But I cannot lie and say I've forgotten or I'm ready to move on."

"I'm sorry. I'm willing to do whatever it takes to work this out," Karen said with sincerity.

"I don't know that we can. All I know is that when I see

you, I see your betrayal. But I haven't been a saint, either. I went to Vegas and had an affair."

Quincy could not believe that Karen had the nerve to be upset over his admission to an affair.

"Who was she?"Karen's voice was feeble.

"Don't even try it. Don't even try to put me in the same category as you. I had sex with an escort. That's nothing more than high-priced masturbation. You actually formed a relationship with someone outside of your marriage. There's a difference."

"I'm willing to forgive you; why can't you be willing to forgive me?"

It seemed so simple. We both cheated, so why don't we just start fresh and move on? But this was not something that Quincy could just overlook. He had been humiliated in front of other men at a Retreat. His pride had been destroyed; Quincy could not overlook this infraction. "I guess what I'm trying to say is that I'm going through with the divorce."

"What? But what about this weekend?"

"This weekend only showed me the truth. The truth is that you always came second to my business and I always came second to your ministers. I'm sorry for calling you a whore and for how I've treated you over the past week. You don't deserve that, but I'm too hurt to move on."

Quincy got up and pushed his plate away. He then made his way toward the door.

"He had a vision," Karen yelled.

Her statement stopped Quincy dead in his tracks. He turned to see a mixture of pain and anger on Karen's tearful face.

"Minister Jacobs had a vision that God was going to allow his testimony to change young men's lives. You built your vision without me even being in it. You just wanted me to show up to the appointed places at the appointed times to show me off, but I've never fit into your world."

Maybe Karen was right. Quincy had developed tunnel vision, and during most of their marriage he'd run on autopilot. That still did not give her a reason to go down to a man of God to get a vision to stand behind.

"You were a part of my vision. I wanted to lay everything at your feet and I was willing to do it for as long as you would remain faithful to me."

Quincy lost his stomach for combat. He now had a face of his wife's lover. Between him imagining the minister preaching against sin, and then turning around and sexing Karen up, at that moment Quincy couldn't stand to be in the same room with her. Neither could Karen, because she got up and walked out of the room. There was no attempt to go after Karen and bring her back. No romantic moment, just a husband who had submitted to the fact that his marriage was broken without prayer.

Chapter Thirty

Chauncey did not stay for service on Sunday. He dropped Will off at the church and made his way toward the hospital. His sister had left frantic messages for him to call or come to the hospital. Chauncey did not bother returning the messages. He knew why she was calling, and he preferred to see what's going on rather than hear.

He arrived at the hospital with grayish-purple clouds hovering above. While standing outside of the hospital, Chauncey came to the revelation that he was, in fact, a coward. None of the events of this weekend had developed his ability to face difficult circumstances. He cowered at the thought that as long as he did not enter the hospital, he did not have to face the truth.

Chauncey began to walk toward the hospital tower, and it seemed that his shoes were made of concrete the way that they dragged along. Through the double sliding doors and past the doctors, RNs, and patients, Chauncey entered the elevator. As the elevator went up, his stomach went down. His arrival to the tenth floor brought him face-to-face with his brother lying as still as death on his hospital bed.

"Henry," Chauncey said, as if his words could bring his brother back.

Henry did not look dead, merely asleep. Chauncey touched Henry's forehead. It was cold, but that could have been a result of the room temperature. But Chauncey knew better. All the arguments in the world seemed miniscule compared to this moment. His baby brother was no longer alive.

Henry had died Saturday night, but his deepest fear was not fulfilled. He did not die alone. His sister had been there for him, but his brother was hours away. Pastor Dawkins had been right: this was not a feeling he would want. All of his resentment toward his brother was shallow. Chauncey wanted nothing more than to see his brother alive again.

The tears his sister must have cried had dried, and rage took its rightful place on her face. "You selfish son of a . . ." Her words trailed off, engulfed by emotions.

"Nicole, please." Chauncey put his hand up in submission.

Nicole stood up from the corner of the room, walked toward Chauncey, and stopped to size him up. "I spent all Saturday watching our brother slowly pass away and watching the door. I was hoping that my big brother would walk in with his large Bible and spend the evening praying for his brother." Nicole fought back the tears. "But I see now that you can't even be counted on with something as crucial as this."

Chauncey's mental bank was empty of any words. There was not a word in his lexicon that could justify his actions. If he did not know any better, Chauncey would have sworn that God had blocked him from producing any explanation.

"I'm sorry. I had to do God's—"

Nicole completed Chauncey's statement with a slap, and walked out while wiping her eyes.

Chauncey sat in the waiting room and cried like a baby until the nurse came in and brought Henry's belongings. He searched through the St. Mary's hospital bag and found pictures of when he and Henry were in Little League together. He also saw pictures of him and his family during Christmas time. Christmas had not been the same without the entire family being there; and it would never be the same again.

To his astonishment, Chauncey found a burgundy leather-bound Bible in Henry's bag. He thumbed through the Bible only to find certain passages highlighted. Some of them were passages that Chauncey used to quote. In the middle of the Bible was a letter, and ironically it was found right where Jesus talks about setting things right with your brother.

> Dear Brother,
>
> I know I made a mess of things when I was alive, and in the end, I had no one else to blame but myself. I just hope that you can find a way in your heart to forgive me. Our burdens get heavier the longer we hold on to them, and you're too much of a good person to be weighed down. Mom, Dad, and I will be waiting for you on the other side. I love you, brother.
>
> Love,
>
> Henry

Chauncey placed the letter to his face. What little that remained of his brother's legacy lay in this letter.

The measure of a man is in the lives that he touched. Despite the friction between Chauncey and his baby brother, not even Chauncey would have wanted his brother to have such a poor send-off. There was not even a police escort for the drive to the cemetery. Chauncey and Nicole were the only ones who attended Henry's funeral.

Henry had betrayed so many people in his life, that, in the end, no one could honestly stand to even be in the same room as his corpse. Tears overwhelmed Chauncey as he saw the wooden casket lowered into the ground. Neither he nor Nicole could sing, so he imagined someone singing "Amazing Grace."

"We're all that we have, big brother," Nicole said.

"I wasted time," Chauncey replied.

"You're only human, and I know that, deep down, you just wanted the family to stay together."

"Why doesn't it feel that way?" Chauncey asked.

"It'll take time. But one thing I know for sure is that no matter what, we are going to stick together." Nicole hugged Chauncey.

Nicole was right: they were all they had. Chauncey embraced her and knew that his convictions did not have to stand in his way of loving his family.

"I didn't get into the minister's class," Chauncey replied.

"Bighead, have you ever thought that maybe you weren't meant to be a minister?"

That thought had never crossed Chauncey's mind. He had known that he was meant to be a preacher from the moment he got saved. He'd had so many people prophesy and speak into him, that he knew it was only a matter of time before he became a minister.

"Just because you're saved don't mean you have to be a preacher. The man that sits in the pew can be just as effective as the man who stands in the pulpit."

All of Chauncey's efforts had been in vain. He'd strived to obtain something that only God could give, and missed one thing that mattered most in his life: being there for his family.

Chapter Thirty-one

"This is going to hurt me more than it's going to hurt you," Quincy said as he slammed down the domino, causing the table to shake as a result of his voracity.

Will shook his head. Quincy had been scoring points on the regular thanks to Chauncey.

"Lock him up, C!" Will said.

"I don't know how to read the board," Chauncey snapped back.

"That's a darn shame," Jamal said as he slammed down his domino.

Will took a moment to survey the condominium. Will dreamed of having an apartment like this: eggshell white carpet; Baltic ceiling with a winding staircase. Quincy's condo even had a piano in it. More importantly, Quincy had a balcony with a view of downtown Long Beach.

"This is a nice little spot you have here," Will said as he played his domino.

"Yeah, I've been staying here for the last four months until I find a more permanent place. I might have to re-sign for another six-month lease since it's hard to find a place in this recession."

"You haven't talked to Karen?" Jamal asked.

"Nope!" Quincy slammed down another domino and disrupted the T-pattern of dominoes.

"I still can't believe you went through with the divorce. God is not for divorce," Chauncey said.

"It's time I started being more concerned with what I want and less with what God wants. If God didn't want me to divorce my wife, He shouldn't have let one of his ministers sleep with her," Quincy said.

Quincy's entire situation reinforced why Will was cool on marriage and females all together. Quincy had everything a female could possibly want: money, homes, cars, and a flair for the finer things. Why would his wife cheat?

In the hood, Will always heard how men were dogs and how they thought with the wrong head. Will knew that was a lie. Today's female was just as capable of treachery as a man was. Will blamed this on a warped sense of women's empowerment. These women saw Michelle Obama, Oprah, and Tyra Banks, and thought that if they could thrive in a man's world, then why couldn't they themselves? Of course, Will's train of thought was disrupted by the fact that Chauncey still had not played another domino.

"C, you need to focus on what you're doing. You're the slowest domino player in the world." Will turned his attention back to the game. "I feel you though, Q, you don't need a girl like that!"

"Do you really think that Karen was out to hurt you?" Chauncey asked as he played a domino.

"No, I know she made a mistake. I just don't think I can get over it," Quincy replied.

"You can do all things through Christ Jesus," Will said, and when he looked up, he had everyone's attention. "What? I do read my Bible. I'm trying to better myself; it's just that when I get home, it's a war zone. I mean, the devil really be on me and my family."

"How's barber college working out?" Quincy asked.

"Great. I got an interview with Platinum Cuts this week. It's hard, because since my father's been locked up, I've always been the one to go out and get money. Now that I'm saved, I haven't been hustling and my family has been struggling."

Will knew that he had come to both love and admire these men. Four months ago, he would not have disclosed with men so much of his deep, personal turmoil. Of course, four months ago he was a high school dropout. Now he had just gotten a GED and was ready to conquer his dream. But for four months he had been ducking and dogging D-Loc and his gang. He spent most of his nights with Jamal. That made it even harder for D-Loc to catch up with him.

"Will, you got to stay the course. Your blessing is on the other side, just hold on," Jamal said.

"I know, that's why I'm nervous about this interview," Will said.

"Just remember, God does not give you the spirit of fear or timidity, but of love and of power and a sound mind," Chauncey added.

"What are you wearing to the interview?" Quincy asked.

Will found Quincy's question to be peculiar; this entire time Will had been thinking about what he was going to say and not about what he was going to wear.

"I don't know. I got a polo shirt and some khakis. I guess I'll wear that." Will shrugged. He continued to play, but he noticed that Quincy started to stare at him in a way that made Will uncomfortable.

"What size are you?" Quincy asked Will.

"I'm about an extra large in T-shirts and about a thirty-two to thirty-four in pants."

"Come with me." Quincy put down his dominoes, got up, and walked toward the back of the condo.

Will followed him, not sure where they were going. He walked along the condo and observed unique African paintings of tribesmen and women. They entered Quincy's massive walk-in closet, and that's when Quincy officially became Will's hero. This closet looked more like the men's suits section at Macy's. He had suits of every different color, from navy blue to buttercream to jet-black with pinstripes. He had an entire section of shoes still in their boxes. Quincy even had a leather seat in front of a display table filled with ties.

"Wow, you got yourself some clean suits, fam," Will said.

"Monday through Friday, my dad used to be covered in dirt from his job in construction. But when Sunday came, he would step out in the finest suits. I vowed that when I got older, I would dress this good every day." Quincy pulled a silver-gray suit from the rack and walked over to Will. "Try this on." Quincy took the jacket off the hanger and handed it over to Will, who walked over to the mirror in the back of the closet and put the jacket on.

The material was as smooth as silk. Will felt like and looked like a new man.

"You look good, we can have it tailored." Quincy said with a smile.

"Thanks." Will was not used to receiving compliments from another man.

"It's all about dressing for where you're going and not for where you've been. You've been through the gutter, but now you're heading for higher ground and you have to be ready for where God takes you."

Will knew his friend was hurt and upset with God, but the fact that he could still acknowledge God gave Will hope. He wished he knew enough about the Bible to help his friend, but if Jamal and Chauncey could not offer any comforting words and they were Bible scholars, then maybe Quincy's situation was beyond everybody's understanding.

Quincy went around to the tie rack in front of the suit rack and pulled off a tie that matched the suit. He held the tie up to Will's jacket. "You know how to tie a tie?"

"No," Will said. He felt sort of ashamed, because he'd always looked at ties as a sign that a man was soft, but since meeting Quincy, he knew he was wrong.

"Every man has to learn how to tie a tie. That's part of his passage from boyhood to manhood," Quincy said.

"I never saw it as important. I mean, there are no occasions other than funerals that call for me to wear a tie. And I stopped going to funerals a long time ago because I saw them as bad luck. One minute you attend a funeral, next minute, folks are attending yours."

"Well, now you're preparing for your career. Here, let me show you." Quincy tossed the tie over Will's neck. He lined the tie up and started to overlap one end with the other until he formed a knot that resembled a tie.

"Now, when you're in the interview tomorrow, try to make it more of a conversation than an interview. Get the person to talk about why he's with the company. The entire point is to get him to see you as an employee already. Tell him what you bring to the company. It may be a barbershop, but it's still a business."

Will was overwhelmed by all the kindness Quincy was showing him. Even though his life wasn't turning out the way he'd expected it to, the man was still taking his time to make sure that Will's did.

"Q, I can't thank you enough for all you're doing. I'm not used to people showing me love like this."

"I want you to succeed, and I believe you have what it takes. You just have to be in an environment that can help you."

Will knew that what Quincy was saying was true. He was closing in on leaving his past behind him. He had become a Christian, he had gone to school, and yet everything he had worked hard for over the last four months was still in danger of being lost on account of his environment. Will did not know if it was God or the pull his father had, but Will was glad to be free. Will stopped hanging around his old spots and only went home when his instincts told him to. He focused on getting his GED. He focused on going to church and he focused on getting his barber's license. That plan had worked for a while, but you can't hide in Long Beach for too long without someone spotting you.

"Listen, Will, I know that you got a tough situation at home, and if you want, I got an extra bedroom. You can stay with me until you get your feet squared."

"Man, I can't stay here," Will said, declining the offer.

"I'm barely here, I'm usually working. You can stay until you get a place of your own."

"I can't thank you enough," Will said.

"Don't thank me. I see you as an investment, but the deal is for you only," Quincy said.

Will knew not to expect Quincy to extend the offer to the entire family, but if Will could at least get his brother out of the house, then Will would have peace of mind.

"I appreciate that, man. I mean, seeing you and everything that you're doing is inspiring."

"It takes hard work to have success and to maintain the success."

"Yeah, it's like what Billy Dee said in that movie *Mahogany*; success is nothing without someone you love to share it with." Will let out a smirk, thinking that Quincy would appreciate him being able to quote a Black classic like Mahogany. Instead, Will found a stunned look on his friend's face. It was like he was mulling over what Will had just said, and a light switch had gone on.

"You're absolutely right, Will," Quincy finally said.

God evidently had a plan for Will in spite of his mistakes, and if Will accomplished nothing else with his life, he was determined to try to understand why God loved him so much.

Broken glass crushed underneath Will's black-and-white tennis shoes. He pulled up his black jeans as he walked along Atlantic Avenue. He walked the route home that took him past a storefront church called Zion Temple. He also passed by a Nubian Beauty Salon.

Will entered a beige apartment complex that faced the end of the street and sat next to a liquor store. Upon entering the apartment, Will was greeted by a putrid smell of spoiled milk. Dirty clothes covered the maroon carpet as SpongeBob SquarePants played on the TV.

His mother sat in a green recliner, motionless, with her eyes open, barely alert. His little sister crawled around as she reached for her pacifier on the floor. Will removed it from her hands before she could put it in her mouth. He picked her up and put her in the crib next to the TV.

Will looked in the refrigerator to find only a box of cereal, baking soda, and a little bit of fruit punch.

"Can you cut my hair?" his brother, Joshua, asked as he turned around to show the condition of his head.

Will closed the refrigerator door and pointed toward the chair next to the dining room table.

"What happened to the money I gave you yesterday?" Will called out to his mother. He was concerned that he had given her sixty dollars and did not see any evidence of his money today. It had been foolish of him to think that a dopefiend would miss an opportunity to get high.

"Where you been?" his mother asked.

"I've been out with friends from church. I got a nice little spot in downtown Long Beach."

"You ain't got no spot in Long Beach. I don't know why you even lying."

Little Elisha started crying, and Will knew that it had to do with her probably needing to be changed or needing some food or just needing some love. Her screams were interrupting his mother from watching her court shows.

"Stop crying, stupid!" His mother reached to smack his sister, and Will rushed over to grab her hand.

"You don't have to hit her every time she cries. She's a baby! She don't know how to ask for something, so she cries when she don't get what she needs."

"Don't tell me how to raise my child. I've been doing this long before you were even thought of. Who you think raised you? She's just spoiled, that's all."

"How can she be spoiled when we're broke? We don't have nothing because you're always smoking it up."

Will was sick of the abuse and the manipulation. Both entities had run rampant in his life, and now he no longer wanted to tolerate it.

"I want to take my brother with me," Will said, to the delight of his brother.

"He ain't going nowhere," his mother snarled.

"All he's going to do is get himself killed. Let me give him a chance to have a normal life," Will pleaded.

"You can go wherever you want. You've already abandoned your family when you started hanging around those church folks. But your brother is going to stay right here."

Will knew he was fighting a useless battle, but he was determined to not give up.

"I'll come for you when I get situated. Just stay strong until
then," Will whispered in his brother's ear.

A knock on the screen door sank Will's heart. D-Loc was
known for his three knocks. That was his way of making his
presence known. Will was amazed at how well he'd dodged
his gang for the last several months, but now he was caught.

"What up, playboy," Will said as he opened the door.

"What's up with you?" D-Loc did not wait for permission.
He opened the screen door and walked in. D-Loc gave Will a
fist pound. He then turned to Will's mother. "How you doing, Mrs. Tate?"

Will's mom responded with a slight nod. This was the first
time Will had seen D-Loc since the Retreat. Will had been
up front with his decision to give his life over to the Lord,
and while everyone disagreed, they had decided to back off of
Will, figuring it would be a matter of time before he returned
to the streets. But Will knew that too much time had passed
and D-Loc's visit was prompted by his need for Will to put in
work.

"Can I holler at you a minute?" D-Loc pointed toward outside.

"Sure." Will walked out and closed the screen door behind
him.

They lived on the second floor and there was a black metal guardrail in place to keep anyone from falling over. Will
followed D-Loc downstairs, where four members of the Untouchables waited for him.

J-Rock was the same size as Will. His boy, Nonsense, had
the same high-yellow complexion as the baseball bat that
rested on his shoulders. Then there were the twins, Deshawn

and Damian. They both were over six feet tall, and 200-plus pounds. It did not take a genius to know that these guys were not here just to talk.

"So what's up, man, are you still with the whole God thing or what?" D-Loc asked.

"Yeah, man, I'm on a new path and I ain't turning back for nothing," Will said with conviction.

"So you're just going to turn your back on your family like that?"

"Look, D-Loc, I appreciate everything that you tried to do for me and my family, but I'm out the game."

"We tried to give you some time to get your mind right, but you not being here is messing with our money." D-loc extended his fist. "We can't just let you up and leave. You made a pledge to the set."

At the time, it had not seemed like a strong pledge when Will pledged his life to the Untouchables. His life was not worth anything to him then, and either way he did not see himself living long, so why not make a lifelong pledge? This whole time he had been feeding off of the devil's pie, going for seconds. He had given up his birthright for the sake of being able to say that he belonged to something.

"Man, I made a new pledge. I'm turning my life around, and if you can't get down with that, then I don't know what to tell you," Will stated firmly.

Will had only one play to make and that was to threaten to go to his father. But at this moment not even his father could save him. Only God could deliver him from what was about to happen. Will would hold his ground on the scripture promise that God had not given him the spirit of fear and timidity.

"Well then, we got a problem, because the only way out

of this is through death." D-Loc opened up the left side of his brown leather coat and flashed his chrome glock. This was the same gun he used to rule the Untouchables with an Iron Fist. The stories associated with that gun made Will even more pensive.

Was this the end? Was Will allowed only a few months of peace before he was killed in broad daylight in front of his family? Oh well, at least Will would get a chance to be with his Lord, and if he was going to die for something, then it might as well be for his beliefs and convictions.

"If I wasn't scared to die when I was out in this world playing tag with Satan, then what makes you think I'm scared now?" With those words, Will got into combat mode. With his fists balled and his body ready to absorb any impact of a bullet, Will waited.

D-Loc pulled out his gun and pulled back the handle. Will froze, and knew he'd missed the opportunity to snatch the gun away. D-Loc had been a god to him, and to challenge his former god was irrational. The sound of a honk spooked everyone involved, including D-Loc. Will looked over D-Loc's shoulder to find a familiar Range Rover. God was still in the miracle business.

Quincy hopped out of the Range Rover, wearing the same polo shirt and slacks he'd had on earlier at his condo. Jamal hopped out of the passenger seat and proceeded to open the door behind him, where he pulled out a scared, timid Chauncey, who did not want to get out of the car. The three men made their way toward Will, with Chauncey keeping a safe distance.

"What up, Will? Just thought you might need help moving," Quincy said.

"Good looking." Of course, Will was referring to more than just the help with moving.

"Still up to the same thing, Devin?" Jamal asked D-Loc.

Will had never known D-Loc's real name, nor had he even bothered to ask. He never thought that Jamal would know who D-Loc was, which was even more shocking.

"You know, I got to do what I got to do," D-Loc replied.

"You and I both grew up in the same neighborhood and watched how gangs and drugs tore our community down. Now you're here perpetuating it?"

Will had never seen D-Loc intimidated before. If he did not know any better, he would even go as far as to suggest that he was scared of Jamal.

"Look, Devin, I don't know what the deal is with you and Will, but what I do know is that Will is trying to get his life together and I need you to let him do that."

It was like Jamal slayed the tension in the air. Will thought he might make it out without any bloodshed.

"This ain't over." D-Loc signaled for his boys to come along with him and he left.

"J, I'm trying to figure out what just happened," Will said.

"Man, I used to go to school with that dude back when his older brother was running things. We got into a fight once, and I mopped him up. He knows that I'm not scared of his gun and that I could knock him out long before he pulls the trigger. The last thing he wants is to get beat down in front of his crew again."

D-Loc's final words echoed throughout Will's ears. Yes, he had been set free by God's grace. Yes, he had just dodged a bullet, but D-Loc was not the type to forget. He would try to get payback and it was up to Will to figure out how.

But Will knew without a doubt, as long as he put his trust in God, that everything was going to be okay. He would not have to spend his days looking over his shoulder, because God had his back.

Chapter Thirty-two

Pastor Dawkins waited for Grace as she emerged from the Relaxation Spa looking more radiant than ever. Grace started to show up to church after the Men's Retreat, and Pastor Dawkins decided to give her a chance to see if there was something more between them than just a spark. This marked their fourth date they had been on since the Retreat. He'd debated whether a trip to the spa was too much of a gift to give to someone he'd just started dating. Regardless, he just loved to see her smile, and wanted to do his part to keep one on her face.

"I got a Kahlúa pedicure and my feet smell like coffee," Grace said.

The Kahlúa pedicure was to cap off a hydro-bath with rose petals, and a one-hour pebble massage. Pastor Dawkins would always preach to the men that if they wanted their wives to love them like no other, then they had to be willing to keep the romance in their marriage and not be cheap. Since he'd never had a wife, Pastor Dawkins wondered how his relationship advice went with the guys. It was easy to give advice when he was not even in a relationship.

"Thank you so much." Grace gave Pastor Dawkins a big hug.

"The restaurant is in walking distance; I figured it's a nice day for a stroll."

Grace did not even wait for Pastor Dawkins to finish. She just started walking. He followed alongside her. He remembered that a gentleman walked along the outside of the curb to protect the woman he was with.

"The men still seem to be on fire in the church. I'm sure that you're happy to see so much growth among men," Grace commented.

"I realized that the strength of Greater Anointing lies in us getting the men together. If we can encourage men and make them feel good about being men, then they will become better fathers and husbands."

Pastor Dawkins took a moment to admire the Pike. Despite all of the expansions of new businesses and shops, he could still see the place where he spent the summers of his youth, running along the pier and riding the Ferris wheel and other carnival rides. The Pike was evidence that the more things changed, the more they stayed the same.

"I'm curious. All this time you spend thinking about everyone else, when do you find the time to do you?" Grace asked.

Pastor Dawkins laughed, because if he had a dollar for every time he was asked that question, he could buy the Staples Center and hold church. They both stopped at a light and waited for the crosswalk to give them permission to walk.

"I really don't, but God has been so good to me that I can't complain about my lot in life."

They finally crossed the street and entered a cozy little Thai restaurant. Pastor Dawkins was pulling out all of the stops. He felt the desire to give her anything, like a parent gives to a spoiled child; except Pastor Dawkins did not believe that this gift from God would spoil. He knew that Grace would accept every gift with humility.

They sat next to the window and ordered their food. To

pass the time, they played a game where they tried to guess what was going on in the lives of the strangers who passed by the restaurant. It was not long before their food arrived.

"You know, I remember one Bible Study when my former pastor talked about the purpose of a wife. He said that a wife was there to help God complete the work in her husband," Grace said.

"I'm sure that roused up some of the independent women at your church," Pastor Dawkins said.

Grace laughed as she wiped the food from her lips. "You know it did. Then he went on to say that it wasn't about giving up who you are, but using the gifts to help your man be all that God desires him to be. In essence, a man cannot fulfill God's will without a woman." Grace concluded her statement with a snap of her fingers, as if she had just heard some good spoken word poetry.

"So are you saying I'm outside of God's will?"

"I believe so, because God has a blessing staring you right in the face and I believe it's time that you accept it."

Pastor Dawkins was leveled by her beauty and her strength. She flirted between the lines of confidence and conceit. At this moment he would give her everything that she desired and pray to God for more. How could a pastor date a woman? How could he fall in love?

"You don't have to be afraid around me. I'm not out to get you, and I'm not interested in the title of first lady. I just want to know the man behind the sermons, and if that's too much, then I don't know what we're doing here." Grace returned to eating her food.

Pastor Dawkins knew what he was doing. He was falling in love, but he could not help but wonder if he was worthy of a woman like Grace.

"Why are you so scared to give yourself a chance to find someone? It's not like you are priest," Grace said.

"Watch out now, I'm not scared. I just don't want to put myself in a compromising situation. Part of the success of our ministry lies in the fact that there hasn't been any scandal regarding me and some sister at the church. I couldn't live with the shame of letting my God down."

"I'm not looking to put you in a compromising situation." Grace took another bite of her food.

There were a lot of things that made Pastor Dawkins enamored with Grace. One of those things was her directness. Grace knew how to be unabashed without being abrasive. She challenged him, and for that he felt inclined to be just as straightforward.

"What you have to understand is that I can't afford to have my integrity questioned. If one of the brothers or sisters of the church walked by and saw us laughing and having a meal together, things would get so twisted that folks would think that I lost my salvation."

"Didn't you just preach a sermon where you said not to care about what others think? Be more concerned with what God thinks?" Grace concluded her question with a wink and a smile.

Pastor Dawkins responded with a chuckle. "Do as God says and not as I do."

Grace pointed her fork at Pastor Dawkins as if to shame him.

"Look, the church is under attack right now with all of these pastors going through a divorce or getting caught up in scandals. I believe that it is not my season to explore new relationships."

"If that were true, then you wouldn't be here. I know that

you carry with you a strong anointing, and you would not be on a date with a woman God had not preordained you to meet."

Pastor Dawkins felt it was wrong to carry such a strong emotion for a woman who was not his wife. He felt that those emotions would one day lead to his downfall, and he could not risk being yet another case of a pastor who could not live up to the standards he preached.

"Look, I'm not trying to put any pressure on you. All I'm saying is don't cut something off for no reason. If you're happy and you didn't have to compromise to achieve it, then go with the flow." Grace touched Pastor Dawkins's hand.

Her hands were soft and warm. He was tempted to kiss them, but that would have been inappropriate. Instead, Pastor Dawkins inhaled the chocolate scent from her fresh nail polish. He had resigned a long time ago to being single, but now in order for him to truly be happy, he would have to let go of his preconceived notions.

"Who's next?" Eric, the barber, said as he shook off the hair from the previous client. Platinum Cuts gave Will a job sweeping up hair, with the promise of a new job upon Will's graduation from Smith's Barber College. For the first time in his life, Will was gainfully employed. He was going to school to get his license. Quincy allowed him to stay in his condo, and he was making decent money to send to his brother.

Will had not given up on trying to get his brother away from his mother. Will's mom was inflexible.

"Hey, boy!" his father said with a big smile on his face.

Will had heard that his father was getting early parole. He'd stopped treating the news as a special occasion, because from Will's standpoint, it was only a matter of time before he went back to prison.

"Hey, Pops!" Will gave him a big hug. He loved his father, Will was just tired of being disappointed.

"I heard you moved out?" Odell asked.

"I had to; I would've ended up shot or in prison like you. I want more for my life."

"More? More? What, you got a new hustle?" Odell said with his eyes bulging.

"I guess you can say that. I decided to get my life straight with the Lord. A friend from church got me a place out in Long Beach and I'm going to school to become a barber."

Will was sure that his father would laugh at his son's plan to become a barber. Instead, Will's conversion caused his father to put his head down in shame.

"So that's it? You're just going to walk out on your family? I thought I raised you better than that."

"Listen, I'm not judging you, and I know that what you did was for me and the family. I just wanted to find my own way."

"Now, look here, I'm supposed to be teaching you and you're over here teaching me." He patted Will on the shoulder. "I'm proud of you, son. Now, stick with it, because I don't want to see you going down the same road I went down. I'm tired of going back and forth to that cage. I'm too old for that."

"I know."

"I'm sorry that I missed out on so much of your life, and, like I said, I just wanted to provide for you guys."

"You don't have to apologize to me, I know. But you still got Joshua and Elisha and they need their father. Josh needs you to show him how to move through life and not get caught up."

"I think Josh already has a good teacher to show him how." Odell wiped his eyes.

If God never did another thing for him, Will was thankful that God at least gave him a break from his past.

"Dad, I want us to do things the right way. If God can do a work in me, then I know He can do a work in you."

Odell started to shake his head and more tears started to appear. "No, it's too late for me. I'm glad you got out when you did, but I, on the other hand, ain't got nothing left."

"Your best days are ahead of you and you don't even know it. And you ain't too old, either. That's why God still got air in your lungs, so you can turn and change. It's not too late."

Will had never spoken so sternly to his father before. Will always saw himself as the good son who followed orders without questions. He never questioned his father's wisdom, but now he could see his father for what he truly was: scared.

He was scared to start over. He was scared to be alone and, overall, he was scared that he would die having failed at being a man. Will knew the reason he was doing all of these things in his life was because of the people in his life, people who wanted to see him do more than just become a statistic. He wanted to give his father the same gift. Will could not give him time back, but he could help his father look forward to the time he had left.

Chapter Thirty-three

The Holy Spirit had convicted Jamal over the last four months. This was the first time Jamal had visited his father since the infamous Sunday barbeque brawl. If his father even allowed him to walk into the house, Jamal would consider it an accomplishment. He heard the squeak that came from his father's recliner. Then he heard the sound of his father's heavy feet pounding the hardwood floor until he got close enough to the door, where Jamal could hear his father breathe, until finally the door opened.

"What you want?" his father asked from the other side of the door.

"I'll tell you this much, I ain't interested in round two."

"You gave me a sucker punch; we know how round two would turn out." His father said as he opened the door.

Jamal's father stepped aside to allow Jamal to enter the living room. The Chargers were playing, and since LA did not have a football team, San Diego was the next best thing. Jamal took a seat on the couch next to his recliner. They spent the next twenty minutes in silence. The only words that were spoken were frustrated grunts of Philip Rivers and his struggles to move the Chargers into the end zone.

"I hope you're not here to make up, because I've already turned the other cheek," his father finally said.

"I'm sorry. I shouldn't have lost control of my emotions,

and you're my father. I should have never put my hands on you."

"Especially over some tramp who got your nose wide open."

The same anger that was present at the barbeque had returned. That same anger that existed throughout Jamal's childhood was now present.

"I didn't hit you because of Chantel. It's because so many men would kill to know who their fathers are, and I've got a father I'm not even proud of."

His father sat up in his recliner and put the game on mute as he turned around. "Did I keep a roof over your head?"

"Yes."

"Did I keep you in a warm house over the winter and a cool house in the summer?"

"Yes, you did." Jamal nodded.

"You always had plenty to eat, and I mean real good, too. Steak, pork chops, and potatoes." Otis sat for a minute to let his words sink into his son's head. "I didn't put no Payless shoes on your feet, either; you had Nike and Adidas and the best sports equipment. And you ain't proud of me?"

"I'm not saying that I'm unappreciative of what you did, but I'm saying that it takes more to be a father than just providing stability. That's part of it, but I learned it's who you are when nobody is around that defines you."

Now the TV was completely off, and his father's bronze eyes were staring dead center at Jamal. "Well, since you're the wise, know-it-all son, tell me, what makes a father?"

Jamal never thought that he and his father would get to this point in their relationship, where he could tell him how he felt and what he had learned over the years.

"You want to know when I was most proud of you as a father?" Jamal took his father's silence as a sign for him to move on. "It was those last two weeks before Mom died. It was not the women you ran out on her with. Don't get me wrong, you had some dime pieces on the side, but for those two weeks you treated Mom like she was the last woman alive." The memories of his mother dying of ovarian cancer were still hard to shake even after all of these years.

"You treated her like your life would end just as soon as her life would end. You fought with the doctors to make sure that Mom's life mattered, and that was the man I wanted to grow up to be like. How you are in the storm is how I want to be twenty-four seven. In the storm you're a man of integrity, of courage, and you're willing to fight for those you love. I don't know why that man is not good enough for you the rest of the time."

"It's because I had no one to show me how to sustain it," his father replied. "I stood by your mother those two weeks because I wanted her to forgive me. I didn't want her whole marriage to be a joke."

Jamal could never understand why death brought the best out of some and the worst out of others. "How could you love my mother and cheat on her?"

"I mean, we lived in a different time. Lots of guys cheated. That was just something we did. We didn't see it as a big thing," Otis put his head down, and then, moments later, he lifted it up. "I'll tell you this much, seeing the man you've become and seeing that I did not have any hand in it, at least, not a positive hand, that drives me crazy."

This entire time Jamal thought that his dad viewed the way he lived as a sissy. Jealousy was not what Jamal expected to be the reason for his father's harsh actions.

"Dad, do you remember what you told me when I first entered junior high school?"

Jamal allowed his father to search his faded memory bank for the answer.

"Son, honestly, I said a lot of things back when you were in school."

"You told me that if I ever got into a fight, I better not come home unless I've won, because if I lost, then I would have a second beating when I got home."

Otis nodded in agreement. "Yeah, I remember that because that was the way my grandfather raised me. That makes you a man."

"That's what makes me self-conscious of what people think. To do something because you're afraid of what someone might say or do is not a passage into manhood, but a passage into slavery."

"You may not be proud of me and I deserve it. I am proud of you, even if I don't say it."

Jamal achieved showing his father that Jamal's way was not the way of the weak, but the way of the strong. "Dad, I want us to go to church together."

His father started to shake his head. "Oh no, I don't go in God's house and He doesn't come into mine."

"That needs to change, because the only way you're going to get the peace you need is from Him." Jamal pointed up at the ceiling.

It was as if his father had placed a huge "S" on his chest and sent him out to save the world. Only Jamal needed to go save his family.

Jamir slept soundly as Jamal and Chantel hovered over him. One day he would be strong enough to understand all of the drama surrounding his entrance into the world. Jamal hoped that Jamir would be strong enough to understand that, despite the fact that his parents were children pretending to be adults, he had been conceived out of love, and his life represented a changed life for all parties involved. He was their caveat into adulthood, but not all of them had made it. Jamal followed Chantel out of Jamir's room as he closed the door. Chantel took a seat on the couch, and Jamal sat Indian style right in front of her.

"Can I ask you something?" Jamal waited until he had Chantel's complete attention. "How often have you thought about the night that Clay died?"

"At least a million times," Chantel said.

"I've tried to replay the scene over and over in my head and figure out which version would bring the right results. But in the end, I can't live with the best scenario because that leaves me without you."

Chantel looked up with her eyes full of life.

"I've loved you since high school," Jamal said.

Chantel rubbed the side of her face in disbelief. Jamal noticed something different when he told Chantel that he loved her. He did not feel guilty, but it felt natural, as if he was where he was meant to be all along.

"How come you never said anything?" Chantel asked him.

"Because part of me felt like I was betraying Clay."

Chantel wrapped her arms around Jamal's neck. "I want us to at least give it a try."

"Yeah, let's give it a try. At least for him." Jamal looked toward Jamir's bedroom. "You know we're going to have to tell him the truth when he gets older," Jamal said.

"We'll do it together," Chantel stated. "Now that we have that settled, I guess I could reap the benefits of that promotion, because if Clay has taught you anything, it's that I'm high maintenance."

The extra money from the promotion had finally allowed Jamal to get some peace between him and his bills. He still managed to see Jamir, though not as often as he'd have liked. Jamal realized that he did not have to sacrifice his career for the sake of family. He just had to keep things in their proper perspective. His boss did not like that Jamal was not a weekend warrior like some of his other coworkers, but he could not deny that Jamal brought excellent results from his work. If he'd learned anything from Quincy's situation it was that family had to come first in a person's life.

"Oh, I know," Jamal replied.

The last piece in Jamal's puzzle was completed. He had the only woman he ever wanted, and he had a chance to still be a father in Jamir's life.

"I know Somalian children who eat more than you do," Quincy hissed at his daughter, Sasha, as she swallowed up her father's sarcasm with a big wide smile. They decided to sit outside of a local Italian restaurant and enjoy a hot lunch.

"What? I'm not hungry!" Sasha said sheepishly.

Her reddish-brown skin was passed down from her mother. The beauty of Karen had been transferred to their one and only offspring. "So how are things at UC Santa Barbara?" Quincy took a bite of his fettuccine alfredo.

"You were right; going to a college near a beach is too distracting. But I did okay this semester."

Sasha was in her sophomore year of college. She'd decided, against her father's better judgment, to major in medieval literature. In 2009, Quincy did not know what people did with comparative lit degrees, but he did know that they did not get paid.

"How's your mother?"

"She's good. She looks great, but she misses you."

How that statement penetrated Quincy's wall was a mystery to him. He did not spend too much time thinking about Karen, but when his thoughts were centered on her, he noticed that his resentment started to decrease more and more.

"How are you, seriously, Sasha?"

"About as well as any child could be who lived through her parents getting a divorce. The only difference is that I do not feel like it's my fault. I just feel like I've been the only grown-up in the situation."

"You got me there. I could've handled the situation better, but what can you do? Emotions run high. I'm only human."

Sasha leaned back and crossed her arms as she stared at her father. "I remember when I did not used to believe that. I used to think you were invincible. I never saw you get hurt. I never even saw you get so much as a cold. I still believe you are my hero, Dad. I just wonder where he is."

"He's gone, sweetie. He was my alter ego." Quincy took a sip of his water. "You're going to have to settle for the real me."

One of the reasons Quincy gave up going to the movies was because there was a lack of originality in the films. Everyone seemed busy remaking older movies. That became even more apparent as he surveyed the New Releases section of Max's Video store. Being an action buff, he started to get discouraged, until he shot a glance over to the comedy section only to find a familiar face.

A slimmer Karen examined the back of a DVD. She wore a hot pink butterfly-collared shirt with a gray undershirt. Quincy had every intention of walking over to her, but first he wanted to admire her silhouette from afar.

Six months had passed since the Retreat, and four months since the last time he'd seen Karen. It was amazing how lost two people could become in one city. He approached her gingerly, not knowing if she was going to embrace him or slug him.

"Hey, you!" Quincy called out.

Karen turned with a pleasant smile as if he was the one who'd undergone a physical change over the past six months. He had developed a beer belly from massive alcohol consumption.

"Hey, no work today?" Karen asked.

"I decided to play hookie. My golf buddy wasn't available, so I decided to grab a movie and maybe a pizza. And you?"

"I called in sick." Karen gave a naughty smile.

"I'm telling!" Quincy said.

Karen grabbed Quincy's hand as her eyes enlarged and she flashed a big smile. It had been a while since a woman who Quincy had a history with touched him.

"No! Don't. Maybe I can buy you lunch in exchange for your silence."

"You're a good negotiator. What were you about to rent?"

Karen showed Quincy the Coming to America DVD and burst into song. "'She's your queen to be . . .'"

Quincy checked to see if the entire store was watching this scene unfold.

"Okay, okay, okay. Simon Cowell is probably gouging his eyes out right now. You've seen that movie a million times," Quincy said.

"Some things never get old." Karen took Quincy by the hand as she headed toward the cash register. "Indulge me. Come watch a movie with me."

He could not recall his wife ever being this sexy before, and he felt powerless against her.

The house had undergone reconstruction on the inside. Earth tones gave the house a calming feel. A blank canvas stood in line, waiting to be painted.

Karen led Quincy to an oil painting of a woman cradling a Bible. The words "The Holy Bible" were illuminated.

"I see you still got talent," Quincy said, admiring the painting.

"You know I got a little something-something." Karen shook her hands to signal her talent was so-so.

She had a glow back. After almost fifteen years, something that had dilapidated over time came roaring back. Quincy was amazed at how she was able to reinvent herself.

"But this one is my prized possession." Karen pointed to a painting next to the white staircase.

Quincy felt a gravitational pull toward the painting. It was of a man and a woman as black as sable. The woman had on a gold robe and a gold head wrapping. The man was shirtless, but he wrapped his arms around the woman, who formed her hands in a prayer.

Karen was not finished with the painting. Looking at the unfinished masterpiece caused her to pick up a brush and start to work the outside of the woman's robe.

Quincy followed her and linked his hands with hers as she guided the brush up and down. He inhaled her cocoa scent and fought with every fiber of his being not to kiss her shoulder. Karen would live and die a hopeless romantic; this was one thing that Quincy was certain of, and he envied her for her optimism.

"You never signed the paper," Karen said.

Quincy had never been a quitter, even though he quit on his marriage.

"I wasn't ready. I just let everyone think that I did," Quincy said.

"You haven't called or come by." Karen put the paint brush down and took a seat on the bottom steps.

"I wasn't ready for that either. I needed time to put things together, and even now, I'm still confused," Quincy said. He looked at Karen, who signaled with her eyes for him to continue. "I don't like to lose anything, no matter if it's a business deal or a poker game or a marriage. When I lost you, it made me feel like I wasn't good enough for you; like I wasn't man enough for you."

"But you were good enough for me."

Quincy placed his finger over his lips to signal for Karen to stop talking. "I didn't know that, and as a result I went into a spiral of bad habits. Drinking and gambling. But none of those things brought me closer to you. Everything I did I did for you, because you made me feel like I could do anything."

Karen walked over and embraced Quincy. He could not continue to fight the truth. The truth was that everything he did was for his wife and nothing mattered without her.

"I missed your embrace," Karen confessed.

"I've missed holding you too," Quincy said.

Tears started to well up in Karen's eyes. "When you stopped holding me, I started to help out in ministry. When you stopped making love to me, I joined the choir." Karen started to cry.

"You got more involved in church because I wouldn't spend time with you?"

"I said that I would never hold you back and I didn't want you to feel that way. So I suffered in silence while you built your skyscrapers. You promised to provide for me, and you did, but that wasn't enough."

The last six months had finally put Quincy in a state where he could bear to hear the truth spoken and not bail out or get angry. Quincy chose to sit beside his wife on the bottom steps.

"From the moment I found that cell phone, I've been on a mission to reclaim what I've lost. I thought I lost the adventurous side of life. Really I lost the most precious side, which was you," Quincy confessed.

Karen leaned her head on his shoulder and Quincy gave her a kiss on her forehead.

"It's a long journey to get back to where we were," Quincy said.

Karen gave him a kiss. Quincy was overwhelmed with desire for Karen. She lay back on the stairs and Quincy kissed her neck. She let out a moan and then Quincy knew he had reclaimed what he had missed.

"I'm not ready to give up on us just yet," Quincy admitted.

"You had a change of heart?" Karen asked quizzically.

"No, that's just the thing; my heart has always belonged to you. I just got distracted."

Karen continued to kiss Quincy. Those kisses were more than just simple acts of pleasure. What Quincy thought he had lost had resurfaced. It conveyed that this time things would be better. That this time things would be different. That this time, they would go the distance.

Epilogue

Eight months later . . .

Drew Brees was an awesome quarterback, and with Jamal controlling him on Madden, Brees became spectacular.

"Can I see?" Jamir reached for the remote.

"Naw, little man, Daddy is playing right now. First rule in life: don't ever interrupt a man while he's playing Madden."

Jamal could tell from the confused look on his son's face that he did not understand what he was saying, but Jamal knew that years down the road he would find the wisdom in his father's words.

"Babe, what do you think about these invitations?" Chantel held up two different designs of invitations.

"They're beautiful, babe." Jamal continued to play.

"You ain't even looking!" Chantel nudged Jamal with her elbow.

Sure enough, she was right. Jamal was unaware that Chantel had sat next to him with the wedding invitations in her hand. Everything was moving so fast for him. He and Chantel went from being parents to Jamir to being engaged in the same breath.

Jamal could not question God's timing and he felt that he had everything he wanted. He had his relationship with God, his relationship with Chantel and Jamir, and finally his career at Pinnacle Sportswear. Of course, at the rate that Chantel was spending money on their September wedding, Jamal hardly saw a dime of his new salary.

"What are you thinking about?" Chantel asked.

"Nothing!" Jamal sounded irritated.

That was a knee-jerk response for all men. The truth was that so many things were running through Jamal's mind at once that he did not know how to process it, let alone articulate it to Chantel. "Nothing," was a less complicated response, and Jamal felt the need to be less complicated, especially with the Saints being on the ten yard line about to score.

"Babe, can you pause the game for a second?" Chantel requested.

Jamal paused the game to avoid an argument. Soon after he and Chantel announced their engagement, they enrolled in marriage counseling. Neither one of them had had great examples of a healthy marriage growing up. One of the first things Jamal learned in marriage counseling was not to deliberately do something that would annoy his spouse. That seemed like common sense and practical enough.

"All right, babe, what's going on?" Jamal placed his arm around Chantel's shoulder and she rested her head on his shoulder.

"I keep waiting for the bottom to drop out. Happiness like this is too dangerous. It makes you careless and it leaves a bunch of broken hearts in its wake."

"It can't rain all the time. Let's just keep God first in our marriage and family, and trust that God will always bring us back to this place of happiness whenever we get lost."

Jamal reassured his fiancée with a kiss on the crown of her head, while Jamir got a hold of the remote and un-paused the game.

"Oh, no!" Jamal snatched the remote from Jamir.

He would have chastised Jamir about playing with Daddy's remote, but he did not have the time. He and the guys were supposed to hang out tonight, which was the occasion on virtually every Friday night. Chantel got up and walked over to the dining room table with her invitations in hand. The only things on Chantel's fingers were her French-manicured nails. Not many women would accept being engaged without a ring to show for it.

Her bare hands were the spark of many conversations throughout the church, but Jamal did not care what the congregation thought. Chantel knew that he was saving up money to buy a townhouse for her and Jamir. Chantel would have accepted a ring from the candy machine as her engagement ring. But he had a better idea.

"Babe, I got you some Cracker Jacks," Jamal said to Chantel.

Chantel jumped up and ran to the pantry next to the kitchen and pulled out a large box of her favorite snack. Chantel stuffed her face with the caramel popcorn. Jamal could barely contain himself from laughter. She even managed to hand some down to Jamir, who ran over and extended his hands toward his mother. It was like he was trying to catch raindrops.

Of course, the moment Jamal had waited for arrived when Chantel noticed that the ring that served as a prize was not a toy. With her mouth full of popcorn, Chantel opened the small velvet box to reveal a three-karat princess-cut diamond engagement ring. Timing was everything, and Jamal always said that he would give the ring to his fiancée when she least expected it.

Chantel covered her mouth with her free hand and started to jump up and down. Jamir started to jump up and down in reaction to his mother.

"Oh my God! But how?" she screamed with excitement.

"It's like that song says: 'if you liked it then you should have put a ring on it.'"

Chantel started to mimic the dance from the famous Beyoncé video, and at that moment, Jamal knew he would regret saying something as corny as that.

Chauncey was having a wonderful time in the Lord on his date with Nina Mosley. She was the head usher at Greater Anointing. They had just attended a gospel concert with BeBe Winans as the headliner, and they decided to partake in dinner at a local seafood restaurant.

"I just love the Apostle Paul. I mean, he was a soldier and a prisoner of the Lord," Chauncey said.

"My favorite person in the Bible was Esther," Nina replied.

Chauncey found that peculiar, since Esther was in only one book in the Bible. To be honest, Chauncey questioned the importance of having this book in the Bible, since he did not get any great revelations from it. Of course, Chauncey would never say this out loud. He would leave his objections to the story of Esther for his private consumption. The Apostle Paul, on the other hand, had authored the majority of the New Testament; why wouldn't anyone find him fascinating?

The server brought out their dinner. Chauncey kept his Southern tradition of eating fish on Fridays. Nina had some shrimp and some scallops.

"This looks delicious. Let us pray over this wonderful meal that the Lord has blessed us with." Chauncey reached for Nina's hands, but she pulled back and put them up as if she were being robbed.

"I don't believe in physical contact on dates. I'm not trying to let the devil get his foot in any doors," she warned.

Okay, now Chauncey felt offended. He would not even entertain the idea of doing anything inappropriate with this sanctified woman, even though she wore a V-cut gold blouse that revealed her breasts. Chauncey had to remind himself of his head-to-neck rule: look at a woman from her head, but do not go past the neck. Instead of getting into a purity debate, Chauncey decided to just pray over the meal without holding hands.

"So, how is it doing the great work of the Lord as an usher?" Chauncey asked enthusiastically. He took a bite of his food.

"It's okay." Nina took a moment to devour a shrimp. "I mean, you wouldn't believe the nerve of some of these members. Here it is, people show up late and they want a seat up in the front next to the pastor. The nerve of these people."

"Humph, humph. God's not going to put up with this foolishness. They just don't teach any respect or church etiquette anymore," Chauncey agreed.

"I know." Nina put her fork down, reached down into her purse, pulled out a full-sized Bible, and opened it right on the table. "It says right here in the Word that everything has to be done in decency and order."

Chauncey could not believe that Nina had pulled out a Bible and placed it between her silverware and Caesar salad.

"Will there be anything else?" the waiter approached and asked.

"Check!" Chauncey said.

"Cheesecake!" Nina said.

Chauncey was not even interested in making it to dessert. He had met some crazy so-called Christians in his lifetime. Especially when he attended a church that believed in casting out devils through smacking people with the Bible; now those were some crazy folks. Chauncey even heard people refer to him as crazy in certain circles, but he knew that was a lie from the pit of hell.

"You don't want dessert?" Nina asked, and leaned forward so that Chauncey could get a good look at her heart-shaped face and bug eyes.

"No, I think I'm going to have to give the benediction on this date in Jesus' name and go on with my evening."

Nina was visibly hurt from his words, and Chauncey wished he could have said things in a different way, but the truth was that he did not want to stay on this date any longer.

"Well, okay. Am I going to see you at church on Sunday?"

"Yeah, I'll make sure not to be late." Chauncey got up and paid the bill. "I really enjoyed the concert."

"Yeah, me too. I'll see you."

He thanked God that they had driven separate cars, which was a further indication of how he was not trying to pull any funny business. Chauncey made a beeline toward the exit, and decided that he would give his little sister a call.

"Hello, Bighead! How was your date?" Nicole asked.

"A true Holy Roller."

"You mean you met someone more spiritual than you?"

"It's almost like she's waiting for Jesus, literally."

Chauncey knew that comment would warrant chuckles from his beloved sister.

"Well, maybe that's God's way of telling you that you can't be so heavenly minded that you're no earthly good."

Chauncey saw firsthand how his superior Christian attitude could be a turnoff for most people. He realized that his faith had to be lived out and not spoken. He spent too much time talking about how awesome God was, instead of demonstrating it in his actions.

"I don't know if this dating thing is for me. I think it's best if I stay single." Chauncey rubbed his forehead as he walked along the curb to his car.

"Don't give up. Everybody deserves to be happy and have someone to share their life with. I haven't given up on the idea that there is someone out there for me, neither should you."

"You're right." Chauncey entered his car.

"So, where are you going now?" Nicole asked.

Chauncey looked at his watch and realized he still had time to meet up with the guys. He knew that their inquisitive nature would inquire about his first date in seven years. "I'm going to fellowship with my brothers."

It had been a long time since Will studied math. He revisited math when he'd prepared for his GED exam. Now, with his GED, Will found the math applicable to helping Joshua with homework. It felt good for Will to have something positive to offer to his brother other than a hustle. He arranged with his father and mother to let his brother stay with him on weekends.

"Now carry over the one," Will said to Joshua, who was stuck on a particular problem.

Usually, Will would spend Friday nights with the guys, and Saturday mornings he took his brother to the park to play basketball. Sundays was church and Fatburgers before he took his brother back home.

Will was also learning that it was okay for his brother to struggle with math. The struggle helped make him stronger, and if that philosophy worked in the streets, than why couldn't it work in the classroom?

"All done." Joshua finished the last problem.

"All right, let's get ready to turn in." Will rubbed Joshua's head.

Quincy's old condo was a blessing that Will would never stop thanking God for. Quincy subsidized the rent and made it dirt cheap so that Will could still feel like he was paying his way. He had a steady flow of clientele at the shop, and he was known as the barber who did not sit around and socialize with the other barbers, but he handled his business and went home. While he'd seen more money as a car thief, nothing could compare to the feeling that honest work brought.

"Man, I want to roll with you one night. I love hanging out with the guys, especially Jamal. I think I can get him in NBA Live," Joshua stated.

"Man, don't rush to be grown. Enjoy only having to worry about homework and bedtime. Speaking of which, it's nine-thirty and way past your bedtime."

Will ushered Joshua into his bedroom, which was next to Quincy's old wardrobe closet. Will did not change a thing when Quincy moved out. Quincy left Will a few start-up suits and ties.

The room was not filled to capacity with suits and ties, but Will had a vision that one day it would be. He would work hard and little by little, he would build. Joshua's room resembled a mini-sports bar. The only things missing were the bar and the chicken wings. He had posters of LeBron James, Kobe Bryant, Ray Lewis and Manny Ramirez. He also had a computer desk next to his bed. Will pulled out the desk chair and placed it next to his brother.

Before Will became a Christian, he used to listen to a rapper named DMX, and this guy used to have some deep prayers on his albums. Of course, the songs that preceded the prayer set a record for the use of the N-word. Even still, Will felt he could relate to DMX, and when he became a Christian, he vowed to keep his prayers real and honest.

"Lord, keep a watch over all of us. Keep me and my brother from falling because there are many temptations out there, and in the end we're only human. Lord Jesus, we love you and pray that you can give us the strength and courage to live for you in a corrupted world. In Jesus we pray, Amen."

"Amen," Joshua followed.

"I love you, bro." Will kissed his brother on his forehead, and placed the chair back under the computer desk as he made his way toward the door.

"Love you too," Joshua said as the lights turned off in the room.

Will did not think that he and his brother could become any closer than they were, but it was possible. A year ago, he would not have told his brother he loved him; that was considered sissy talk. He lived in a world where love was implied and not shown. He definitely would not have kissed his brother, either. Such displays of affection would cause someone to question Will's manhood.

Over the past year Will had learned that so many of the myths surrounding manhood were birthed out of insecurities. Life was too short and he understood that better than most. He was going to tell his brother that he loved him because there would come a day when he wouldn't be able to tell him.

Will turned most of the lights off on his way out the door. He left the light on in the living room so that his brother wouldn't get scared. A spacious three-bedroom condo could be intimidating to anyone at night. Will grabbed the keys off of his kitchen counter and made his way toward his coat closet next to the door. Will removed his leather jacket and helmet as he exited his condo.

They say riding a motorcycle is the closest thing to flying without leaving the ground. Will could not disagree; he would add that the only thing better than riding his bike on a cool Southern California day was riding it at night. The bike was another one of Quincy's toys that he'd decided to part with; maybe Quincy had come to grips with the fact that he was a little too old to ride motorcycles. In any case, Will was grateful for his bike. Will cautiously exited the parking lot before he began to ride along the street. As soon as he reached the first light before a long straightaway, Will adjusted both his helmet and gloves. He waited for the amber light to turn green, and when it did, Will was off, flying along the cool Long Beach night.

Quincy knew that he did not have a whole lot of time to kill. He had not had a thing to eat since breakfast. He had inhaled a bagel with strawberry cream cheese. Karen usually had a nice hot meal waiting for him when he got home on Fridays. Quincy would catch a little bit of the game before he headed out with the guys.

"Hey, babe, I'm home! What's for dinner?" Quincy said before he even had a chance to set his briefcase down.

Karen emerged, still in her T-shirt and sweats. She looked refreshed, as if she had just woken up from a two-hour nap. "Hey, babe, how was your day?"

"Fine," Quincy grumbled.

"You hungry?" Karen asked.

"Yeah, what's for dinner?"

"Well, I wanted to cook steak, but I forgot to take it out in time, so I did not even bother to try to cook it. Then I was going to cook chicken, but I thought about it and I realized that we've been eating a lot of chicken lately, so I thought that you might be tired of it."

"So what are we having for dinner?" Quincy asked.

Karen dropped her arms from her sides as if in submission. Quincy was not trying to annoy his wife; he just wanted to know what they were having for dinner. He spent the entire day talking and trying to analyze the meaning behind people's words. He just wanted to come home and have chicken or steak.

"I ordered a pizza." Karen nodded toward the pizza that sat on the dining room table.

"Sweet!" Quincy rushed over and opened the pizza box. He pulled two large slices out and cupped them in his hand as he made his way toward the living room.

"So, anything exciting happen today at work?" Karen asked.

"No, just a regular day."

That was a lie. The truth was it had been a very active day; Quincy just did not feel talking about it with the Angels playing.

"Well, today my boss went off on every single person in our department. I mean it was a hot mess."

Karen's voice started to fade and the sound of baseball and the consumption of a pepperoni and sausage pizza became the dominant sounds.

"Did you hear what I just said?" Karen asked

"Yeah, baby, of course I did." Quincy shrugged.

"What did I just say?"

"Something about today at work."

Quincy must have answered wrong because she responded with a slap on the shoulders.

"I earned that," Quincy said.

"You sure did. I listen to you go on and on about architecture and that is not the most fascinating thing to listen to."

Quincy and Karen had enrolled in marriage counseling as they tried to save their marriage. Quincy would have been lying if he said that he did not suffer an occasional blow to his ego every time the affair was mentioned.

Every day he was getting stronger and every day the Lord was teaching him lessons in both humility and forgiveness. Quincy even felt empathy for Minister Jacobs, who had to step down from ministry until he could resolve some of his personal issues.

"I'm sorry, babe. You know how I am on Friday nights," Quincy apologized.

Karen lay down on Quincy's lap and started to rub his shins. "I wish you didn't have to go."

"I know, but I'll be back before you know it."

Karen sat up and looked Quincy in the eyes. In truth, she did not have to say anything; her eyes told the entire story.

"Thank you for not giving up on us," Karen said.

It would take some time, but Quincy would convey to her just how much her faith in God had saved him.

"You about to get handled in this game," Will said as he fired his cue ball into the triangle of pool balls. Will managed to knock in a few striped balls, but the majority of the balls remained on the pool table.

"I see I'm going to have to educate the rookie." Quincy placed chalk on his stick, then he fired a shot and landed a solid green ball into the corner pocket.

"All right, now, don't get too cocky. Remember what happened the last time we played?" Will reminded them.

"I don't know what you're talking about; I was just playing around with you." Quincy fired a shot and missed a ball.

"I guess you was just playing there too? Huh?" Will asked.

Jamal and Chauncey sat at a table next to the pool table and shared a bowl of nachos.

"Didn't you have a date tonight?" Jamal asked Chauncey.

"Yeah, it didn't go so well. Some people are so heavenly minded that they're no earthly good," Chauncey replied, stealing his baby sister's line.

"Well, I'm sorry to hear that. So what are you going to do now?"

"I'm just going to continue to be single and on fire for God, and I'm going to have a little talk with Jesus."

"That's fine, so long as you're not having a little talk with 'Palm-olina,'" Quincy said as he took another shot.

All the men found Quincy's comment hysterical except for Chauncey. He had a noticeably perturbed look on his face.

"You know what, Brother Page? It just don't make no sense for you to be a Christian and say the type of things you say," Chauncey commented.

"That's why I go to church. I ain't right and God knows that, but He also knows my heart. You wouldn't go to a hospital and expect folks there to be well, now would you?"

Quincy's comment received both laughter and applause. He promptly bowed to both.

"Get your victories in now, because when I get on, it's a wrap," Jamal said with his mouth full of nachos.

This was the way their weekly pool meeting went. After the Retreat, the four had made a pact to stay connected. Their Friday nights were not just about playing pool. They encouraged one another to pursue their goals, and they eagerly awaited the next Men's Retreat.

Reader's Group Guide Questions

1. Was Quincy right in his assessment that the pastor had an unhealthy relationship with the female members of the congregation?

2. Was it appropriate for Pastor Dawkins to meet a woman at a Men's Retreat?

3. How was each character affected by his or her father?

4. Did the male-dominant view of the story give you a better insight into the male psyche?

5. Does Will stand a chance of surviving without the support of his gang and family?

6. Were you surprised that Chauncey did not leave the Retreat to be by his brother?

7. Do Jamal and Chantel stand a chance of surviving their tumultuous past?

8. Did Quincy overreact to Karen's infidelity?

9. Was the Men's Retreat a success from the characters' standpoint?

10. Did the story show a clear contrast between a man defined by society and a man defined by scripture?

Urban Christian His Glory Book Club!

Established in January 2007, UC His Glory Book Club is another way to introduce Urban Christian and its authors. We are an online book club supporting Urban Christian authors by purchasing, reading, and providing written reviews of the authors' books. UC His Glory Book Club welcomes both men and women of the literary world who have a passion for reading Christian-based fiction.

UC His Glory Book Club is the brainchild of Joylynn Jossel, author and Executive Editor of Urban Christian and Kendra Norman-Bellamy, author and copy editor for Urban Christian. The book club will provide support, positive feedback, encouragement, and a forum whereby members can openly discuss and review the literary works of Urban Christian authors. In the future, we anticipate broadening our spectrum of services to include online author chats, author spotlights, interviews with your favorite Urban Christian author(s), special online groups for UC His Glory Book Club members, ability to post reviews on the website and amazon.com, membership ID cards, UC His Glory Yahoo! Group and much more.

Even though there will be no membership fees attached to becoming a member of UC His Glory Book Club, we do expect our members to be active, committed, and to follow the guidelines of the book club.

UC His Glory Book Club members pledge to:
- Follow the guidelines of UC His Glory Book Club.
- Provide input, opinions, and reviews that build up, rather than tear down.

- Commit to purchasing, reading, and discussing featured book(s) of the month.
- Respect the Christian beliefs of UC His Glory Book Club.
- Believe that Jesus is the Christ, Son of the Living God.

We look forward to the online fellowship.

Many Blessings to You!

Shelia E. Lipsey
President
UC His Glory Book Club

**Visit the official Urban Christian His Glory Book Club website at www.uchisglorybookclub.net